HONEY IN THE ROCK

Christine van der Mark

HONEY IN THE ROCK

TORONTO/MONTREAL
McCLELLAND AND STEWART LIMITED

Copyright © Christine van der Mark 1966

All rights reserved. No part of this book may be reproduced in any form without permission in writing from the publisher except by a reviewer who may quote brief passages in a review to be printed in a magazine or newspaper.

The Canadian Publishers
McClelland and Stewart Limited
25 Hollinger Road, Toronto 16,
Canada

PRINTED IN GREAT BRITAIN BY
BRISTOL TYPESETTING CO. LTD.
BARTON MANOR - ST. PHILIPS
BRISTOL 2

Chapter One

1

At half past seven of a September morning in 1936, Dan Root got off the train at the little Alberta prairie hamlet of Ulna. On one shoulder he balanced a bedroll, while in his hand he carried a heavy suitcase, these two pieces of luggage representing all that he possessed in the world. After a few grey bags of mail and some crates and boxes had been flung down on the platform beside him, the train gasped and spluttered, pulled itself into order with a crashing of coaches and boxcars, and moved slowly off, blowing a few forlorn hoots as it gathered speed across the prairie.

Setting his things down on a bench, Dan straightened and looked about him. A man with a dray and a team of horses took the bags of mail and crates from the platform. He seemed about to drive off when he hesitated, looking speculatively at the newcomer.

"Waiting for someone?" he asked.

"Yes," said Dan nervously. "Someone named Gottlieb Zwick was supposed to meet my train. I'm the new teacher for the Lily of the Valley School."

"Ah-huh. Gottlieb Zwick, eh? Well, if I was you, I'd come over to the hotel and wait there. Just throw your suitcase on the dray. I'll take you across."

The morning had a cool freshness under a perfectly blue sky. Perched on the dray, swinging his legs as they lumbered along, Dan shivered a little in his thin jacket. Three enormous grain elevators overshadowed the scattering of houses and outbuildings, the stores, and the ugly, square, weather-beaten hotel. Beyond, lay the prairie, the pasture lands, and the patchwork quilt of dark fallowfields, fields of stubble, and fields of yellow uncut grain or those which were scenes of furious activity where late threshing was in full swing. The towering windmills, their arms revolving against the blue sky, stood like sentinels at wide intervals. Great clouds of dust rolled on the roads, following the passing of every tractor, truck or car.

In the hotel waiting-room with its ancient leather upholstery, its smell of beer mixed with furniture polish, and its general air of dreariness, Dan set down his luggage again, and stood at the dirty window, looking out into the street. He was a tall, thin, wiry young man of not quite twenty years old, dressed in baggy, grey-flannel trousers and a rumpled threadbare tweed jacket that sagged on his narrow shoulders. He had dark, untidy hair and thin knobbly nervous hands with the fine nails broken and abused. Except for the intelligent eyes with their depth and pathos and tenderness, his youthful face with its snub features and wide unsmiling mouth, had a slightly cynical cast in which bitterness had too soon overlaid a nature basically sweet.

He could not help being apprehensive of what awaited him here, if the past were any guide as to his capabilities. His summer job had been with a farmer who had worked him until he had dropped. Then as he had lain in the horse stall, unable to get up, he had heard the harsh voice of his taskmaster, " If you can't work, go back where you come from. I'll get somebody who can! "

Taut and nervous, Dan could not keep still, but walked about, constantly looking out of the window and glancing again at his watch. But I'm not a farmer, he thought. It wasn't a fair test. I'm like my father, a student, a bookworm. He sighed, thinking how his father had died of heart break, worn out at fifty, a petty book-keeper laid off when the company had installed machinery to do his work. He had never found another job. There were no jobs! There was no money, either. Engrossed in his books and music, Dan had not known there was no money. At his father's death, his mother had taken in boarders. And with his newly acquired teacher's training, Dan had tried to get a job. For a whole year he had washed dishes in a café, ushered in a theatre. And then the farm.

The farm had been Big Bill's idea. Big Bill, their best paying boarder. They'd be married by now, Dan thought. Mother and Big Bill!

" But *why*, Mother, *why*?" he had asked her, coming home sick, defeated, to find her wearing a diamond ring!

"He's kind," his mother had said, turning her face away. "He's a genius as a mechanic. He's got his own business."

"'Big Bill's Body Building'!"

"There's nothing disgusting about it. There'll always be cars to repair. And I've got to think of your young sister. Peggy's only fourteen."

Dan had wanted to say that he would take care of them, that he was the man of the family. But there he lay, weak as an infant, unable to keep down anything but crackers and water.

His mother had turned to him, suddenly tense and desperate.

"I'm setting you free, Dan," she had said. "You must go and make what you can of your own life."

And at lunchtime, Big Bill had flung a letter down on his pillow, a letter post-marked *Ulna*.

"Maybe it's a job," he had sneered. "Maybe you can show us what's the use of all your fancy education. Playing the piano... Ye gods!"

But I know I can teach, Dan thought fiercely, pacing up and down the waiting-room. At least it's a chance to see. He whirled around as weighty footsteps came rolling down the protesting hotel stairs, and Joe Weiman appeared, shirt sleeves rolled up, waistline sagging, his smile as oily as his hair.

"Well, stranger, looking for a room?" he asked genially.

"I'm waiting for Gottlieb Zwick," Dan answered with another glance at the window. "My name's Dan Root. I'm the new teacher for the Lily of the Valley School, and a certain Gottlieb Zwick was supposed to meet my train. Do you know where I might find him, by any chance?"

"No, I don't know that," said Joe slowly, looking the new teacher up and down with some amusement. "But I sure do know one thing. If I was waiting on Gottlieb Zwick, I'd sit down. Here, have a chair."

Abruptly, Dan sat down, while Joe leaned against the desk, idly smoking.

"So you're the new teacher for the Lily of the Valley, eh? Have a cigarette?"

"N-no thanks."

"Don't drink neither?"

"No."

"Well, if you don't smoke and drink, you'll do all right out at the Lily of the Valley. They're all Brethren in Christ out there, and it's real strict."

"Brethren in Christ? I've never heard of it."

"Oh you get lots of those there around here. Real Bible punchers. Take today. It's Saturday, but that'll be their Sabbath. They'll all be off at church today."

"You mean they're Seventh Day Adventists?"

"I don't mean nothing of the kind. They're Brethren in Christ. And they keep Saturday for their Sabbath. And boy, are they strict! But not so strict as the Town Brethren we get in Ulna. Out there in the Valley you get the Dancing Brethren. The ones in town don't even dance. Or play cards. All they do is have lots of kids."

Joe winked meaningfully. "But the Dancing Brethren, anyways they have dances, so a person can have some fun. Know any German?"

Dan shook his head.

"They all speak the Low German out there. Some of the old folks don't speak no English. Course the kids will speak English."

Dan looked again at the window and down the street.

"Maybe Gottlieb Zwick is at church then?" he suggested.

Joe snorted with laughter.

"Not him. Not by a long shot. If I was you, I'd just relax and take a snooze. Gottlieb, he'll show up when he gets here." Lowering himself into a chair opposite Dan, he stretched out in comfort. "It's a funny district you're going to," he confided. "The Zwicks and the Leniuks, they pretty well run everything."

"It was a Mr. Herman Ries who wrote to me," said Dan, producing a letter from his jacket pocket.

"Oh him! He's just the secretary. He's got nothing to say. It's Jud Zwick and Jonas Leniuk who runs things. They been out in that country more than thirty years. And funny thing is, they both got newspaper wives!"

Dan looked blank.

"Don't tell me you never heard of newspaper wives! Well, you take this Jud Zwick, Gottlieb's old Dad. See, he was married to a sister of Jonas Leniuk, but she died when Gottlieb was born. So I guess it got pretty lonely out there on the homestead, with a kid to look after and the farm to run. So Jud put an ad in the *Prairie Messenger* for a housekeeper, object matrimony. You know the way they do. So this old bag Florrie turns up, and Jud marries her. Seven months later she had a baby boy! Born out there on the homestead. That's the young kid they call Reuben.

"Sounds all right, don't it?" Joe laughed softly. "Well, the fact is, this Florrie was a fallen woman. Mrs. Fox worked in the post office then, and she used to steam open all the letters so as to get the gossip. And she was wise to old Florrie. Jud's ad said, 'No objection one child.' And one of the letters Florrie wrote, she says, 'There'll be one child.' But when she come, she come in alone. The child gets here seven months after! Mrs. Fox sure had a good laugh when Jud come in here to register his new son! But the laugh was on old lady Fox after all. Seems Florrie had some big shot of a relative down east, and he got Mrs. Fox fired."

"Only poetic justice," murmured Dan.

"Mrs. Fox's daughter Ada Pearl works in the post office now, though. Never heard nothing about her steaming open letters. She even went around with the kid Reuben in high school when he came into Ulna to do grade twelve."

"Just the same, I think I'll invest in some sealing wax," Dan declared.

"Good idea . . . Well, then there's Jonas Leniuk's wife. She's out of the newspaper too. She don't speak a word of English yet. Hell, she never gets off the place except to go to church. A year after Jud got his wife, Jonas gets this woman clear out from Russia. A Russian-German woman. A Bolshevik. A widow. Got her through the Brethren's paper, *The Everlasting Light*, it's called. Out she come with four kids, all girls. Right away Jonas Leniuk married her and adopted the kids. So they're all Leniuks now. What d'you think of that?"

Dan's head swam with weakness. Still not fully recovered in health, he had made the crazy journey which had begun at one in the morning, the train jolting and shunting and rattling along until half past seven, to cover the one hundred and sixty-seven miles from Calgary to Ulna. Slowly he framed the remark:

"Either he's a very altruistic person, or else he acted in the spirit of desperation."

"Jees! Talk English, can't you!"

Dan flushed.

"Maybe this Jonas Leniuk was just lonely," he suggested.

"Lonely! Looney's more like it. Even a looney man, just imagine taking in five women! And know what? After a while, she had a baby, this here newspaper wife from Russia, Jonas's baby that is. And what d'you know? It was another girl!"

Something infectious in Joe's chuckle made Dan smile.

"You can laugh, boy. But you better watch your step out there at the Lily of the Valley with all them Leniuk girls. Yep, there's Sarah, she's the oldest. Getting on, Sarah is. She's Gottlieb Zwick's intended. Been his intended since they was in school. But hard times, you know. Of course that Herman Ries you mentioned awhile back, he's sweet on Sarah too. But nobody could get Sarah away from Gottlieb. Herman Ries, he's a real Hun. Come out from Germany after the war. Fought on the other side from us."

"Your name sounds German too," Dan observed, looking critically at the sign over the desk.

"Sure, but hell, my folks was born here. It makes a difference! Anyways, to get back to the Leniuk girls. After Sarah, there's Leota." He grinned. "Keep hands off Leota. She's mine."

"I've no time for girls," said Dan wearily. "I'm saving up to go to university."

"Oh I heard that line before. 'I got no time for girls.' But love gets in the way, Teacher, you'll find that out. This your first school?"

"Yes," Dan admitted.

"Just what I figured. Boy, you'll see the love bug will get you out there on the lone prair-ee."

Dan looked out once more at the deserted street.

"Is there a general store in this town?" he asked.

"You bet! A Jew store. Just a block down there and turn left. Zimmerman's."

"Do they—do they give credit?"

"Sure! Zimm's always give credit to the teacher of the Lily

of the Valley School. The teacher gets paid at that school."

"Well, that's a relief. If you'll excuse me, I think I'll go over to this store and get a few groceries. I'm going to be baching at the teacherage, so I'll need them."

"Go ahead."

Dan glanced anxiously at his belongings. "Would it be all right if I leave my things here?"

"Sure thing. I'll put them down behind the desk. And if I see Gottlieb, I'll tell him where you are."

At the store, the screen door squealed open at his touch. Along one side, the shelves held groceries of every description, while dry goods and clothing, boots and shoes and notions, were arranged in orderly groups on the other, and at the back hung harness and leather goods. A square of tin nailed to the floor just inside showed where the stove would stand in winter. Behind the food counter, a small dark woman with greying hair and a pleasant tired face, looked up and smiled as Dan came in.

"My name is Dan Root," he said shyly, glad she was old enough to be his mother, rather than young and terrifying. "I'm the new teacher for the Lily of the Valley School. I was just wondering—could I charge some groceries here until I get my first cheque?"

"Of course," she answered. "I'm pleased to meet you, Mr. Root. Now just what did you want?"

She spoke good English with a slight accent he could not place.

"It's silly, but I don't quite know. I should have made a list."

"You'll want a few staples," she suggested. "Flour and sugar, tea and coffee, and some canned goods to fall back on. I'm sure they'll supply you with milk and eggs and butter and fresh vegetables out in the country." She smiled at him encouragingly out of odd foreign eyes.

"That sounds about it," he said gratefully.

As he watched her getting the things ready, he began to feel strange. Sounds became fainter, and Mrs. Zimmerman seemed far away. He swayed where he stood.

"Are you all right?" he heard her ask. "Here's a chair. Sit down."

He sank into it, his elbows on the counter, his head in his hands. " I'm all right," he said, his voice muffled. " It's just I've been ill, and the journey was so—"

" That terrible train! " She put a string around the box, tied it expertly and broke it off. " There. Now, Mr. Root, you come with me."

Numbly he followed her into a cheerful apartment behind the store.

" You sit on the couch," she said, " while I make a cup of tea. Did you ever have tea out of a samovar, Mr. Root? With a slice of lemon in it?"

" No, I haven't," he answered, reviving.

" Well, I'm going to fix you some right now. Too bad Nathan isn't here this morning. He went off early . . . How are you going to get out to the Valley?"

Dan sighed. " Someone named Gottlieb Zwick was supposed to meet my train. But he didn't show up, so I went along to the hotel. I met the proprietor there I guess. A man named Weiman."

" Oh yes. Joe Weiman."

" He was telling me all about my new home."

Mrs. Zimmerman set out thin pretty cups.

" You don't want to pay too much attention to what Joe says," she advised. " How about some oatmeal cookies? They're just about as good as breakfast."

" I don't want to be a bother."

" You're no bother at all."

" So that's a samovar?" Dan admired its size and its silver sheen where it dominated the dining-room table.

" Yes," she said proudly. " My late husband and I brought it out with us from Russia twenty-eight years ago." She handed him a cup of tea poured from the little tap. It was fragrant and fresh, with the slice of lemon, just what he could wish for. " Is this your first job?" she asked.

" My first teaching job. I'm as green as grass."

" You'll do just fine," she soothed.

" I want to save up to go to university."

" Just what we wanted Nathan to do. But you know, he just loves this store. He said to me, 'Mother, I love serving the public, and here I'll stay.' Nathan's a good business man too.

Much better than his late father. My husband was more the student type, like yourself."

"I couldn't sell a cup of water to someone dying of thirst on the desert," sighed Dan.

"I'm glad to hear you make a joke. Well, everyone to his own trade. You mustn't take life too seriously, Mr. Root. Have a bit of fun with it all."

"Well, according to our friend Joe, this Lily of the Valley place is pretty strict. Or did he say they are the Dancing Brethren?"

"That's right. They do have their dances out there. You'll have a nice time, I'm sure. They're good people. There's Herman Ries now . . ."

"The Hun?"

Mrs. Zimmerman laughed. "He was through the war, on the German side, of course. But he was only a boy. Hardly as old as you I should think. He's musical. He has his own piano, and he plays all alone out there on the prairie."

"This Joe Weiman talked about Jonas Leniuk and Jud Zwick and their newspaper wives."

"Never mind what Joe told you. You wait till you meet Florrie Zwick. She's a nice woman. It's a good marriage and a happy home. Reuben Zwick was a friend of Nathan's at school here. He has a farm up north from his mother's people, I believe. But he comes home for a couple of months around Christmas. You'll meet him then. He would be nice companion for you." Mrs. Zimmerman refilled Dan's cup, put more cookies on the plate. "And you'll find Jonas Leniuk a very decent man. He always did fight to see the teachers get their pay. The Leniuk girls are all nice. When the women around here want a hired girl, they always try to get a Leniuk. They're good cooks and hard workers, those girls. Pretty, too."

Dan set down his cup, nibbling at the lemon rind.

"Are you feeling better now?" she inquired anxiously.

"I'm fine."

"Do you hear that roar outside?"

Dan listened intently.

"It sounds like a truck that is going to fall to bits all at the same moment, like the one-hoss shay."

"One of these days it will. That's your friend Gottlieb

Zwick." She parted the curtains. " See, there he goes, right over to the station . . . Now he's turning on one wheel and he'll head for the hotel. Don't worry yourself, Mr. Root. He'll be coming this way in a minute."

Dan had a glimpse of a filthy battered red truck as it flashed past the buildings near the hotel, churning up clouds of dust in its wake. After a short interval of quiet throbbing it gave a furious roar, tore back on its own tracks, and turned groaning towards the store.

"Come along, Mr. Root," said Mrs. Zimmerman mildly with her tolerant wise smile, " I'll introduce you."

2

The screen door squealed wildly and banged shut upon the entrance of a man in a dirty work shirt and denim pants as stiff as stove pipes. He was short and thick-set with broad shoulders and lean hips, his face black with dust and streaked with sweat. Having made his dramatic entry, he stood relaxed and slouched, his thumbs in his belt, watching Dan coming in nervously behind Mrs. Zimmerman.

" Here's the new teacher, Gottlieb," said Mrs. Zimmerman. " This is Gottlieb Zwick, Mr. Root."

" Happy to meet you," Dan murmured.

Gottlieb nodded. They looked at each other in silence for a difficult moment.

" Well, come on! " Gottlieb rasped. "What are we waiting for? I haven't got all day. Looked for you at the station and the hotel too before I could locate you." He spoke with an attractive accent and lilt.

Dan thought it best not to waste time in pointing out that he had been waiting for Gottlieb since half past seven that morning.

" I'm afraid I left my things at the hotel," he apologised.

" I already tossed them into the back of the truck."

" There's a radio wrapped up in the bedroll," said Dan, aghast.

" What's in the suitcase? Bricks?"

With a sarcastic grin, Gottlieb shoved back his sweaty hat. He exuded sweat and horse and self-confidence. His profile was handsome, the type that would become a nutcracker face in old age, Dan thought, but would undoubtedly be attractive with the grime washed off.

"Gimme some Old Chum and papers, Mrs. Zimm," Gottlieb demanded. "And put it on my bill."

"How's it going?" she asked maternally.

"Been on the tractor since daylight. Fighting with all the brothers about noise on the Sabbath. After that August snowstorm holding things up, I'm not wasting any old Sabbaths. And of course, looking for the new teacher takes more of my time."

"Now Gottlieb!"

"These your groceries?" he asked Dan. "Well, bring 'em along and let's get going!"

"I wish you the best of luck, Mr. Root," Mrs. Zimmerman said kindly, her voice lost as Gottlieb yanked open the door, Dan gasping after him with the box of provisions.

The truck still shook and rumbled with life, standing parked by the board walk, its front wheels turned as though anxious to take to the road again.

As he and Gottlieb got into the cab from opposite sides, Dan saw that a passenger would be sitting between them, a big fresh-faced young woman with sparkling dark eyes and black hair, braided at the nape of the neck. She smiled at the newcomer, showing deep dimples.

"This is Mr. Twig," Gottlieb announced sourly, slamming the door and driving off with his eyes on the road.

The noise of the truck making conversation next to impossible, Dan retired into his corner, silent and nettled. After a time Gottlieb flashed him a teasing look, exchanging laughing glances with the girl.

"I'm sorry!" he shouted. "It isn't Twig, it's Root!"

"My name's Sarah Leniuk," the girl said loudly over the din, moving closer to Dan to avoid Gottlieb's dirty clothes, for she wore a spotless, cotton-print dress with wide, puffed sleeves. Gottlieb's intended, thought Dan. As the rough ride jostled him against her, he could not help noticing that her flesh had a sweet fresh smell, like apples. Her bare forearms were heavy, tanned, and strong, her hands larger than his own and far more powerful.

Gottlieb turned the truck off the road, over a bumpy bit of trail, braking sharply before a tight barbed-wire gate that led into a field.

"Why you don't stay on the road?" Sarah demanded irritably.

"It's quicker. You want to get to church on time, don't you?"

"You'll tip us over."

Gottlieb leaned across Sarah to Dan.

"Mr. Twig, d'you mind opening the gate so I can get through?"

"Of course," said Dan, fumbling with the door handle until Gottlieb shot forth a strong filthy hand that managed it at once.

"It would be better to walk, just about," Sarah complained.

"Well, go ahead and walk. See if I care," said Gottlieb with superb indifference.

Getting out of the cab, Dan found that the sun had become hot. The brown prairie wool scrunched under his feet. Still dazed and weak, he got the gate open and the truck lurched through, leaving him eating dust. But when he fought with the wire and the post to shut the gate again, he could not do it. Sarah came to his rescue, looping the wire over the post with an ease that put him to shame. A bleak stretch of pasture land lay before them, dented by a faint wagon trail. The chirp of crickets rose on the dusty air. Weeds grew knee deep along the fence line, brown and brittle. Balls of Russian thistle lay caught in the wire. The tawny grass was pock-marked.

"Hail done that," said Sarah briefly.

In the distance rose four gaunt hills with strongly marked valleys between them.

"That's the Knuckle Hills you're looking at," she informed him. "Wrist River is down to the right of them, and at the end of that long slope is Ulna where we just come from."

"Come on! Let's get going!" Gottlieb snarled from the cab. "He can look at the beauty spots all winter!"

Handling the truck as though it were a spirited horse, Gottlieb rushed along the almost non-existent trail, making his passengers leap and jolt against each other on the hard seat, his wicked grin flashing in his dark earth-grimed face. At length a group of buildings came into view on a crossroad, a farmstead with house and barns and tilled fields, a church with its cross rising starkly into the sky, and a school with the sun shining blindingly on its wide row of windows. Sarah pointed encouragingly ahead. She and Dan had another gate to cope with. A stretch of road. And the truck stopped with a flourish inside the schoolyard beside a two-roomed shack.

Feeling battered and bruised, Dan got stiffly out, while Gottlieb darted to the back of his truck, unceremoniously flinging down the suitcase, the bedroll and the box of groceries, all unrecognisable with dust.

"Why you don't come to church once?" Sarah asked him, watching, while Dan winced as each of his possessions struck the ground.

"You say a prayer for me!" Gottlieb cried gaily, getting into the cab and backing the truck out of the yard.

3

"Well, here's your teacherage," said Sarah resignedly, as the truck rolled off, clattering and banging. "The women scrubbed it all out for you and the key is hanging on that nail by the window."

While Dan unlocked the door, she picked up the heavy suitcase as though it were nothing.

"You shouldn't be doing that," said Dan, shocked.

"It's quite a nice little place." Sarah took the suitcase inside without hearing him. "See, here's your stove and your food cupboards. Nice table and chair. And in the other room is a bed and drawers. There's coal in the coal shed out back by the barn, and kindling too."

Dan brought in the other things, setting them down on the clean floor. The place had been sweetened with soap and whitewash. He longed to get settled and go over to the school and take stock of things. "You better come to church," Sarah suggested. "It's just time."

"I wasn't thinking of going to church. I—I don't belong to the Brethren."

"I know that." Sarah smiled, her dimples softening her expression. "But this way you could meet everybody. They'll

sort of expect it, now they seen you coming here in the truck."
He felt an unexpected motherliness in her.

"You think I should go?"

"You don't need to go every Sabbath, Mr. Root. But this first day, it would be nice."

"Well, I'm ready if you are," he told her.

At the churchyard, people were arriving by wagon and truck, or on foot. The yard, marked by a fence of barbed wire, contained a small graveyard with weathered wooden crosses. Beyond this stood a little frame house separated from the church by a hedge of brown winter-killed trees.

"The preacher lives there, Philip Jebson," Sarah explained. "But he isn't here today, and Jud Zwick will do the preaching."

At the gate a man met them, a tall man with big shoulders, thinning fair hair, and gold-rimmed spectacles.

"Hello Herman," said Sarah dimpling. "Here's your new teacher."

"Good morning, Sarah," Herman greeted her, his eyes lingering on her face before he turned to Dan. He had a fair complexion, the kind that never tans, but burns to a permanent dull red. His high colour had deepened.

"Well," Sarah laughed, "I got to get in there. I play the organ, and I want to be ready." She left them.

"You're Mr. Ries?" Dan asked politely, reaching for the letter again, thinking, So this is the Hun. The one who is sweet on Sarah.

"Pleased to meet you," said Herman, thrusting out a strong hard hand. "So Gottlieb got you here all right!" He spoke with a strong Germanic accent. "I'll introduce you." He drew Dan along into the crowd. Soon the new teacher was shaking hands with the various parents of the children he would teach, the children themselves looking on, full of curiosity. "And here comes Jonas Leniuk, the chairman of the school board," Herman told him. "And his wife too."

Jonas Leniuk came through the gate a bit ahead of his wife, speaking briefly to neighbours as he passed them, quickly coming to Herman and Dan to be introduced. The other introductions had not really impressed Dan; he felt too tired to remember names and faces. But this was a man whom he would never forget. Jonas had removed his cap, showing the grey hair that grew thickly on his big rolling head. His face was dark, scored with lines, and lighted by greenish eyes in which the sun struck a yellow note. His English came thick and slow, but his gaze pierced Dan through and through.

"Thirty-six pupils you will have," he said slowly, measuring the young teacher. "You think you can handle?"

"Yes, of course."

"Six in high school. Your record from high school is good, good. Some beginners, not speaking the English yet. Then twenty-five children in other grades. You take a stick to them sometimes, maybe?"

"That is not the modern method."

Jonas smiled a little, turning as his wife came up beside them. "My wife, Kazmiri. She does not speak much of the English."

She nodded, touching Dan's hand with her fingertips and moved on. The Bolshevik woman, he thought with a thrill of excitement. A beautiful woman with a face of sorrows.

"And this is my daughter Fenna," said Jonas as a pretty young girl paused by them, looking shyly up at Dan, her bright hair shining, her skin glowing rose pink. "Last year she took some of Grade eleven. Now she wants to go on with it. But I am not so sure. She's growing up."

His own daughter, Dan thought. Yes, she looks like him somehow. The same eyes. But he's an ugly old coot, while she's —she's—lovely.

"Oh I do want to go on with school!" she pleaded. "I want to go right on and be a teacher."

Jonas looked thoughtful. "Well, we'll see about it. Where are the others?" he asked her.

"There's Prolet now with Mrs. White."

Briefly Dan met a small dark girl with a disarming grin and frizzy hair flying in the wind.

"Here's Naomi too," said Fenna as another sister came on the run, fearful of being late, stopping long enough to give Dan a slow smile, and drawl, "Pleased to meet you." Leota came last, climbing down from a wagon with another family. Keep hands off Leota, she's mine! Joe had said. But Dan saw that she was as shy as he himself.

"Well, we go in now, or we come late," said Jonas with a nod, going to join his womenfolk inside the church.

Dan slipped into a back seat at the end of a pew, glad of the coolness and the quiet. Almost at once, from the pulpit a voice like thunder gave out the hymn in German and in English. Dan looked up, startled, at the face of Jud Zwick, the lay preacher. This man, then, was Gottlieb Zwick's father. He had the same thick-set figure, but it was even thicker, especially through the chest and shoulders. The features were much the same too, but the nose looked as though it had been broken, more than once, Dan thought, and perhaps various teeth had been knocked out at the same time. Because he wouldn't fight back? Dan wondered. A roguish twinkle often passed over Jud's face with its crooked smile.

"*When Sang the Morning Stars!*" he boomed.

Dan opened the hymn book and found that it was in German and in English both. At the pedal organ, Sarah played over the air with strength and vigour. The congregation rose and sang. Dan had never heard such singing in a church. There was no choir, but the people themselves sang the parts, the rich bass notes, the high soprano, the tenor coming in sweetly, the alto a deep undertone of women's voices. Dan could sing well himself, but he stayed silent, listening, moved by the harmony and by the sincerity of the singing.

When the hymn was over, since the service proceeded in German, Dan let it wash peacefully over him. From where he sat, he could see the Leniuk family in a row on the curved pew. He studied them unobtrusively. The mother, the woman from Russia with her fine patrician face. The girl Leota looked like her, with the same delicate bone structure and tender mouth. He saw how the light caught Fenna's bright hair. Suddenly he caught Naomi watching him, and looked away, feeling his face flush. I'm scared stiff of a girl like that. Too sophisticated for me. Anyway, I haven't got time for women.

After another hymn, a long prayer followed. Then Jud Zwick began to speak in English. That must be for my sake, Dan thought, growing hot with embarrassment. The sermon told of Moses leading the Children of Israel through the wilderness, of the manna and the quail, of Moses striking the rock to give the people water.

"But food and water's not enough," said Jud tenderly. "That don't feed the soul. But the land that's promised is a land of honey too. Even if the land seems like a rock," he roared, "a desert rock, still there's honey in it. We've got to find that honey. We must open our eyes and see it. The honey is there all right, but it's up to us to find it. Even in the hardest life," said Jud as gently as a mother to her child, "Brother, Sister, there's sweetness!

"Now we'll sing a hymn about this honey. *There's Honey in the Rock.*"

Dan stumbled out into the hot sunshine, intending to get away, to escape to his teacherage and sort out his thoughts. But at the gate he felt a firm hand on his arm.

"Well, Mr. Root," said a cheery woman's voice behind him without a trace of an accent, "welcome to the Lily of the Valley District." He turned. "I'm Mrs. Zwick. But just call me Florrie. Everybody does." She took his hand in a warm clasp. She came only to his shoulder, a plump vigorous woman in her sixties, with many laughing lines creasing her freckled face, wisps of reddish grey hair blowing out from under a crazy straw hat jammed down on her head. The fallen woman, he thought, his heart racing. But anyone who looked less like a fallen woman he could not imagine. "How about coming over to our place for Sabbath dinner?" she asked.

"Oh, I don't want to be a bother, really."

"You're no bother! I put the whole dinner in the oven before we left, and it'll be cooking like mad. Come home with us in the wagon, and Gottlieb will run you back in the truck this evening."

"Gottlieb?" Dan swallowed. "But I'd be a nuisance."

"A nuisance, eh? We'll see about that. Come on, I'll bet you're hungry after that awful trip."

"Well, I—"

"We'll just wait a minute for my better half. He'll be right along . . . Leota . . . Naomi . . . God go with you . . . And with you . . . Did you meet these girls, Mr. Root?"

"Yes, I did," he answered hurriedly.

"I'm sorry Reuben isn't home right now," she said. "He's our younger son. He'll be coming around the beginning of November."

"God go with you," said Jonas, taking Jud's hand in farewell.

"And with you," Jud answered.

"It was a real nice sermon, Jud," Florrie declared as her husband untethered the horses and climbed up into the wagon. "Real nice." She looked over the desolate land, brown, dried out, hailed, soil-drifted. "True, too," she smiled. "Just as true as anything can be."

"Welcome, Teacher," said Jud with his crooked grin. "Welcome to our country, and to the honey that's in it!"

Chapter Two

I

DURING the first two months of school, varying reports about the new teacher drifted home to parents in the Lily of the Valley District. That he was sure strict. That he made the children work. That he liked singing and had actually written them a song of their own, words and music. That he was no good at baseball, and that he frequently forgot to eat any lunch. From his thirty-six pupils he gradually had won a grudging respect, even a secret liking.

It was Fenna who told him about the Hallowe'en Party.

"We always have one in the school, every year," she said smiling up at him with her bright look. "It's to get the young people together, after harvest."

"A dance?" he asked nervously.

"Well, games and then dancing too."

Herman came to be the chaperone, and a big crowd turned up, taking over the school and the teacherage. The girls brought staggering heaps of sandwiches and cake. A washtub of water boiled on the teacherage stove for coffee. All five Leniuk girls arrived with Gottlieb in his wagon, bringing cakes more tempting than any others. With some trepidation, Dan had prepared funny tricks and games. And eating apples from strings, a couple at each apple. He felt rewarded by the laughter and fun. For blind-man's buff, a blindfolded Gottlieb made the girls run shrieking before him until he captured Naomi in a great sweep of his arms, taking her off into the darkness of the cloakroom for a forfeit. At lunchtime, the teenage girls of the school did the serving, each intriguing in a little black mask that just covered the eyes. Then Billy White began to strum his guitar, and two of the Gerlizt boys tuned up their fiddles. It was time for dancing.

Even in a crowd, the Leniuk girls stood out. There was a great family resemblance between Sarah and Leota, both with sleek, dark hair parted in the middle and drawn back into an elaborate braided knot, both with dark eyes and upward slanting brows. But while Sarah's colouring glowed richly on cheek and lip and her dimples were deep and her figure ripe, Leota was pale, slender, and withdrawn. Yet her face had strong beautiful lines. In her left cheek there lurked the trace of a dimple which showed but rarely.

Naomi's dark hair curled richly to her shoulders, with little tendrils escaping across her forehead. With the same bold colouring as Sarah's, she had a smiling, good-natured, slumbering look. Although a large safety pin held her gaudy dress closed at the side, and holes appeared in the heels of her stockings when she walked, yet she looked as vivid as a wild tiger lily or an Indian paint brush. " Naomi's best in the fields," the women said of her, " and Leota's best in the house. But Sarah's best in everything."

Prolet sat alone, the coppery shade of her dress with its gold buttons, making a splash of colour on the bench. Her short hair grew thickly, like a bush, in a tight, dark, frizz that stood out from her head as though it possessed a life of its own. In her small pointed face with its gallant turned up nose, her large mouth showed rather fine but prominent teeth whenever she spoke or smiled. Glasses, with the cheapest of round metal rims that money could buy, lay like a deformity across her face.

Even in her black mask, Fenna attracted attention. The brassy overtones of her hair caught the light wherever she moved. She wore it in two braids at the sides, caught at the back of her head with a clip. The braids brought out the various lights and shades of her hair, while the rest of it hung to her shoulders, slightly waving at the ends. Although her features were nothing to be compared with Leota's, her complexion was lovely, and such a shining look lighted her face as to make almost everyone believe her to be breath-takingly beautiful.

As soon as the dancing began, Herman at once claimed Sarah for a partner.

"When are you going to marry me, Sair?" he asked, guiding her expertly among the dancers.

She dimpled, laughing easily. "You must get tired asking."

"I never get tired asking," he assured her seriously.

"I wish Reuben was home," said Leota to Naomi as they stood on the sidelines. "He's just a kid, but he always gives me a nice dance or two."

"Listen!" Naomi's eyes glistened. "I think I hear a truck. Maybe it's the Ulna gang."

A few minutes later, with shouts and ribald laughter, a new group of young people invaded the cloakroom. Uncertain on his feet, with beery breath, Joe Weiman appeared among the dancers, searching for Leota, while his companions looked about for entertainment. Wally Lunt, the stationmaster's son, made straight for Naomi. With a shrill laugh, Ada Pearl Fox clapped Gottlieb on the shoulder.

"Long time no see!" she cried.

"You got the wrong brother there, Ada Pearl!" shouted Joe. "You gotta wait for Reuben!"

"Oh *him*!" Ada Pearl shrugged. "Reuben's not coming home any more," she said loudly. "I just had a letter."

Shrinking back in her corner, Leota felt her heart contract. She looked curiously at the girl from the post office with her carefully made up face and her unnaturally golden hair; and picturing Ada Pearl opening a letter from Reuben, she found the idea intolerably painful.

"Leota!" shouted Joe at the other end of the room.

Just then Nathan Zimmerman came in. Slight and dark, with hooked features that would have looked well stamped upon a coin, he seemed alien in the crowd, yet distinctive and quietly strong. His eye fell upon Leota.

"Like to dance?" he asked softly.

Suddenly Philip Jebson, the young preacher, filled the doorway. His eyes flashed with a fanatical light. Wordlessly he exchanged an understanding look with Fenna. She came to him as though she had been called.

"I heard the truck and the yelling clear over to the manse," he explained. "Thought I'd better come and see if I was needed."

She gazed raptly up at his handsome face, his perfectly controlled curly fair hair.

"We had a wonderful time," she told him, "until the Ulna gang came."

His glance scorched her from head to foot, taking in the intriguing little black mask, and the vivid green dress which she had made over from one of Sarah's to fit her own trim figure.

"I'm surprised, Fenna," he muttered. "Your appearance is —well, it's very worldly. Very worldly."

She hung her bright head.

"Mama thought it was just right for a young girl."

"You have to take care, Fenna," he said low and intensely, as dancing couples brushed past them. "I've just come home from performing a most distasteful marriage. A baby on the way. These young people should realise that love comes *after* marriage."

"Oh yes," whispered Fenna, unstrung at the mention of babies and marriage.

"Fenna!" Mr. Root called.

Quickly she went to the teacher.

"I thought we'd feed them, and perhaps that will quiet them down," Dan said, setting a large pot of coffee down on the desk. "Please get some sandwiches out of that box and put them on plates. There are still clean cups in the cupboard. Maybe coffee would sober them up. There's plenty of cake left."

"We'll let them dance a bit," Herman suggested coming by. "Then I'll wave the lantern and holler for the Home Sweet Home."

Watching the others, Prolet wondered how her evening would turn out. When she saw Nathan Zimmerman asking Leota to dance, she felt glad for Leota's sake that Joe had not yet found her. But then just as they glided near Prolet, Joe thumped Nathan meaningfully on the shoulder to make him relinquish Leota. As he did so, Nathan turned, to find himself face to face with Prolet. It would have been most ungracious of him to have gone in search of another girl, and it was not in Nathan's mannerly old worldliness to be ungracious. Smiling, he bent towards her.

"Will you give me the pleasure?" he asked.

Delighted, she rose, reflecting that it was truly wonderful to dance with someone slender and slight, not too much taller than herself; for often she got landed with a kindly person like Herman who insisted upon taking pity on her, but who towered so huge that she had difficulty in dancing with him at all. Nathan was just right.

"You're Prolet, aren't you?" he smiled.

"That's me."

"It's such a different, pretty name, I always think."

"Maybe you wouldn't think so if you knew where it came from," she remarked, looking over his shoulder at Joe and Leota dancing near.

"Where does it come from, then?"

"It's short for proletariat," she laughed. "See, Papa turned Communist when I was on the way, so that's why he named me Prolet. There wasn't much grub around neither when I was coming, so that's how I turned out the runt of the family."

"But that's fascinating!" cried Nathan. "Your folks were in Russia, weren't they? My father was in the University at Kiev during the riots of 1905. He actually knew a man who named his daughter Dima after Dialectical Materialism."

"If I ever have a little girl, I'll call her Rose or Violet," Prolet declared. Then she rushed on, "Well then, see, Papa didn't like being a communist when they started taking away his land. So he tried to change back. So then, he got killed."

"Look, they're giving out coffee," said Nathan, holding her tightly by the arm. "Let's go and sit over there and have some."

"Well, of course, I did have lunch you know."

"Have some more."

"I was hoping I'd see you soon, one of these days," Prolet confided as they sat down. "See, I have an idea I want to ask you about."

As a matter of fact, the idea had flashed into her mind with the speed of lightning at that very moment.

"Ask away," Nathan invited, accepting two cups of coffee from Dan, and handing one to his partner. "What's up?"

"When I was in town the other day," she said, slowly stirring the coffee, "I couldn't help hearing your mother talking to Mrs. Gerlitz."

Nathan stared at her in astonishment, waiting for her to continue.

"Your mother says, 'I won't be able to go on in the store much longer,' she says. 'It's my feet. And you know, I'm just so tired.' Then she says, 'These high school kids helping after school, that's not enough. We need someone full time,' she says." Prolet took a deep breath. "I was just wondering, would someone like me do for the job?"

She saw him taking a good look at her, at the awful glasses, the flying frizzy hair, the small insignificant figure. She waited, her whole future at stake, thrilling to her wonderful idea, wondering why she had not thought of it before, when Fenna suddenly appeared with a plate of sandwiches, Fenna looking like a lovely spring flower, bewitching in her little black mask.

"Don't you know me, Pro?" she asked. "It's me, Fenna."

"Well, thanks for the sandwich," said Prolet tensely.

Nathan didn't seem to notice Fenna at all, and when the music started up again, the younger girl moved away with the plate.

"It's something I can't decide all in a moment, just like that," he said as people around them got up to dance. "Mother and I really thought of getting a man."

"But a girl, a girl might be better with the—the women customers," suggested Prolet.

"That's quite true, especially when Mother retires . . . Let's dance, Prolet. We can talk better that way."

"It's a two-step," said Prolet. "We'll have to talk pretty fast to keep up!"

"We'll take it slow," he told her, gliding into long steps while couples all around them bobbed around like so many grasshoppers.

"Someone like you might be able to help me with the buying," he said, thinking out loud while they danced. "Mother always got just cotton house-dresses, but I started a little rack of nicer dresses for parties, you know the kind of thing. You'd be surprised how fast they go." He held her at arm's length a moment. "Now that dress you're wearing, I'd say really has style. You'd know what to pick."

"I'd love it!" cried Prolet.

She could see that he was considering, weighing things up,

being infected with something of her own excitement.

"And you know, another thing is," Prolet put in, "if a dress won't fit a customer just right, I know how to make it fit."

"Of course you have to remember we sell a lot of other things besides dresses. Everything from soup to nuts. And I don't mean just the nuts you eat."

"I know all about nuts. And bolts. Everything on a farm I know about," said Prolet confidently.

As the two-step ended, they stood absently clapping their hands.

"Home Sweet Home Waltz!" Herman called, going outside with the lantern. "Home Sweet Home dance!" he shouted again in the darkness.

"He's sure breaking it up fast," said Nathan ruefully.

He seemed to take it for granted he would have the last dance with Prolet.

"Listen," he said as they waltzed off together. "I'd like you to come and have supper with Mother and myself sometime. Soon. Then we can talk it all over. I know she's going to retire, but she'll want to be consulted. How about it? When could you come?"

"Friday," Prolet decided quickly. "The day after tomorrow. That is, if I can catch a ride into town."

"Catch a ride, nothing. I'm coming to get you in our old car."

"Coming to get me?"

"Of course. What time would suit you best? Four o'clock?"

"Yes, four o'clock would be just right."

They smiled at each other like conspirators, Prolet for the first time becoming aware of the warmth of his slender hand holding hers, and of the softness of his gaze.

When Joe saw coffee coming, he gripped Leota's wrist and led her over to the sidelines. She thought it best not to make a scene, but to go with him and sit down sociably. She wished he would let go of her wrist for she hated his touch, but he held on, with his coffee cup in his other hand. She also took a cup, but her mouth still felt dry, and an odd pressure on her chest made it difficult to breathe.

She was glad to see that Prolet was having coffee with

Nathan. Ada Pearl and Gottlieb had their heads close together while Sarah danced off haughtily with Herman. Fenna helped to serve, and Naomi was nowhere to be seen. Leota felt alone and desperate.

"Well. Peaches, long time no see," Joe was saying.

Scalding her mouth on the coffee, Leota did not answer.

"I tell all the guys," Joe confided loudly, "I tell all the guys, keep hands off Leota. She's mine!"

Nervously the girl set down her cup.

"Boy, I know how to pick 'em!" Joe boasted, smacking his lips.

"They're going to dance," she pointed out, as the boys began playing *Red River Valley*.

"You wanna dance?" he asked with a great show of gallantry. "Sure, kid. Anything your little heart desires."

He was a good dancer, and dancing, she did not feel quite so conspicuous. But if only there were someone to whom she could give a look of entreaty. If only Reuben were home! He was just a kid of course, but an awfully nice one, and so quick to understand. But there wasn't anyone. And Joe held her so disgustingly tightly. He would kiss her right on the dance floor if he got a chance.

When the foxtrot had ended, Leota managed to slip away through the crowd. She could hear Joe shouting, "Get your partners for a two-step!" while Ada Pearl shrilled, "Atta boy, Joe! Put some life into this old party!"

Leota darted through the door, running lightly past the front steps and around the corner of the building. The chill of the October evening penetrated her thin dress. In the darkness she could not see ahead, and so collided with a couple who stood together kissing. With a little cry of dismay, she turned back a few steps, only to meet Joe face to face. She knew it was Joe because he wore a white shirt with the sleeves rolled up, and the shirt stood out in the dark. Her own dress, a pale blue with a round neck and puffed sleeves, was an easy mark for him.

"Trying to hide on me, eh?" he laughed, wrapping his arms about her. "Come on, frozen face!"

"Let me go! Let me go!" Leota gasped frantically.

"Sure, I'll let you go. In a minute."

She fought like a wild thing, but he held her fast with one arm, his free hand mussing her hair while he laughed and talked in a soft oily voice.

"Real wild cat, ain't you?" he said admiringly. "Real little wild cat." And his hand slid from her hair to her shoulder, and then to cupping her breast. In a flash her teeth sank into his arm, while she kicked out with her sharp-toed slipper, giving him a cutting blow on the shin.

"Jees!" As his hold loosened for a fraction of a second, she slithered away.

"Home Sweet Home dance!" yelled Herman, waving a lantern along the path.

"Breaking it up awful early, ain't you?" Joe asked, coming innocently into the arc of light shed by the lantern.

"Well, just a kids' party, really," said Herman, taking Joe back into the schoolhouse with him.

From the shadows, thankful to be hidden from curious eyes, Leota saw the two men disappear. Crying quietly, she stumbled over the uneven ground to Gottlieb's wagon, shivering as she waited for the party to be over. It was Fenna who appeared first.

"Oh Fen," Leota whispered, leaning over the wagon box, "please go get my coat for me out of the cloakroom."

"Why you don't get it yourself?" Fenna asked sulkily

But she was still too much the youngest sister to raise many objections. Presently she returned with the coat. The other sisters arrived too, yawning and talking, while Gottlieb went to fetch the horses from the barn.

2

In the darkness of the prairie night, the wagon went lurching and rumbling along the hard ruts of the road, the clip-clopping of the horses' feet, the jingle of harness, the noisy clattering of wheels, the knocking of iron on stone, echoing over the wide countryside. In the heavily clouded sky only a few stars shone, giving scant light, but Gottlieb knew the trail well. The horses trotted briskly occasionally breaking into a canter when he struck the wagon box with the ends of the lines. Beside him Sarah sat on an upturned wooden crate, for she was taller than

Gottlieb, and seated, she felt small and protected. They talked together low and intimately, while behind them, in the hay spread out on the floor of the wagon, the other four Leniuk sisters chatted and laughed, or broke into snatches of song. Now and then, far away in the distance, some farm dog barked his disapproval of their passing at so late an hour, but otherwise they were a little moving world to themselves with the dark empty land stretching out on every hand.

"We better shut up now," remarked Naomi. "I can tell by the slant of the hill we're nearly home. Don't want to wake up Jonas."

"Oh, he'll wake up. But it's all right if we go with Gottlieb and Sarah," Fenna argued. "He said it was all right."

"Fen! Get down and open the gate!" Sarah commanded from her seat beside Gottlieb.

"Oh you! I always get the dirty work!" Fenna protested, climbing down over the wheel.

"Leave it open!" Gottlieb shouted. "I'll shut it when I go back."

With Fenna catching a ride clinging to the end of the wagon box, they drove into the yard. She had scarcely jumped down when Leota, Prolet, and Naomi joined her, hurrying to the dark house, by tacit agreement leaving Sarah alone with Gottlieb. They entered at the back door which opened on a level with the ground to a little platform inside, with steps leading downwards to the basement and upwards to the kichen. In silence, making only the softest scuffing of shoes on the stairs, they crept in one behind the other up to the kitchen, and through the curtained doorway where stairs led to their bedrooms in the loft. Then not a sound stirred the stillness of the house.

Deftly, Gottlieb turned the wagon in the yard, heading the horses towards the gate again. Making the lines secure, he reached into the breast pocket of his jacket for a cigarette.

"It was a nice party," said Sarah.

"Kid stuff," Gottlieb answered, cupping his hands around a lighted match.

By the flame's light, Sarah saw his face, the face of the man she loved, the strong, black lashes lowered, the hard line of the lips holding a cigarette, and beyond him, blackness. Sometimes she almost hated him, but at other times, as now, just the sudden sight of him would set her heart throbbing. The match blew out in the wind.

"Damn," he muttered.

"I must go in," she said without moving.

In the darkness he kissed her hard on the mouth, until she was breathless, his right arm tight about her neck, his free hand holding the cigarette. Covering his face with kisses, she flung her arms about him, but they found no hold on the slippery back of his windproof jacket.

"Oh Gottlieb," she faltered, "why you don't always be nice to me? You was flirting like everything with Naomi and Ada Pearl tonight."

"I wasn't doing nothing of the kind!"

Detecting the familiar irritable note coming into his voice, she said swiftly, "I'm glad Mr. Root's here. He makes things different. And it was nice, just like when we was kids with the girls in the back of the wagon, singing . . ."

But even as she said it, sadness came with memory. When you start looking back, then you're old, she thought.

"Well, I got to shove off," Gottlieb said brusquely, disentangling himself from her arms. "Mind shutting the gate for me, Sair Girl?"

Stifling her passion and hurt, she climbed out of the wagon. His goodnight kiss had softened her, even though it left her more wounded than comforted. He does care, she thought as he drove through. He wouldn't kiss me like that if he didn't.

"I won't be seeing you for awhile," he called down in the gloom. "Be pretty busy up at Bronson's for a bit. Couple of weeks maybe?"

"O.K.," she answered, trying to sound cheery.

"Be seeing you."

Over the rattle of the wagon, she could just hear his last words, which brought her a little reassurance. Replacing the post and the wire loop that held it, she walked slowly to the house. A wandering wind, crisp with the hint of frost, fanned her hot cheeks, while the enormousness of the prairie night covered her. The vast acres seemed to breathe and sleep, and stir in their slumber. The banging and clattering of the wagon wheels was extraordinarily loud in the quiet. At the door she stood listening to the sounds, for they brought Gottlieb close. Then she went in like a shadow, removing her shoes at the entrance, stepping softly in stockinged feet up to the kitchen.

Inside, the light of a lantern struck her in the eyes, and she beheld Jonas in his long underwear, staring across at her.

"You scared me," she gasped, dropping her shoes with a clatter.

Even in his underwear with the top two buttons undone, showing the black hair on his chest, Jonas had a certain presence. He rolled his big grey head in her direction, his light eyes taking in every detail about her. Eyes like Gottlieb's. Like Fenna's. He saw her flushed face and proud defiance, the large cheap, gipsyish hoop-earrings that swung and glinted in the lantern light.

"Didn't hear no wagon going back at first," he explained. "Heard somebody come in . . ." He shrugged, lowering the wick in the lantern, preparing to blow it out.

"You don't need to get so suspicious," she hissed in a whisper.

Sarah was the only one of the girls who dared to talk back to him, and when she did, she felt as though she fought a battle for the whole family, Mama included.

"I never got suspicious of you yet," he said, his patience giving way. He turned up the flame again. "What I want to know is, did Gottlieb speak to you about getting married?"

"That's my business!" answered Sarah, outraged.

"It is my business what goes on in this house," said Jonas, staring her down. "Ten year now he courts you. Why he don't marry you?"

"The—the crops, they're always so bad. You know that. We can't get married till times get better."

Completely unconscious of his appearance, Jonas took a chair back between his great hands.

"This year Gottlieb done pretty good, Jud told me. With his wheat and his pigs. He could fix up that granary for a place to live. A start. Make it tight for winter."

"He's going to work at Bronson's for the winter," said Sarah contemptuously. "Old man Bronson can't find a better man for all those horses and cattle. And he pays twenty dollars a month cold cash."

Honey in the Rock

The chair looked frail in Jonas's hands as he gripped it.

"Bronson's got a house for the hired man," he told her. "Always Bronson likes best a hired man to be married and bring his wife."

"It's not your business," said Sarah tersely, feeling on the point of breaking down.

"If he don't mean marriage now, you bust up with him," Jonas ordered, letting go the chair and picking up the lantern.

"I won't!" she defied him.

"He's not coming round here after you no more," said Jonas, his face dark in the shadows. "If you don't tell him to go, I'll tell him."

"You can't stop me seeing Gottlieb!"

"He's not coming round here after you no more."

"I'll go get another job!" cried Sarah desperately. "Now Prolet's left Mrs. White, she needs a girl, with another baby coming along."

"That's up to you," said Jonas.

Standing before him, struggling for self-control, Sarah felt a great wave of loneliness. She alone of her sisters understood the loss of their own father, for she alone had really known him. Certain vivid memories remained in the back of her mind to leap out unbidden at times like this. Disdaining the figure in the long underwear, she saw instead her handsome laughing father, young and gay, singing a catchy little song to a lute-like instrument. She saw him talking impressively to a roomful of important people. She saw him embracing Mama, coming home after a journey with gifts for them all. She had been his favourite, the precocious eldest, following him everywhere. That he had died for his beliefs, leaving a helpless woman with four daughters to fend for, only rendered him more wonderful in Sarah's imagination. Papa, she thought, refusing to weep before this loutish tyrant her mother had married. Oh, Papa.

"So I got to marry Gottlieb or get out!" she cried. "You just want to get rid of me!"

She rushed past him, through the curtained doorway and up to the loft.

Chapter Three

I

"I THINK I hear a car now."

By the sitting-room fire, Kazmiri lifted her head in the lamplight, letting her knitting lie in her lap.

"I'll look out the kitchen window!" Naomi sprang up, going into the darkened kitchen.

"Let's hope they get here soon, or Jonas might come," said Leota nervously.

Embroidering a cross-stitch design on a white bath towel, Sarah shook her head. "They've lots of time yet."

"There's a car all right," Naomi called from the kitchen. "But it isn't coming in here. It's turning off. I guess that wasn't them yet. She must be having a good time, eh?" she added, coming back into the sitting-room. "Having dinner with Mama Zimm."

"Prolet looked nice, anyways," Fenna remarked, turning the pages of her history book. "In my best silk stockings, Leota's nice red blouse, and Sarah's gold beads."

Sarah held up her embroidery needle like a weapon.

"It's fine about the beads," she declared. "Just so Prolet has a good time on her first date."

"And the blouse too," said Leota.

Naomi scooped another shovelful of coal on to the fire.

"With his mother along, she's sure to have a good time."

"It's quite right, to see his mother," said Kazmiri, going on with her knitting. "If I had a son, I'd want to see the girl he takes out."

"Oh Mama!" giggled Naomi, seating herself on a cushion on the floor. "Don't be so old-fashioned."

The click of the kitchen door as it closed made them all jump.

"Who is it?" Kazmiri called, keeping her voice calm.

"It's me."

Drenched and dripping, with a man's suit coat thrown over her shoulders, Prolet came into the room. For a moment, they all stared, stricken into silence.

"So he tried to drown you!" Naomi cried at last. "Look at her! She's been in the creek. Have a nice swim?"

"Prolet!" Mama came towards her, trying desperately to understand.

"My best silk stockings!" wailed Fenna. "Look at them. The whole knee gone, and runs all over!"

"I've got a pair you can have. New ones," soothed Leota, holding back the young sister.

"What happened? Tell us what happened!" shouted Sarah above the hubbub.

"Yes," agreed Mama. "What has happened to you, Prolet? Get these wet things off right now. Naomi, bring that blanket off my bed. She'll catch her death of cold."

"For gosh sake tell us what happened!" cried Sarah.

"I fell into the creek," Prolet stated flatly, coming in to the warmth of the fire.

"You fell in the creek." Sarah sighed with exasperation.

"Your beads, Sarah. I'm so sorry. The string broke . . . They're all at the bottom." Prolet shivered with cold.

"They cost fifty cents." Sarah waved her hand, dismissing the beads. "Let them go, but tell us what happened!"

"Here!" Naomi put the blanket round Prolet's shoulders. "Now sit down here on my cushion, that's the warmest place. Tell us all about it. Why did he want to drown you?"

Prolet sat down by the fire, looking up at them, her untamable hair shining with drops of water. Leota spread out the wet things to dry.

"Be careful of the coat!" warned Prolet. "It's *his*!"

"I'll treat it like a crate of new-laid eggs," Leota promised, going to find a hanger.

"Listen, Prolet," said Sarah severely, "here you go off on a date in Fenna's best stockings, in Leota's blouse and my beads . . . You come back wet like you took a swim in the creek, and you don't tell us what happened!"

Prolet laughed shakily.

"I told him not to drive into the yard, because Jonas might be on the way home and see the lights. So I says, "Just cut off on the turn here, and I'll walk the rest of the way."

"I seen the car turning off," Naomi said. "I figured that it couldn't be you."

"Then we got out to walk across the field," Prolet went on, "and I don't know what happened. I just slipped into the creek, walking too near the edge."

"It must be love," said Fenna with an exaggerated sigh.

"Maybe it is," Prolet agreed. "Only he'll think I'm such a nut. Maybe he won't never come back."

"He'll come back to get his coat," Leota comforted her.

"He said he'd come back. He says, 'I'll be back Sunday night for sure'."

"Before you fell in the creek," said Mama, taking up her knitting again, "was it nice with him? Did you have a nice supper?"

"Yes," said Naomi, "how was it with Mama Zimm?"

"Awful nice." Prolet thought for a moment, gazing into space, the light of adventure and happiness shining in her face. "See, I never told you what this date was all about, did I? I asked Nathan at the dance if I could work at the store."

"At the store?" Sarah echoed.

"See, I heard Mrs. Zimm one day saying how her feet was so tired, and how they needed someone full time. So I figured I could do work like that. Much nicer than milking cows. So at the dance, I asked Nate."

"But why you didn't ask Mrs. Zimm herself?" asked Sarah.

"Well, I figured, if I'm going to be turned down, I'd sooner it was him than her."

"I'd feel the same," said Leota.

"So Nate said he'd take me to have supper with his mother and we'd talk it all over."

"Oh, it was that kind of a date!" said Fenna disgustedly. "Here I thought you really had a date. Borrowing my best silk stockings and ruining them!"

"Did you get the job?" Naomi asked eagerly.

Prolet pulled the blanket around her shoulders.

"I—I don't know. I'm not sure."

"What did she say?" Sarah demanded with energy. "You should speak up for yourself, Pro,"

"Was she nice to you, Prolet?" Kazmiri asked anxiously.

"Mama, I never knew a woman so nice to me. We had the best little supper. They got it fixed up so pretty behind the store there. Mind you, even a refrigerator! And such pretty dishes. So we ate our supper, and then I helped with the dishes, and we talked all about this and that."

"About the job in the store?" Sarah asked.

"Oh, no, not about the job."

"But you said you was going to have supper with his mother and talk all about it."

"I know. But we didn't talk about it. After supper and dishes, then we sat in the sitting-room and had coffee. I felt just like a lady with the radio on, and music. Well then it got time for Nate to get the car started to take me home. So when he went out, I says to Mrs. Zimm, 'You know I wanted to work in the store.' And she says, 'Just you wait, dear, Nate will tell you all about it on the way home'."

"So then he told you he wasn't too sure?" Leota asked.

"First of all, he didn't say nothing. We kept on driving. Then we got to that long road by Gerlitz's pasture. So we turned in to the pasture apiece where the fence is down. Then we parked."

"You parked!" Naomi struck herself on the forehead with the palm of her hand. "She sat in a parked car, in the dark, with Zimm!"

"Hush!" said Mama.

"So I says to him, 'Do I get the job!' Well, he just sat there and didn't say nothing. Then I says, 'I guess I'm just too ugly'."

The girls looked at their sister in sympathetic silence. But suddenly Prolet's laughter bubbled up.

"Then he says, 'Stop saying you're ugly! You're not ugly,' he says. 'You're not ugly at all.' Then he says, 'You used to come into the store with eyelashes half a foot long. What happened to them?' he says. He took my glasses off and I told him about that guy in Ulna that cut off my eyelashes. 'See, they didn't fit under the glasses,' I says. And he says, 'You mean to tell me that guy cut off your eyelashes, lovely eyelashes like that?' he says. 'With a pair of nail scissors? I could kill him! That guy just don't know nothing about giving proper glasses'." Prolet removed the offending spectacles, looking at them critically. "He tells me in Calgary you can get glasses that don't touch your eyelashes. Nice ones without any rims, that hardly show they're on."

"They would cost lots of money, too," said Sarah.

"Well, then I says, 'It must be my hair that's wrong.' And he says, 'There's nothing wrong with your hair.' He says, 'I got ideas about your hair. A good hairdresser in Calgary could fix that so nice all the girls would be jealous!'"

"*He's* got ideas about your hair!" cried Fenna in shocked tones. "What kind of a guy is he?"

"He's been around," said Prolet.

"How's that good hairdresser going to fix it?" asked Naomi.

"Well, he says I should get it cut off real short, clipped, he says. And then have little curls close to my head all over. He says I got the right shaped head for it."

"How could he tell about the shape of your head with all that hair sticking out the way it is?" Sarah demanded.

"Oh, he could tell, with his hands."

"With his hands!" Leota gasped, blushing.

"He took her in his arms, like this!" said Naomi, embracing a pillow. "Just like in the movies! Did he kiss you too?"

"Mind your business!" Prolet retorted, turning her back.

"But what about the job, Pro?" Mama asked.

"Well, I says, 'If I got my glasses and hair all fixed up, would I be O.K. to work in the store?' Then," said Prolet, looking around at their startled faces, "then he asked me to marry him."

"Oh no, Pro!" said Sarah. "You got it all wrong. A man don't ask you to marry him after dancing three times with you, and one date."

"What did he say, Pro?" Mama asked quietly.

"He says, 'Will you marry me?' I couldn't get that wrong, could I? He says, 'See Mother and I figured we'd get a man. But if it was you,' he says, 'and Mother goes to Calgary to live with her sister like she wants to, well, then we'd really have to get married, Prolet,' he says."

"Oh that kind of a proposal," said Fenna. "He just wants you for help in the store, and no pay!"

"It's just business!" cried Sarah angrily.

"But he held her head in his hands," hummed Naomi.

"He's nice," said Leota. "Gentle, sort of. He'd be a good husband."

"Did you tell him 'yes' right away?" Fenna asked scornfully, while Mama gazed thoughtfully at Prolet.

"No," answered Prolet. "I says to him, 'Look', I says, 'I got to tell you I'm not strong like Naomi and Sarah. I pretty near keeled over working at Mrs. White's milking all them cows and doing that big garden, so I could buy my glasses. And,' I says, 'having a whole lot of kids like that would just about kill me.' So then he says, 'Don't be silly,' he says. 'No need to have a baby every year. There's family planning'."

"You talked about having babies!" asked Fenna in horror.

"Well, if you're going to marry somebody, you can talk about babies. What's wrong with that?"

"What is this—this family planning?" asked Mama.

"He says it's just that you have a baby when you're good and ready to, not every nine or ten months like some."

The Leniuk sisters held their breath as one, tense and silent. Mama rocked in her chair.

"It wasn't like that in my time," she said. "In my time, we got married and then the babies came."

"So then, you said you'd marry him?" Sarah asked, her cheeks flaming.

Prolet huddled down in the blanket. "No. I says, 'Well, I know I'm not good looking. Even with decent glasses and my hair fixed, I wouldn't be pretty,' I says."

"Why you didn't just say 'Yes'?" Fenna demanded.

"I don't know," said Prolet. "Honest, I don't know. I sure wanted to."

"You wanted to be sure he meant it," suggested Leota.

"Yes, that's right," said Prolet. "Maybe I wanted him to coax me a bit."

"Did he?" asked Naomi.

"He says, 'You look O.K. to me just like you are,' he says. 'Only if you want to get decent glasses and your hair done to make you feel better, that's all right with me.' 'Well then,' I says, 'but would it please your mother?' And he says, 'Yes, she likes you, I could see that.' Well then I says, 'But you'd have to speak to Jonas. We couldn't get married without telling my folks!'"

"What did he say to that?" asked Naomi excitedly.

"He just couldn't come and tell Jonas, 'Can I marry Prolet?'" Sarah groaned, thinking of her own predicament.

"Tell us," urged Mama.

"I says, 'Course I know I'm free, white, and over twenty-one, but when you get married you don't want to just go off like that.' And he says, 'No, I got no intentions of just going off,' he says. 'When you get married it's nothing to be ashamed of. You can tell the whole world,' he says. He tells me he don't mind talking to Jonas. He says Jonas is a decent respectable man that always pays his bills. Even when times get hard. Not like some. And he's coming on Sunday night to speak to Jonas."

"Wheeee!" Naomi let out a long breath. "I'm gonna be right here in the front seat to see what happens!"

"I can't believe it," said Sarah. "After three times dancing with you, and one date."

"Just for a wife to work in the store," scoffed Fenna, going back to her history book with a great show of nonchalance.

"Oh Pro," Leota breathed. "I hope it all turns out right."

"How can it turn out right, with Jonas?" sighed Sarah.

"Would it please you, Mama?" Prolet asked meekly.

After knitting a few stitches in silence, Mama said, "Well, it seems he's honest and doesn't mean wrong. But I don't know Pro. You don't really know this young man. You want to marry someone that you—that you love, don't you? It seems he wants somebody in the store, and it would be very sensible for him to marry like that. But what about *you*?"

"I love him," said Prolet firmly. "I love him."

"And he is a—a Jew," Mama added.

"I love him," Prolet declared.

"How can you be so sure?" Sarah demanded.

"I'm sure," said Prolet, falling into a dream with a smile on her lips.

"What will Jonas think, Mama?" Leota asked.

"We have to wait to see that," said Kazmiri carefully. "But I'd be glad, Prolet, if it would make you happy."

"Only she fell in the creek and ruined everything, maybe," Fenna reminded them sharply.

"He'll think I'm such a nut," Prolet giggled. "Slipping into the creek like that. Just didn't see where I was going! But he says last thing to me, he says, 'I'll be back Sunday night for sure.' See, he couldn't come tomorow, because Saturday night's the big night in the store. So he had to wait until Sunday."

"He'll come," comforted Leota. "He's got to get his coat back, you know."

"Is it drying up?" asked Prolet, getting to her feet and pulling the blanket around her. "He'll be so cold driving home without it."

"Sure, he'll die of pneumonia on the way, and you'll never see him no more," teased Naomi.

"What about your nice new brown suit you made?" Leota asked. "That's real wet still. Don't you care about it?"

"Oh that. It's good stuff. It won't shrink. I better put these things away before Jonas comes." She took Nathan's coat into loving hands.

"Are you all warm again, Pro?" Mama asked.

"Never so warm in my life." They heard her laughing as she stumbled over the tail end of the blanket on her way upstairs.

2

"Do I look all right?" Prolet asked anxiously, twirling before the small mirror of the dresser in the lamplight of the loft bedroom. "It's my prettiest dress, and anyways, it's the one I wore to the Hallowe'en party when I first met him. He says it has style."

"You look lovely," Leota assured her.

"You need just a bit of lipstick," Sarah advised. "Let me put it on for you. There!"

"What about some perfume?" Naomi asked. "Here's some stuff they call *Heart Throb* out of the catalogue."

"Get away with that!" Sarah cried. "You'll knock us all dead with the smell."

"Did they finish their coffee?" Prolet whispered as Fenna appeared at the top of the stairs.

"Oh yes. They went out to the barn to talk about the money for the Christmas concert. That's what Philip and Herman came over for," Fenna explained patiently. "My gosh, d'you have to go and put on your party dress?"

"Of course she does!" snapped Sarah. "You mind your business."

"My hands are like two dead fish!" Prolet held cold fingers against her burning cheeks. "I near died when Herm and Philip had to come over. They sat there hours with a cup of coffee. I figured they'd still be there when poor Nate comes to speak his piece to Jonas!"

"Well, they went out to the barn now," said Fenna, brushing her hair.

"Oh, I hope Jonas gets back in before Nate comes." Prolet wrung her hands.

"Don't worry. He'll come the minute the car drives into the yard." Leota got up quickly. "I'll go down and set the sitting-room straight now the men are gone."

"Just so long he don't bring Philip and Herm back in!"

"Stop worrying." Sarah peeped into the mirror at herself, patting her hair. "Let's all go down now," she suggested.

"There he comes!" cried Naomi, pointing through the window at the headlights of a car. "See, he's opening the gate . . . Now he's driving through! Come on, Pro. Don't look like you was just going to have your tonsils out!"

They clattered down the stairs and into the sitting-room, where Kazmiri appeared wearing her Sunday dress, her grey hair freshly brushed and combed into its neat knot.

"Oh Mama," whispered Pro. "You look so nice, all because of me!"

"Where's Jonas?" Sarah asked abruptly.

"He comes, in a minute," her mother answered.

"Someone's knocking!" Naomi held up her hand. "Listen!"

Everyone looked at Prolet.

"I'll go, if you like," Fenna offered.

"No you won't," said Sarah. "Let Pro go."

Prolet turned a white face to them. "Yes, I'll go," she whispered.

In utter silence they waited, their hearts beating rapidly.

Prolet dropped the curtain between the sitting-room and the kitchen. They heard her open the back door and descend the stairs. Footsteps. A low voice. A laugh from Prolet. They were in the kitchen now, whispering together.

"I think I heard a kiss," said Leota, blushing hotly.

The curtain lifted, and the young couple stood framed in the doorway. With his arm around Prolet, Nathan smiled.

"Good evening to you all," he said. His slight accent in the Low German was charming, his self-possession a relief. "I brought a little something for you ladies after our accident the other night," he told them, showing a package. "I'm so terribly sorry I didn't look after Prolet better than that, so she had to put ladders in the best silk stockings of her sister." He glanced down at Fenna. "Maybe this will make up for it."

"What is it?" Fenna asked, starting up with her radiant look.

"Bring it over to the table," Prolet suggested.

The girls gathered around.

"A pair of silk stockings each!" exclaimed Leota.

"How did you know our sizes?" asked Sarah in astonishment.

"Whenever a lady comes to the store to buy a pair of stockings, I write down her name and her size," Nathan explained. "Then if someone else in the family comes to buy her some stockings and can't remember the size—" He bowed. "I can tell them."

"Oh you wonderful guy!" said Naomi, digging him in the ribs.

"And here," said Nathan, taking a small parcel from his pocket, "is our special line for the mothers." He stood before Kazmiri. "For you," he said. And then he spoke to her in Russian, words that made all the girls look up, startled. None of them understood. Only to Sarah were those accents familiar, yet strange. Again she stood in the presence of her own father, and felt the prick of tears. Their mother stared at Nathan, a look coming into her face which her daughters could not remember ever having seen. A youthful look which had not been hers since she had left her own country nearly twenty years before. She spoke to him in the same language, taking his hand, her voice deep and affectionate, moved.

Nathan shook his head ruefully.

"I'm getting rusty," he told her, switching to Low German. "Mother and I haven't spoken Russian very much since my father died."

"You speak it very nicely, very nicely. I love to hear you speak it." She added. "But I haven't opened your gift."

"This is a warmer line of hose," he said sitting down beside her. "Silk and wool, but still quite dressy."

"I didn't know you had these nice silk stockings in the store," Sarah declared. "You could only get the cotton or the lisle when I asked."

"I just started getting them in. I thought perhaps, sometimes when a girl is getting ready to go to a dance, she springs a run, and then it's too late to send for new ones in the catalogue."

"Good for you! But Nathan, you didn't need to get me silk stockings. Prolet didn't ruin my stockings."

"She broke your beads, she said."

"Oh that." Sarah dimpled. "Well anyway, thanks a lot."

The others murmured their thanks too, Naomi whispering to Prolet, "He courts you with silk stockings!"

"Thank you very much, very much," said Kazmiri, smoothing the silk and wool with a roughened hand.

As heavy steps thudded on the outside stairs, and the kitchen door opened, banging shut, silk stockings and their tissue wrappings magically disappeared. Kazmiri and Leota took up their knitting while the others sat still and nervous. Prolet found herself sitting beside Fenna. Quietly she rose, choosing an inconspicuous seat behind the stove. With a sweep of his hand, Jonas flung aside the curtain, putting in his big head.

"Just wondered who drove in now."

Nathan got up at once, his hand outstretched.

"Good evening. Mr. Leniuk."

Wonderingly, Jonas took the proffered hand.

"Evening." He opened the stove, poking at the fire. "You're a long way from home tonight?"

"Yes, I came to see you," said Nathan, casually putting a foot on the fender.

The women tensed, trying to look normal.

"I was just outside," Jonas mumbled, "talking to Herm

and the preacher about the Christmas concert. Don't owe you nothing, do I?"

"Oh no."

"The girls been running up bills?" Jonas demanded, looking around severely on them.

"Oh no! The Leniuks always pay."

"Well then—" Jonas shut the stove, straightened up, and looked suspiciously at the young man.

Nathan straightened up too, gazing steadily back at Jonas.

"I want to marry Prolet," he said quietly. "If that's all right with you."

"Marry Prolet?"

Kazmiri stirred. "Come and sit down, Jonas," she said cajolingly. "You too, Nathan. That's how it is, Jonas," she explained. "The young man wants to marry Prolet."

But how awful, awful, Sarah thought desperately. How can he do it, I don't know. Gottlieb wouldn't. He just wouldn't. Maybe that's why he never asks me to marry him. He'd have to face Jonas like this.

"When did you meet with Prolet?" Jonas asked, sitting down at last.

"At the Hallowe'en dance," Nathan answered, easing himself into a chair.

"Then you don't know her to marry!"

"With your permission, I could get to know her better."

Jonas passed a hand over his grizzled head.

"She's a Russian-German girl, you know. You speak the Low German pretty good, it seems."

"I speak the Low German, the High German, Yiddish, some French, a bit of Russian, and some words of Chinese. And English of course."

Jonas laughed, rubbing his hands.

"You know our religion. We keep Saturday for Sabbath. You know its different from most."

"In my religion, we keep Saturday for Sabbath too," said Nathan smiling. "But with the store, it's difficult. Saturday is the big day for the store. But our Sabbath is Saturday just the same."

"Why you don't marry a Jew girl?" Jonas demanded, suddenly hard.

"Naturally I've thought about this," Nathan replied. "But you know, we are the only Jewish family around here. In Calgary we've got relations, friends. But those girls don't want to leave the city and come out to the bald prairie to live. The store is my life. I love it. My father built up the business and the good name. I'd be a fool to leave."

Jonas nodded. "How's business?" he asked.

"Well, we manage. I've been keeping close accounts, and things are picking up. Not too much, mind you. But I can make a living."

Leota thought, He's doing all right. She sent Prolet an encouraging smile.

He's not near so good looking as Philip, Fenna thought. With that nose like an eagle's beak, and the way his hair grows in a point on his forehead.

"Your father gave a lot of credit when times was bad," said Jonas thoughtfully. "What you going to do with all those bad debts?"

"Before my father died," Nathan replied, "he said to me, 'Collect what you can, and let the rest go.' He said, 'Times will get better again, and somehow, we lived through the worst, and they lived. So just let the rest go.' What else is there to do?" he asked simply.

"That is very—Christian," nodded Jonas, satisfied.

"Also very Hebrew," smiled Nathan.

"How old are you?" Jonas asked.

"Twenty-four last August."

"So you would be running the business now?"

"Yes. I guess you could say I am. Mother wants to retire. She is lonely here now, and she thought she'd go to Calgary and live with her sister. She has plenty of friends there."

"Then you would marry Prolet, and she would work in the store too?"

"We could run it together."

"So it is for the store you want to marry her?" asked Jonas harshly.

The women leaned forward. Prolet's hand went to her cheek.

"I said the store was my life," said Nathan. "So wasn't I lucky to fall in love with someone who likes the idea of the store? Prolet likes it. And I think, together, we could have a very happy life. She has ideas for the store too."

Jonas looked keenly at the young man.

"This religion," he said, changing the subject completely, so that the women breathed again, "what would you do about the religion?"

"Prolet could do as she likes. There is her church in Ulna too, you know."

"But how can you marry up, then? Our preachers wouldn't marry a—a Jew and a believer."

Nathan stayed quiet a moment. He had qualities which Jonas had never contended with before. Some vein of his ancestry had given him the ease, the perfect outer equilibrium, the infinite patience of the Oriental trader. His face remained an enigma, with interest, charm, respect, alert on its fine hooked features.

Jonas bent forward, looking down at his hands.

"What will your mother think now?"

"Mother loves Prolet already."

Kazmiri moved a little, her eyes wet.

"But how will you marry up?" Jonas repeated.

"I think that we could find a place in Calgary where they would marry us."

"Away from home?" Kazmiri faltered.

"I am so sorry." Nathan turned to her. "But it would be a way out for Prolet and me."

"Go to Calgary alone, to be married?" Jonas shook his head.

"Mother would, of course, chaperone us."

"Mama Zimm again," Naomi snickered under her breath.

Jonas shot Prolet a quick glance. Then he looked at his wife. Silently, Kazmiri pleaded with him.

"Are you pleased, Mama?" he asked.

"Yes, very pleased," she said quietly.

"But it is for Pro to say. Does she want to marry with this young man?"

Nathan rose from his chair. "Do you, Prolet?" he asked, before them all.

Shyly she came out from behind the stove. She had been ready to defend him against an army of Jonases, but he had

D

needed no defence from a woman. In that hour he had grown in stature before her eyes. She had no doubts.

"Oh yes!" she said.

"You don't know her so well," said Jonas. "When you want to get married?"

"Early in December, if it can be arranged," Nathan told him. "After that, the Christmas rush gets too much, and I must be there. I could get someone to take over for a few days."

Jonas got up.

"Then come here to court her till you get married." He shook Nathan's hand. "God go with you on your wedding day."

"I give you my blessing," said Kazmiri warmly, coming to shake hands.

Fascinated, Leota watched Nathan and Prolet sit down together, holding hands unashamed in front of everybody.

"It must be wonderful," sighed Fenna enviously, "to be young, and in love!"

"What a proposal," muttered Naomi under her breath. "Now you know what we all got to go through to get our man."

He really cares about her, Sarah thought. You can see it in his eyes he loves her. After dancing three times with her, and just one date! I can't hardly believe it, she thought, wondering at the sudden pain that filled her heart. She could hardly keep back her tears. Of course, everybody cries at weddings and things, she told herself. But I never figured I would. At the sight of their joined hands, she turned away as if blinded by too dazzling a light.

"I'll put the kettle on and we'll have something!" cried Naomi. "Even in love you got to eat!"

Chapter Four

I

"Ming and Ting went," Leota announced, coming into the kitchen after doing her morning chores. "Broke down the fence and crossed over the creek. Guess I better go look for them."

"How will you go?" asked Naomi. She and Prolet were busy shredding cabbage for the winter's supply of sauerkraut, while Fenna had gone to school.

"I'll take Zoe," Leota answered, running up the stairs two at a time.

She found Sarah packing a small suitcase.

"I'm off to White's," said Sarah briefly, turning her face away from Leota. "I told Jonas to let them know when he went past."

"Take your holiday first," Leota pleaded. "It's such hard work there."

" I can't stand the love birds." Sarah kept her voice even, her back to her sister. "I'm not—not jealous of Pro. But they can sit there, holding hands, and Gottlieb isn't allowed to come in the house, even."

"Maybe Jonas would get over that, whatever the trouble is."

"He won't!" Sarah snapped shut her case. "Naomi could bring me my box next time she goes by with the team. I won't skin my face asking Jonas!"

"We'll get your box over."

"Anyways, Gottlieb can come to see me there."

Watching through the window her sister's lonely figure trudging along the road, Leota made a few sandwiches with thick slices of homemade bread. She had not had time to do up her hair, and it hung in two black braids on her back, tied at the ends with bits of ribbon. She looked like a schoolgirl let loose on an unexpected holiday.

"Not coming for dinner?" Mama asked, kneading dough with floury hands.

"Well, I don't know. It might take quite some time to find them, and it's near eleven now."

"Wear a jacket," Mama advised. "It's going to snow I think. It doesn't look so good. Better take a pail and make yourself some tea if you get cold."

"You look real nice," said Prolet, munching a piece of cabbage. "You got the right figure for slacks and sweater."

"She can't say nothing nasty," Naomi remarked. "Life is just all sweet for Prolet now."

Laughing, Leota picked up her lunch and a work jacket and went off. Tethered in a stall of the barn, stood Zoe, a dependable old brown workhorse. Although possessed of a shocking gait, being large and clumsy, she had the virtues of stolidity, endurance, and good sense. Leota put Jonas's stock saddle on Zoe's back, tying on the coat and lunch and a tin pail for tea, as well as a halter for Ming when she should find her. With a feeling of adventure, she rode forth, following the hoof marks until they disappeared into the dry prairie grass. Then she turned Zoe towards the hills, slapping the brown rump occasionally with one end of the reins, singing to herself as she went along.

The huge pasture spread out to the Knuckle Hills in shadowy coulees and rough contours. In good summers, springs of water gurgled among the rocks, saskatoons ripened profusely in the more sheltered places, and the grass was lush. As though remembering all this, Jonas's horses often looked longingly over the prairie to the hills, blue in the distance; and whenever they found themselves free, some instinct would draw them back there. Winter had not yet come to the prairie, but it would soon be on the way. The sky, overcast and grey, was sombre; the breath of the wind held the freshness of snow.

After a time, Leota left all sign of habitation behind, riding at a steady trot along a faint trail that hugged the side of a hill, then dipped into a little valley. Here, Leniuk's land adjoined that of Zwick's with a common fenceline for nearly a mile. The hill cut off her view, but she distinctly heard the rush of hoofs in the distance. Pulling Zoe to a walk, she turned in the saddle, listening and looking about. Suddenly, on the horizon a horse appeared, running wildly, its tail streaming like a flag, a rider sitting as determinedly as a burr on its back. She recognised the horse at once. It was Darkie, a mare Jud had bought, getting her for a song from a cowpuncher who had turned a highly-strung nervous creature into a crazy hysterical animal, trying to break her with cruel beatings. He had not broken her spirit, though he seemed to have ruined her for riding. But Jud had rescued her with gentleness. He's always a sucker that way, Leota thought, watching Darkie galloping straight for the fence.

But who could be riding her? Leota reined Zoe in anxiously, for it appeared Darkie would be crazy enough to go straight through the barbed wire. Zoe tossed her head like a disapproving grandmother as Darkie and her rider flew gracefully through the air, sailing over the fence like a poem in motion, landing lightly on the Leniuk's side, and continuing a mad race. Nudging Zoe with her heels, Leota moved slowly forward, the dimple that so seldom appeared in her cheek, showing now. For it was Reuben, Reuben come home for Christmas after all.

He went in a wide arc, gradually getting the horse under control, coming back towards Leota at a brisk nervous trot.

"Pretty good riding!" Leota greeted him as he rode up beside her. "Good as going to the Calgary Stampede, just about."

"You'll never believe I didn't do that on purpose," laughed Reuben. "I could see you a long ways off. Just thought I'd come and say Hello, when this darn critter got scared and started running."

"I didn't see you."

"No. I was up on top. Where you off to?"

"Looking for Ming and Ting."

"I know Ming's your little cayuse, but who's Ting?"

"She's Ming's new filly. They went off this morning, broke down the pasture fence by the creek. I'm looking for them."

"You better start at the beginning and tell me all the news. I just got back last night."

"We heard you wouldn't be coming."

"Seems I came, though."

She glanced across at him as he struggled with Darkie who did about six dancing steps to every long stride of Zoe's. He wore Jud's oldest cowboy hat, the one with the bullet hole in the crown. "A hat ain't a hat without a bullet hole in it somewheres," Jud would say. Under the hat, Reuben's face was deeply tanned, not good looking, but mature and resolute, with hidden reserves under its humour. He was alert and competent with a fearless intelligent gaze that missed nothing.

"We had a Hallowe'en party Wednesday night," Leota told him.

"So I hear."

She coloured under his look, fearing that he had also heard all about her encounter with Joe.

"What else can I tell you?" she wondered. "Well, I don't know if you're interested, but Prolet is engaged to Nathan Zimmerman."

"Prolet!" Darkie danced sideways, mincing and prancing.

"Nathan came last night to ask Jonas, right in front of everybody. They're getting married next month."

"Cripes!"

"They met at the Hallowe'en party, and it was love at first sight."

"Must have been quite a party."

"They just danced together three times," Leota said shyly, "then they had one date, and now they're engaged."

"Well, take me, for instance," said Reuben seriously. "Never laid eyes on Darkie till this morning when Dad tells me to give her a workout. She hated me on first sight, and now . . ." He paused as Darkie stood up on her hind legs before a large hummock at the side of the trail. "And now she's just crazy about me . . . Steady Girl!" He eased Darkie to a walk.

Leota watched him, smiling. It was funny how he could be so much like Jud without being any blood relation. It was in the way his eyes would fill up with laughter before a muscle of his face twitched. It was in the set of his shoulders and the tones of his voice. The same traces of German accent clung to his speech, and some of the odd turns of phrase that Jud used.

"I can't think where Ming and Ting could've got to," Leota said, stopping on the top of a little knoll and searching the countryside.

"If you ask me, they'd go right to the Knuckles," Reuben suggested.

"There's three gullies. I just don't know which one to try first."

"Try them all. I'll come with you if you'll have me."

"You think Darkie will be O.K?"

"The best thing for her."

"Then I'd be glad of your company," she said, prodding Zoe.

It seemed odd to feel shy of Reuben after knowing him from childhood. But then, he had been away so much during the last few years. At high school in Ulna. And back and forth between his relatives at Red Deer and his folks at the Lily of the Valley. Though he always came to dance with her at the dances when he was at home, she could not remember having been alone with him like this before. He was both familiar and strange to her. But he's only a kid, she thought as always. And an awful nice one.

They came to the entrance of the first valley between the two lowest of the four hills.

"There's no horses," said Leota.

"Ride up the valley a bit," Reuben advised, "and then there's a path round the face of the hill. Down here there's too many rocks for horses."

He led the way, Darkie arching her neck and snorting, Zoe plodding after her. Skirting the next hill, they found no horses in the second valley either. It was deeper than the first with steep rocky banks on either side. In its shelter, scrubby bushes grew, bare now of leaves. Underfoot lay the pebbly bed of a small stream fed by a spring from above.

"Why we don't have lunch?" Leota suggested. "Over there under those rocks, out of the wind."

"Sure thing. You didn't bring tea, I suppose?"

"Yes!" she cried. "And I could sure do with a cup right now."

"Good. We'll get a fire going."

Dismounting, he tied Darkie in a quiet level place, leaving to go in search of firewood, and to fill the pail at the spring. Leota untied the lunch and her coat and loosened the saddle on Zoe. She brought her share, too, of dead fallen branches and brittle sticks. With the grey rock wall behind them, they sat on Leota's old jacket and set the sticks alight, piling the wood on over the blaze.

"It's nice," said Leota gratefully, warming herself at the orange flames. "Here's the sandwiches. They're a bit squashed."

"They look wonderful to me."

She sat back against the rock, while Reuben stretched out beside her, casually leaning on one elbow. The rocks and the fire shut out the lowering sky and the dead brown landscape. They might have been alone in the world together, the girl thought. A good thing he isn't like Joe. When the water boiled, she made tea, and they drank it turn and turn about from her one tin cup. It surprised her, the pleasure this gave her.

"Pro and Nathan," said Reuben, as though he must have been turning the idea over in his mind for some time. "I'm so glad."

"We're glad too." Leota helped herself to another sandwich.

"She's getting a good husband. Nathan and I were always friends . . . the bastard and the Jew."

He felt her sympathy in the quick look she gave him.

"It used to hurt," he admitted. "But now I know how lucky I am. Luckier than most . . . But if I don't watch," he teased, smiling up at her, "if I don't watch, who knows who'll be gone next when I come home! It's a wonder to me it wasn't you Nate picked on. But I'm awful glad it wasn't you, Leota," he said warmly.

"Go away with you!" she murmured in confusion.

He gazed at the flickering fire.

"Only I don't suppose I'll be coming back much after this year. When I'm twenty-one in March, the farm will be mine, and then I want to really take over and run it right. I was awful lucky, you know. When Ma's uncle heard she'd got a baby in her old age, he was so tickled, he fixed his will so I'd get his farm."

"What's it like up there?" Leota asked eagerly.

"Oh it's a good farm all right. More trees than here. And we get rain. The buildings are pretty old, but they're solid. The old uncle really knew how to build. And it's a good half section."

Honey in the Rock

The wind flung a handful of sleet at them. The fire hissed and spat as arrowheads of ice struck the hot glowing bed of embers.

"Cripes!" Reuben leapt up. "We better get going. This'll never find Ming and Ting!"

"I don't think it'll be much." Leota began covering the remains of the fire with dust. "Just seems like a little shower."

"Yes, it's passing over. But we better get cracking, Leota." He helped her put out the last few sparks.

Leota called Zoe, who came at once.

"Darkie's going wild."

Reuben went to his horse cautiously as a cold wind sprang up, bringing a few more needles of sleet. Though Darkie quivered and snorted, nervously backing and circling, Reuben was deft and sure, quickly getting her under control and mounting her, while Leota rode ahead.

"You're a good little rider," he said admiringly as Darkie cut a few capers. "You should show horses in the ring. Good light hands, straight back, good seat..."

"Reuben!"

"It was supposed to be a compliment. My cousin Ruth shows Uncle's horses. She sits there like a sack of flour."

"I hope we find Ming and Ting in the next valley," Leota said anxiously, pretending to ignore his remarks, but keeping them to savour in secret.

They rode across the face of the third knuckle, the highest of the four hills, and brought their horses to a standstill, looking down over the steep cliff side. This valley was the deepest of them all with a sheer cliff dropping down below them. Brush grew thickly along the sides, and the wind moaned eerily through the cleft.

"There they are," said Leota suddenly, pointing. "Right at the end of the valley. We'll have to ride down the hill and get round them."

Ming and her filly had not bothered to climb any distance. They stood together, sheltering by a little slope near the bottom of the great knuckle, their manes and tails lifting gently in the breeze as they bent their heads to graze.

"Go down zigzag," Reuben suggested. "That should bring us just about level with them."

The wary Ming heard them coming. Tossing her head, she started off up the gorge, the filly at her side. But at every step, she went down heavily on her right fore leg.

"Oh, she's lamed!" Leota cried.

"You hold Darkie, and I'll go on foot."

"Wait, here's the halter." Leota gave it to him, taking Darkie's reins. "Ming isn't wild, but she's mean."

Reuben moved slowly, talking and calling until he could get near enough to pat the mare and slip on the halter. Then he bent down to examine the foot.

"Looks like a wire cut," he called back. "Pretty bad one too."

He led the limping mare over to Leota. "Nice little filly she's got."

While they stood there, Leota trying to take the rope of Ming's halter with one hand, and with the other give Reuben the reins of his own horse, a furious wind suddenly came whistling down the gorge, bringing a noisy shower of sleet in thousands of needle pricks. Ming snorted uneasily, trying to pull away from Leota who held on tightly to the rope, glad that Zoe never panicked. Darkie, however, started to run with Reuben hanging on to the reins. He stopped her, holding her while she plunged and struggled, whinnying with fear. The sudden storm swirled about them.

"I don't think I'll try to ride her!" Reuben shouted. "It'll only waste time. I'll ride with you. Go by the road," he said, leaping up behind her saddle, pulling Darkie along by the reins. "Follow this fence, and then there's a gate."

With horses all around them, Zoe's big feet thudding on the hard ground, and the wind and sleet beating their backs, they made a strange little procession.

"Boy, she sure knocks the teeth out of you back here," Reuben laughed. "What a saddle pony!"

At the gate Leota put on her coat and tied a scarf over her head.

"We still got quite a ways to go," she remarked. "Down this road, past White's and the school, and then home. I guess I'm not much of a horse wrangler, taking so long."

"You do all right," he said, putting a comradely arm about her shoulders.

Ignoring the gesture, she got back up on Zoe. The daylight had begun to fade, what with the greyness of the storm and the shortness of the November afternoon. She was glad of it, for now no one would see them on the road unless they passed very close. She wondered vaguely what the time was. They must have stayed talking by that fire much longer than she had reckoned.

"Come a ki-yi yippee yippee yi yippee yea," sang Reuben, jumping up behind her.

". . . and it looks like rain,
And my danged old slicker's in the wagon again . . .!"

Leota soon joined him. And then they went on from that to "You waited too long to say you were sorry," "Be Nobody's Darling but Mine," and "Bury me not on the Lone Prairie!" She felt him warm and alive behind her on Zoe, his arms at times almost encircling her as he led his cavorting horse by the reins. Looking straight ahead, she sang high and shrill and sweet, giving the words a foreign flavour. Reuben could sing well too. They had both been brought up on hymns, and singing came naturally to them. They sang "Honey in the Rock," "The Wings of the Morning," and all their other favourites. It made the long trail home in the storm seem short, and soothed the animals.

They fell into silence, however, as they passed through Leniuk's gate. At the house, the lamps had already been lighted. The cows had taken shelter in the lea of the barn. Quickly Leota brought the horses inside, while Reuben struck a match to the lantern which hung on its hook inside the door.

"I'll just take a look at Ming's foot," he offered. "Got any disinfectant?"

Leota found the bottle and a swab.

"It's a pretty clean cut, after all," he told her as she held the lantern while he doctored the wound. "Better have Jonas look at it again in the morning." He lowered the quivering foot to the floor.

While Leota threw down hay for the horses from the loft, Reuben unsaddled Zoe. It was nice to work together like this, she thought. A thrill of joy went through her for the few hours spent with an intelligent companionable young man. Smiling she recalled a saying of Jud's: "How a guy treats his horses, that's how he treats his women." But immediately following on her happiness, all the complexities of her life at home and of this present situation rushed upon her. Reuben ought to come in and get warm and dry. Have something hot and nourishing to eat. But if he came in with her, Jonas would ask searching questions. There would be the amusement and remarks of her sisters. And Reuben should borrow a horse to go home on. Darkie still thumped in the stall, starting wildly whenever they passed near, the whites of her eyes showing in the lantern light. Leota did not know what to do.

"You should come up to the house," she said doubtfully when they had finished. "But Jonas will ask us when you met up with me, and how long we rode together. A person can't lie to him. He looks right through you."

"I know all about Jonas."

"But you're soaked." Leota felt his wet sleeve in dismay. "And if Darkie won't let you ride..."

"Oh, I'll get her calmed down."

For a moment they stood together beside Zoe in the stall, while the wind outside blew in furious gusts, blasting the roof and walls of the barn with fine pointed sleet. With a hand on the neck of the patient horse, Reuben looked thoughtfully at Leota, not with the jeering amusement such as she had learned to expect from the men she knew, but with such warmth that she felt as though he had touched her. It came as a shock to her to see that he had not actually moved. She was suddenly shy of him. Though she had known him since childhood, in his presence now she became aware of a disturbing and unfamiliar element which threatened to unnerve her.

"You can't go home like that," she said briskly, attempting to assume the role of an older sister. "Come on, we'll go in and tell them you helped me. We don't need to say since before lunch."

"We should be able to cook up something to tell them," said Reuben. "Say I met you coming home, near the school when I was giving Darkie a workout. And Ming was being mean..."

"Only what would you be doing giving Darkie a workout in a snowstorm?" Leota giggled. She had had so little girlhood, passing swiftly from child to adult. The sheer lunacy of youth had never been hers.

"Let's see now. I was looking for a cow, maybe."

"Cows!" Leota laughed hysterically. "Naomi will be coming soon to milk the cows!"

"If it's Naomi, there's nothing to worry about. She says I'm so slow I'd stop in my tracks if I went any slower."

From the wind and the darkness outside came a shout, the jingle of harness, a hollow clatter as the door rolled open.

"It's Dad!" cried Reuben.

"Hi there!" Jud took off his hat, beating it against the wall to make it shed its snow and wetness.

"Anything wrong, Dad?"

"I'll tell the cockeyed world! Florrie's smashed her hand in the door of Herm's truck in town today. Her right hand, too."

"My gosh! Is it bad?"

"Pretty bad. Lucky that nurse woman was there, and fixed it up."

"How's she feeling?" Leota asked anxiously.

"Well, you know Florrie. She's chipper no matter what. But I come to get Sarah to lend a hand for awhile."

"Sarah went to work at White's, just this morning," Leota told him.

"She did, eh? Well, what about this pretty young lady I'm looking at right now? Florrie always gets Sarah on account of Gottlieb, but if Sarah's gone to White's . . ."

"What about it, Leota?" Reuben asked.

"I—I'll come, Jud," said Leota eagerly. "If you can put up with my cooking, why I'd love to help Florrie!"

"Good girl! Throw some duds into a gunny sack, then and come along!"

"We'll have something to eat before we go," she suggested, her tone warm with welcome. "You and Reuben both. And get yourselves dry."

"O.K. I'll just drive the team round the side, out of the wind."

"I'll get things ready." She disappeared into the darkness.

"Must of been quite a workout you gave Darkie," Jud observed dryly, pulling his hat down over his eyes.

"I met Leota looking for horses this morning!" Reuben laughed. "But it would be better not to tell them up at the house."

Jud twinkled.

"Me, I never know nothing what the young folks do. But just don't expect me to tell lies."

Chapter Five

I

WHEN Dan saw the gathering greyness of that Monday afternoon, he decided to let the children go home early, and he was glad he had done so when later on, sleet began hammering the schoolhouse windows. He lighted a coal-oil lamp, built up the fire in the stove, and went on marking exercise books, with a secure feeling that all the children must have reached home by now. At last he finished, blew out the lamp, and throwing on his coat, went to the pump to draw a fresh pail of water.

Through the swirling snow he saw what seemed a small cavalcade passing on the nearby road. He heard hoofs and the snorting of a horse, and then a high sweet girl's voice raised in song. It was " Honey in the Rock ". A rich male voice joined in, and then both voices and the stamping of hoofs were lost in a blast of wind, while he stood there bareheaded, beaten by the storm, with the pail in his hand. The horses had been heading down Leniuk's road, and Dan wondered which of the Leniuk girls had passed, and who had been her companion. A devastating loneliness took hold of him. When he had made his meagre supper at the teacherage, he sat down with a notebook and pencil. He knew he was not a poet, but at least writing was something to do with the long empty evening.

" Tonight," he said to himself, " I make a prayer."

And thinking of the riders singing out there in the storm, Dan wrote:

Dear God, grant me to taste of the honey in the rock!

> Moses struck the rock
> And water gushed,
> The cool, life-giving water.

Honey in the Rock

Manna fell to earth
And quail hovered near.
Still this is not all.
For the rock holds honey too.
Yes, the sweetest honey
Waiting there for you, Brother,
Waiting there for me, Brother.

Thus says the prairie Prophet.

Others find this honey, so it seems,
While I hold the empty gourd.
Others find poetry
And the singing of birds,
The rose pinned to the silken gown,
The wonder of requited love.

I had a rose, just once,
But it had no scent.
And I loved and had pain in return.
Honey in the rock!
Food not enough;
Wheat does not feed the starved heart
Or body either
When the hail stones smash it flat,
And the sun throbs down,
And the winds tear up the seed.
But not sun nor wind nor hail can blast the rock
And despoil it of its strangest treasure:
The sweetness in it.
So how will I with bare hands?

Tonight
I make a prayer!
Dear God, grant me to taste of the honey in the rock!

He woke on Tuesday morning thinking about his poem, and during the noonhour as he sat in his shack munching a peanut butter sandwich, he wrestled with the writing again. At half past twelve he heard hoarse shouting which no doubt meant that the bigger boys had started a fight in the schoolhouse. Ought he to tell them to go out and start a ball game? But a thin layer of snow from last night's storm covered the ground, and the wind blew bitterly. The smaller children would only sit around getting chilled. Spreading another piece of bread, he read his poem over once more. He wanted to inject as many harsh sounds as possible into the last verse so that the prayer at the end would have a quality of peace. It did not satisfy him. A rush of icy air whipped the papers from the table, scattering them to the floor as the door opened and Philip Jebson entered without knocking.

"Hullo," said Dan, completely startled.

Quickly he gathered up his papers, stuffing them hastily into a book.

"Don't let me stop your lunch," said Philip politely, motioning to the slice of bread with one large bite taken out of it, lying nakedly and plateless on the table.

"Oh, that's all right. I'm finished, really," Dan mumbled, rapidly clearing up. "Won't you sit down?"

"I just figured it was time I paid you a visit," said Philip, taking off his long black coat and looking helplessly around for a place to put it.

"Give it to me. I'll put it on the bed in the other room."

"Thank you. Well, Brother Root, how are you liking it here at the Lily of the Valley?"

"Oh fine, just fine."

Philip sat down ponderously. At right angles to him, Dan saw his profile, handsome, chiselled as though out of stone.

"Of course at the Hallowe'en party, it was not the place to talk, but I was real pleased to know you came to service that first Sabbath," said Philip, rubbing his red hands to warm them. "I do wish we could have that pleasure again."

A frightful din now came from the direction of the schoolhouse. Dan glanced at his watch.

"I'm sorry, Mr. Jebson, but I can't stay long. I really must get back to the school, or they'll be tearing the place down."

"I won't keep you long, Brother Root," said Philip, immobile and determined. "This is important too, I figure. And the intellectuals of the district ought to get acquainted, don't you think?"

E

Dan resigned himself as Philip leaned towards him. Intellectuals, eh? He gave a lopsided grin.

"I hear you wrote a hymn, Brother Root," said Philip.

"It's not really a hymn."

"The reason you got the job, I might as well tell you, the reason we chose you out of two hundred applications, was for your musical qualifications."

"Really? But you know, I'm not all that good. And there's no piano in the school."

"It's the first time in years we got a musical teacher."

Dan did not try to answer.

"What I wanted to ask you, will you bring the children next Sabbath, and let them sing your song in church?"

"But I'm trying to tell you. It isn't really a hymn. I don't know what you might call it. A cowboy ditty, I guess, with some religion thrown in. And it's doggerel, complete doggerel, lines and music."

"Everybody in the Lily of the Valley District is singing it."

"No!"

"You're quite famous. Did you know Billy White is gone to Calgary today with his Dad and he's going to sing your song on the *Lone Prairie* programme at four o'clock this afternoon?"

"I didn't know," said Dan, blushing up to the roots of his hair.

"How come you wrote it?" Philip asked bluntly.

"It was to teach the children to sing in parts. Without an instrument, that's difficult," Dan explained earnestly. "So I wrote this little ditty in parts that are all pretty much the same tune, each one lower than the last. Then there's a fragment or two left over for the better singers."

"You would do a great service if you would bring the children to church and let them sing it there."

"I don't know." Dan hesitated. "Some of the children come from homes where the parents don't attend church."

"All the more reason, Brother Root. If a child is going to sing, parents will come to hear."

"You may only make these people annoyed. And they may feel that I'm interfering. It's your job to get the people to go to church, not mine."

"You got the job for your musical qualifications, Brother Root."

"I took the job to teach school," said Dan stubbornly. "And in the schoolroom, you may be sure I use my musical ability such as it is."

Philip stared moodily out of the window at the desolate landscape.

"I was hoping to have your help," he said. "I want to build up this church and make it strong in case I leave, as I hope to soon."

"Where do you plan to go?"

"I applied to my Bible School in the States, to go out into the Mission field in the East."

"India?"

"At first. Then I want to go to Tibet."

"Tibet! But they don't let missionaries in there."

"That's just it, Brother Root. There'll have to be a first one. I want that one to be me. Philip Jebson."

"Just what for?" Dan demanded rudely.

"What for?" Philip stared at him incredulously. "To save souls, of course. To make converts to Christianity."

"They've got their own religion."

"They're waiting, just waiting, for the message I can bring them. You think I'm crazy? Then you don't know history. At the turn of the century missionaries were converting Indians by the thousand. Think of it. By the thousand. Like Paul in Bible days."

Dan groped in his mind for historical facts.

"But that was surely more an economic situation than a religious one," he protested. "I know that whole villages were converted to Christianity, but it was to their advantage. People as poor as they, what did they have to lose? If they adopted the British religion, they were more likely to reap economic benefits."

Philip shook his head as though at a befuddled idiot.

"Don't belittle the Lord's work, Brother Root."

Dan shot a look at his watch.

"Heavens! I've got to run. They'll be saddling up to go home if I don't hurry."

"The disease of the modern world, hurry!" said Philip

in disgust. " What about the singing next Sabbath? I can count on you to bring the children to sing your song, can't I?" He put a vibrant hand on Dan's shoulder, smiling in a superior way.

" I promised you nothing! " Dan exclaimed, feeling trapped.

" Fenna will play the organ for them," Philip said, as though everything were settled.

" Fenna?"

" She plays very well, you know. Only Sarah overshadows her. Sabbath teaching and music always have went well together for a missionary's wife," Philip brooded. " I have hopes. Reasonable hopes."

Fenna . . . Then this—hunk of granite—hopes to marry Fenna, Dan thought. Tibet and Fenna. Converts by the thousand. It made Dan's head go round. And a stab of pain which he did not recognise for what it was, went through his heart.

" You will excuse me," he said aloud, gathering books and papers together. " My job is to teach, and I must go."

" Your song on the Sabbath, Brother Root?" Philip persisted as Dan dived into the other room to get the long black coat.

Dan was about to shout, " For the last time no! " But Fenna was to play for the children to sing . . . She would have to practise with them. And after all, it might be better to oil the wheels of his existence here, just a little.

" I'll put it up to the children," he said at last. " Those who don't want to come will not be forced to do so. I'll bring along only the ones who want to come and who are sure their parents won't mind. That's the best I can do, Mr. Jebson."

" Well, it's something, at least," said Philip grudgingly.

" Oh, one thing more," said Dan as his visitor made ready to depart. " Please stop calling me ' Brother Root '. Call me ' Dan '. ' Brother Root ' makes me feel as if we're both underground already, pushing daisies together." He smiled, holding out his hand. " If you don't mind! "

No answering smile appeared on Philip's face, only a look of bewilderment and annoyance as he said a curt good-bye. Not a shred of humour, Dan thought watching him go off across the school yard, feeling in himself a flush of embarrassment that his bit of a joke had fallen flat.

He found it hard to concentrate on the afternoon's work, his mind in a turmoil over Philip's visit. Well, at least it had been mentally stimulating! Tibet. And Fenna. He glanced across at her where she sat in a far corner of the room, working diligently. Acutely aware of her as always, it came to him now that lately he had had an empty lost feeling when she happened to be absent, and a sense of relief when he saw her coming along the road. Of course, she was the only one in the class to whom he could talk as to an equal, but he must be careful, he told himself nervously. Again he remembered her at the dance, and it gave him a shock to realise she had been in his thoughts ever since Wednesday evening, a warm vision on which he had nourished his heart. Lines of his poem ran through his mind:

> ... And I loved once
> And had pain in return.

And the impassioned plea:

> Dear God, grant me to taste of the honey in the rock!

Had he written those words because of Fenna? For they were false otherwise. He had never been in love.

Just before closing time, he told the children about Philip's request for the song.

"You must get permission from your parents," he told them. "Then on Friday afternoon, I'll let school out early, and the ones who are going to sing will come to the church to practise with the organ."

"I'll play," Fenna offered.

"Yes, that's what Mr. Jebson suggested."

Fenna came up to his desk when he had dismissed the class.

"It will be cold in the church, Mr. Root," she reminded him. "I get the fire going on my way home from school for Friday night service most times. Maybe I better get it lit at noon hour."

"I hadn't thought of that. A very good idea," he said in a business like way. Self-knowledge, he thought. That's the thing. You can keep yourself from slipping when you know what it is you must contend with in yourself. But she is beautiful.

Even on a dark day like this, she has a shining look with that bright hair. He cleared the books from his desk while Fenna put on her things, chatting to some of the bigger girls. Then they all fell silent, trying to identify a banging and scrambling which came from directly overhead.

"Sounds as if there were some large animal on the roof," Dan commented.

"There sure is," laughed Fenna. "It's Reuben fixing the shingles."

"He climbed up there just when you rang the bell," one of the children said. "Didn't you see him, Mr. Root?"

Dan watched the plaster on the ceiling anxiously while the banging and hammering continued for a few minutes longer.

"Here he comes!" cried Fenna as Reuben slithered down the slanting roof on the seat of his pants with a hammer in his hand, landing lightly on his feet just outside the windows.

"'Scuse the noise," he said, coming in a moment later. "Dad said I better get up here quick and fix the shingles before it really snows."

"Sure you didn't come to get a few crumbs of knowledge?" Fenna asked sarcastically. She was ready to go home now, but stood with her books and lunch pail, as though waiting for the homage due her from the two young men.

"I'll bet I've got more crumbs of knowledge than you have," Reuben retorted. "Tell me where this line of Shakespeare comes from." Taking a comb from his pocket, he began parting his hair, pretending to weep and blubber, and at the same time throwing kisses into the air.

"You're just crazy," said Fenna.

But a hearty laugh came out of Dan.

"'Parting is such sweet sorrow,'" he intoned.

"Right! Now here's another one."

Snatching up two crackers from a desk where someone had left them at lunch, he got down on all fours, snarling and roaring like an animal, stuffing the crackers into his mouth and eating noisily.

"Really, Reuben, you're disgusting," exclaimed Fenna.

"Get it?" he asked Dan.

Dan shook his head. "Not that one."

"It's easy. 'Et tu, Brute.'"

"Just imagine, making a spectacle of yourself like that," said Fenna, who had not understood. "Look at your hands."

"Yeah, just look at them," said Reuben advancing upon her, holding his blackened hands in front of her face.

"Goodnight, Mr. Root!" she shouted, defeated, going off with the last of the stragglers.

"Well, Mr. Root, the name's Reuben Zwick. Pleased to meet you."

"I'm pleased to meet you, too. Come on over to the shack."

"Are you finding the place warm enough?" Reuben asked as they bent against the wind.

"The floor is a bit cold."

"When it snows, just bank it up all round."

"Where did you learn your Shakespeare?" Dan asked, opening the door of the teacherage.

"Oh I took Grade twelve in Ulna. We had a dandy teacher there for three years. Miss Hester. She was nuts on Shakespeare. If we didn't learn anything else, we learned Shakespeare. Was a time I had a quotation for anything that came up. But I'm getting rusty. She wanted to light lamps in the darkness of our minds . . . Say, is it O.K. if I call you Dan?"

"I wish you would."

"Getting along all right?" Reuben asked.

"Sure. Of course the Christmas concert is a load on my mind just now."

"Don't worry about it. They've been fixing about the finances. The women put up the lunch. You just have to put on the programme."

"Yes, I know. I was thinking I might need some kind of platform."

"There's planks and sawhorses up in the loft of the barn. Green curtains too, packed away in the cupboard somewhere. I remember when Ma made them out of flour sacks and dyed them."

"You're a godsend!" Dan said gratefully.

"If there's anything else you need, why just holler . . . May I turn the radio on?" Reuben's eyes sparkled. "If you don't mind listening, I want to tune in to the *Lone Prairie* programme."

"This is CBX, and the *Lone Prairie* programme with the

Lone Ranger saying Hello, Hello, and Hello to you all," came the deep velvety voice of the announcer. Amused and slightly cynical, Dan and Reuben settled down to listen.

"We have quite a list of birthday greetings here," the voice went on. "Here's Happy Birthday to Winona Street, nine years old today, at Box 66 Windfield. And Happy Birthday to Donnie Scot, just turned six . . ."

While the greetings continued to go out over the air waves, Dan's thoughts drifted. Nice chap, he decided, with a glance at Reuben. Intelligent. Looks you straight in the eye. Evidently Miss Hester did a good job; here's at least one mind with a light in it. Competent too. Can't imagine that he'd ever make a mess of anything. Bet he doesn't lie awake at night thinking over the stupid things he's done during the day.

"Well, that's the end of the birthday greetings," said the Lone Prairie Ranger in his oily tone. "Now, who's going to sing for us first? Let's see. This boy over here with the red hair and freckles? Right up here. That's it. Now what's your name?"

"Bill White," came the faint answer.

"Of course! Philip Jebson told me he was going to sing!" Dan exclaimed. "I had forgotten all about it!"

"Now, come a little closer, Billy," cautioned the Lone Ranger. "That's it. How old are you?"

"Thirteen," answered a clear, confident boyish voice.

"Where do you come from?"

"Ulna."

"Way out on the prairie, eh? And what are you going to sing for us, Billy?"

"It's called, *In the Wind Blown Along*."

"And is this your geetar?"

"Yep, and my teacher wrote the song."

"Your teacher? And what's her name?"

"It's not a her, it's a him. Name's Mr. Root."

"Well, well! And I guess Mr. Root's listening in, eh? Now you go ahead and say hello, and then go right into your song. Here's a nice big shiny apple for Mr. Root out there at Ulna. Go ahead, Billy."

"Hello, Mr. Root! Hello everybody out there at Lily of the Valley!" shouted Billy into the mike.

Then loud and sure he struck the chords on the guitar and swung into the song.

> "' I am like the Russian thistle
> In the wind blown along.
> Rolling o'er and o'er the prairie
> In the wind blown along.
>
> Torn up from my watered roots
> In the wind blown along;
> Without a home, without a guide
> In the wind blown along.
>
> He is like the fenceline sure
> Hand outstretched for to save;
> In the dust-storm or the blizzard
> Hand outstretched for to save.
>
> Though I'm an outcast, still He's there,
> Hand outstretched for to save;
> And I'm not too lost or lowly
> For His outstretched hand to save.' "

"Boy, that's a real humdinger!" said the Lone Ranger. "Congratulations to Mr. Root and to his talented pupil, Bill White, out there at Ulna . . . Now we have a little girl here . . ."

"That's all I wanted to hear! You're a genius!" exclaimed Reuben admiringly as he switched off the radio.

"I feel like the darnedest fool. It's just doggerel."

"Even doggerel takes something. I couldn't do it, that's for sure. Billy sang it mighty nice, too."

"It's much better with all the different parts in it. That's what I wrote it for."

"Everybody in the district's singing it! And you're doing fine out here, just fine. They say there's not one person against you."

Dan flushed with pleasure.

"Hope I can do as well in my studying," he said diffidently. "I'm studying Chaucer, nights."

Reuben took the heavy text book into his hands.

"I remember we took some character of Chaucer's with Miss Hester. It was a student of Oxford, I think. Anyway, he would gladly learn and gladly teach . . . Like you," he said laughing. "You're going to go to college, aren't you?"

"Yes, if I can ever get enough money together."

"What do you do all summer?" Reuben asked, looking at Dan with his clear intrepid gaze.

"I try to get jobs. Last summer I worked on a farm."

"Good for you."

"No, it was anything but good for me." Dan laughed ruefully. "I'm not lazy, but then again, I'm not used to farm work."

"I like farming, and I've got my own farm. Just born lucky," Reuben remarked.

And Dan, knowing how he had been born, was startled.

"Got anything lined up for next summer?" Reuben asked.

"Not so far. But it's only November."

"Can you keep books?"

"I know something about it."

"I've got an uncle up north. Dabbles in everything. He has a lumber business, a farm, a hardware store. He builds houses. He's got a finger in every pie. But he can't keep books, and nobody can get him straightened out. He doesn't like city slickers, and in a country place like that, it's hard to find someone who could help. I tried last summer, but I was farming, and in the evenings I was just too tired. Look, I'll tell him about you. Aunt Vere would board you . . . And you wouldn't make him feel ignorant."

"It's awfully decent of you . . . I don't know how to thank you."

"Well, don't thank me. I'm not being anything special. And if I could find a nice friendly white collar guy to help my uncle, why it's all to the good . . . Now, come on home to supper at our place."

"Well, I—"

"Ma says you're to come. We've got Leota Leniuk up there helping Ma. And boy, can she cook!"

"Did you come on horseback?"

"Yeah. Say, do you ride?"

"Well, yes. That is, I sit on the horse. Chief Heap-Big-Jump-Up-And-Clutch-Leather they call me."

"Whites have an old nag named Cyclone. I guess he was pretty fast twenty-five years ago. I'll go over and borrow him for you. I'll just be a few minutes. Throw your tooth brush into a gunny sack and come for the night."

"But I have quite a bit of work—"

"It can wait for one night of your life."

Feeling strangely light and free, Dan paced the floor of his narrow shack, his heart leaping with excitement. A decent summer job seemed almost in view. Calculating what he could save through the winter with what he already had, and a modest appraisal of what the summer might bring, he could perhaps count on starting at the university in a year's time.

When Reuben appeared on the road leading Cyclone, Dan felt a rush of affection for him. He had never had a real friend. He had come to regard himself as a lonely person, marked out by life for loneliness. But it occurred to him now that this was probably not true. He felt a great impetus of energy, as if something of Reuben's strength and balance, the birthright of all Florrie's kin, had entered into him. It's appreciation, he decided. Someone appreciating my own peculiar qualities . . . I'd like to be like that, he thought humbly . . . Lifting up the downtrodden . . . He remembered the riders going by, singing in the storm the evening before. He smiled to himself. I bet that was Reuben. Reuben and Leota. Even Leota wouldn't be shy of Reuben.

He looked again at the poem he had written.

> Moses struck the rock
> And quail hovered near . . .
> . . . its strangest treasure:
> The sweetness in it . . .
>
> Dear God, grant me to taste of the honey in the rock!

He saw it now in all its adolescence and self-pity. His hand moved to tear the page and fling it into the fire. But he stopped himself, a quirk of amusement in the twist of his mouth, his perspective for the moment having leaped ahead ten years into maturity. He snatched up a pencil and scribbled at the end of his poem:

Dear God,
    Many, many thanks for honey suddenly and unexpectedly received.
                Humbly and gratefully yours,
                        D.R.

Chapter Six

I

ONE balmy day in December, while Leota and Florrie were doing the lunch dishes and Reuben was lathering his face at the wash basin, preparing to shave, Gottlieb suddenly opened the back door and came into the kitchen.

"Well, well!" cried Florrie, rushing to enfold him in a warm hug. "Surprise, surprise!" Standing off a bit, she looked him over with her shrewd gaze. "Return of the prodigal! How're you wintering?"

"Gone in like the gophers for the winter," laughed Gottlieb. "Nice and clean you're all getting," he said as Florrie went back to the dishes. "Well, Reuben, when you're all slicked up, what about riding into town with me for company?"

Grinning at him in the mirror, Reuben answered, "Sure. It's train night. I'll see if there's any Christmas mail."

"Should be in now," said Florrie. "It's the twentieth of December. There's things I ordered from the catalogue weeks back."

"How's the hand?" Gottlieb asked, rolling himself a cigarette.

"Coming along. Taking quite some time. But anyways, it meant I had company with Leota here. Nice to talk to another woman, sure is."

"Mean to say you're shaving?" Gottlieb asked Reuben in mock surprise. "How many whiskers you got now? It was just thirteen last time I counted back in the fall."

"Go wan," said Florrie. "He's had quite a beard for some time now. What d'you mean, thirteen whiskers?"

It was really Leota, Gottlieb wanted to tease. She kept her back to him, going steadily on with the dishes. Although she had known Gottlieb for so long, she never felt at ease in his presence. She knew he liked to rile her, make her show temper, or blush.

"What's under here?" he asked, lifting the edge of a spotless dish towel that covered something on the table. "Oh boy! Braided bread with poppy seeds! Ma, I never had a good meal since I left home. Let me have some!"

"Here's the knife," said Florrie good-naturedly. "You can cut yourself a piece. Just one, mind. Here's the butter."

"Boy, still warm," said Gottlieb slicing off a crust. "Jees, Ma, let me give you a kiss for that."

"Get your whiskery chin off me!" cried Florrie, pushing him away. "Anyways, it was Leota made the bread, not me."

"Then I got to give Leota the kiss!"

Her hands dripping, Leota fled, getting the table between them. Gottlieb would have been round it at a bound, but Reuben, with one side of his face still white with shaving soap, seized him in a vice-like grip. Gasping and struggling, they thumped around the kitchen, and finally fell with a crash in front of the stove.

"Listen you two!" shouted Florrie above the groans, grunts and curses from the floor, "if my cake has fell, it'll be all sog for the Christmas party. Leota," she said severely, stepping elaborately over two writhing hands clenched together, "if you ever want to know what it's like in a nut house, all you got to do is stay at the Zwick's place awhile."

"This kid," Gottlieb gasped, "getting too big for his boots. Can't hold him no more. Come on now, kid, say 'Uncle,'" he panted, rising to the top for a moment.

"Say 'Uncle' yourself," grunted Reuben, pulling him down again.

"Gottlieb!" yelled Jud, thrusting open the back door. "Where is he? Hey! Come and get your goddarn horse! He's tromped down the side gate and got the chickens all on the run."

"I'm coming!"

"Got you beat," smiled Reuben getting up off the floor.

"Got me beat nothing," Gottlieb protested. "If I didn't have this jacket on—"

"Quick!" said Florrie. "Go get Patches out of there. Run!"

"Maybe I can get shaved now," Reuben remarked, going back to the mirror.

"That Patches!" Florrie watched through the window while Gottlieb caught his big black and white horse, and Jud tried to wire up the fallen posts. "No matter how you tie him, he always gets away. Figures out every gate. The only way to keep him tight is to shut him in the barn. That's what Gottlieb's doing now," she added. "Close up the doors. That's the only thing to hold him."

"Clever old horse," said Gottlieb coming in again a moment later. "Looks over a situation, and next thing you know, he's gone."

"No looking about it," Florrie argued. "He keeps his eyes right ahead, and figures it all out with his nose and his lips."

"Ma, you make me blush."

"Good thing somebody can still make you blush. Say, got the afternoon off to take Sarah Christmas shopping?"

"Got the afternoon off."

"Coming for supper? I'd just like to know. Jud and me will be out visiting, but Leota will have something here for you and Reuben if you want it."

"Well thanks, Ma," said Gottlieb giving Leota a long look from under his dark lashes. "But I won't be back this way."

"Coming on Christmas Day?"

"Sure. New Year's Day too."

"Good for you. Coming to the Christmas party at the school tomorrow night?"

"Tomorrow night? Sure, I'll be there. Might be late, though. How's Mr. Root and his concert?"

"He's getting skinnier than that starving greyhound like you see painted on a Greyhound Bus," declared Florrie, hanging up the dish-towel.

"They're practising like mad down at the school Fenna said on Sunday," said Leota, wiping out the dishpan.

"Mr. Root and Fenna getting pretty thick, so I hear." Gottlieb licked a cigarette paper, rolling it deftly over the tobacco. "I hear tell he's in love with her."

"Don't believe it," Reuben retorted. "He's got no time for girls."

"It's always been Philip Jebson with her," said Leota.

"Mr. Root better look out for Philip," laughed Gottlieb, his cigarette hanging on his lip while he snapped his lighter. "Philip's a jealous man. Weighs thirty pounds heavier, easy. I bet Mr. Root would groan to make a hundred and twenty."

> "'Let me have men about me that are fat:
> Sleek-headed men and such as sleep o'nights,'"

Reuben chanted into the mirror.

> "'Yon Daniel had a lean and hungry look:
> He thinks too much: such men are dangerous.'"

"He's hungry looking all right," said Gottlieb, "but he's the one who'll be in danger if he don't look out."
"Maybe it's all just talk," said Lecta worriedly.
Florrie sat down on the little loveseat she had once bought at an auction sale for herself and Jud.
"It'll blow over when the party is over." She twiddled with the dial of the radio. "Let's see if there's some pretty music."
"Coming Reube?" asked Gottlieb.
"Sure, right away."
"There's that nice song again," said Florrie, turning up the volume to a blare. "'*You're the only star in my blue heaven.*'"
"'And you're shining just for me,'" warbled Jud, coming in and stamping the snow off his boots, flinging his coat on to a spike driven into the wall. "'You're the only light that guides me through the night . . .' Come on, Leota, let's dance!"
And he whisked her away, nearly swinging her off her feet, dancing her about the kitchen with his powerful lead, singing resonantly in her ear. In the meantime, Reuben had pulled his mother to her feet, and now they were dancing.
"Well, look at that now," said Gottlieb. "Who'm I gonna dance with?"
But he joined them at once, having turned Florrie's broom upside down, using it for a partner, brushing his cheek against its spiky bristles, dancing idiotically with it until the song stopped. Then clutching the broom, he ended with a flourish:

"Oh I love the bearded lady
Cause her whiskers tickle so!
Shave and a haircut, six bits!"

"My cake!" Florrie groaned. "I'm scared to look. It'll be flat as a pancake with all this tromping around!"

Gingerly she opened the oven door.

"Didn't fall a bit," exclaimed Leota, peeking over her shoulder as Florrie gently closed the door again.

"It was your arm done the mixing, that's why."

"Well now I been to visit all the nuts in the nut house," said Gottlieb, replacing the broom, "let's get off to town, Reube!"

"God go with you," said Jud.

"Come on, Pop, it's no use sending a prayer after me," protested Gottlieb. "I'm just the black sheep of the family, but I'll find my way, even drunk. Patches will get me there."

Jud simply regarded him with tolerant affection.

With a superior smile, Gottlieb did up his jacket, put on his overshoes and gloves, considering himself witty and good fun, thinking that he indeed brought something into the dull family circle, especially to the old folks and tame Leota.

2

Gottlieb and Reuben rode into town just as the sun lay on the prairie rim like a ball of fire. An orange glow tinted with purple filled the whole western sky, daubing the snow with hues of mauve. Ahead, the outlines of the grain elevators rose up stark and bare, shoulders to the sky, receiving a tarnished gilding from the surge of colour in the sunset. Sleds and horses moved about in the slush, stood tethered at the stores and hotel, or took off with a merry jingle of sleigh bells for the outward trails.

The two young men put their horses in a stable behind Zimmerman's. As they stepped into the street, Joe approached with his slouching gait down the board walk.

"Hey Reube!" he shouted. "Something for you over at the post office. Telegram from up north. Hope it isn't bad news."

"Hope not," said Reuben. "Well thanks for telling me."

"Going over now?" Gottlieb asked.

"No. I'll give Zimm the list for Ma's groceries first."

"Meet me over at the beer parlour," Gottlieb grinned.

"He ain't old enough," Joe mocked.

"Just for a tomato juice."

Reuben let them joke over him.

"Well, I won't ask for a birth certificate this time," Joe allowed with elaborate generosity.

When they had parted, Reuben hurried at Zimmerman's, wondering what the telegram could mean, mentally going over various of his relatives, hoping that all was well with them. Arriving at the post office, he found the small place crowded, with a long line-up at the wicket waiting for Christmas mail which had come on the weekly train that morning. Ada Pearl was not in her usual place; she had been hard at it all day, and now old Slim Smith had taken over. Pinned to the green bulletin board, among the notices for Christmas parties and dances, Reuben saw a sealed envelope addressed to himself in red ink. Pulling it down, he pushed his way out into the street, impatiently tearing it open. Inside was a neatly folded note.

"Dear Reuben," he read. "A telegram came for you just when I was going off duty. I am taking it home, and the rest of your mail too, and leaving this note. For two reasons. One is that you would have to wait an awful long time in the line-up to get it. And the other is, if it's bad news, I'll be there to hold your hand. As ever, Ada Pearl."

He stood still for a moment, clenching the note in his hand. As the sun slipped below the horizon, the garish colours were quickly fading from the sky. A flood of metallic gold under a layer of purple cloud, swept the whole prairie for a few minutes. Reuben paused, considering. Hunger gnawed at him. He ought to be on his way home now, but he could not go without the Christmas mail. Slowly he set off down the road.

Twilight came with a line of pale yellow in the west. The vastness of the prairie sky, with its torn stained clouds, held a few large stars. The Fox place had a private, secluded situation, nestling into a hill with the town behind it, the sitting-room windows facing Wrist River and prairie sunsets. A gush of oil on their homestead had made them rich overnight, enabling them to build just as they chose. The front steps, lighted on both sides, made Reuben feel exposed as he knocked. The door opened almost at once, and he stood face to face with Ada Pearl.

"Reuben!" she cried. "How wonderful to see you! I knew you'd be in on the last train-day before Christmas. Come in!"

He stepped into the hall, festive with Christmas lights and decorations.

"I just came for my mail."

"Yes, of course." She took his arm confidingly as they passed through an archway. Shaded lamps gave a quiet light to the room with its plush chesterfield and chairs, thick rugs and heavy drapes. Reuben was not completely ignorant of the more refined modes of living. His Aunt Ruth's home in town had all the niceties of this one. She had inherited fine pieces of furniture from her husband's family, well rubbed and lovingly cared for through generations. Therefore he knew something about good quality. Through long association with the Leniuk womenfolk, he also knew how elegance could be achieved out of sheer nothing, with polished lamp chimneys, the nickel plating on stoves kept gleaming, cheap linoleum with a sheen like satin from constant scrubbing and waxing, rugs fashioned of dyed rags braided by hand, and curtains made of dyed flour sacks.

"You're quite fancy out here," Reuben remarked now, sitting down in a deep chair, not in the least overawed by the finery about him, though aware that he must reek of horse.

"Why I don't believe you've ever been out here before," said Ada Pearl in surprise, pleased at his aplomb. "No, we were still in the little old place when I was in high school."

She came to sit near him, hugging one knee with her clasped hands. In the silence, the music of Christmas carols wafted forth from the radio turned low.

"You're quite a stranger," she said with a forced laugh.

He noted changes in her, for he had not really looked at her for a long time. She had slimmed down somewhat in face and figure, and had learned to use her make-up more skilfully. Her blonded hair, no longer frizzled with a cheap permanent, lay in smooth shining waves. Yet for all that, there was a hard look about her. She embarrassed him. He did not know what to say to her, feeling that his own simple humour would sound hoydenish. He came at once to the point.

"I was wondering about the telegram."

"Oh yes, of course, the telegram."

She produced it, watching avidly as he ripped it open and read its contents.

"Well?" she demanded.

"It's not bad news," he answered, putting the telegram away in an inside pocket of his jacket. "Do you mind giving me the rest of my mail? I must get off home."

"But you've only just come," Ada Pearl objected. "Why not stay here for supper?" She rose, leading the way to the other end of the room. Reuben got up too. And then he saw that everything had a look of readiness and waiting. A little table was set for two with a pretty cloth, plates and glassware, and candles. "We're all alone," she said, turning to him. "The folks have gone to Hosanna and won't be back until tomorrow."

"I'm sorry," said Reuben casually, "but I have a date tonight."

"Well, break it then."

"No, I can't."

"Who is it? One of the Leniuk girls?" she asked smiling, trying to read his face. She saw nothing in his expression, not even annoyance. Who does he think he is? she thought to herself, as she so often had in the last few weeks, seeing him striding about town or leaping into the saddle, never bothering about her except for an impersonal greeting as he picked up the mail. Whenever she would try to get him into conversation, he would smile absently, his clear hazel eyes looking right through her.

He used to kiss me, she thought now, fury rising in her at his indifference. I think he was nuts about me once, when we were kids in high school. What did I do that made him change?

"Have a cup of coffee with me, just for old times' sake," she suggested.

Before he could answer, she had hurried through the door into the kitchen. Like a restive horse, Reuben moved about, looking for the mail. With surprising speed, Ada Pearl returned, carrying a tray with coloured paper serviettes, two cups of steaming coffee, and a plate of rich, dark, fruit cake.

"Just milk, no sugar for you. I remember, you see."

"Ada Pearl, I don't want to hurt your feelings, but I cannot stay. Please, I must have my mail and go home."

"I know," she said soothingly, "but you still have time to drink a cup of coffee before your long ride. Do sit down. It reminds me so much of our high school days. We've had lots of cups of coffee together."

"Those days are over," he declared, submitting to taking a cup.

With a little thrill, she recognised a tightening of his jaw-line which could mean a struggle between them.

"I never had such a good time since," said Ada Pearl. "We had great fun, didn't we? The old gang is all broken up now." She sighed reminiscently. "And Nate had gone and married that funny monkey-faced Leniuk girl," she mused. "That was the biggest surprise of all."

Reuben was silent, sipping the coffee.

"Nice?" she asked.

"Yes, thank you." He knew he had tasted better around the Lily of the Valley way, but he did not say so.

Inwardly she was wondering when Reuben would ask for his mail again, but he said nothing. Setting down the empty cup, he waited, unrelaxed and wary.

"Remember the old Shakespeare Miss Hester used to sling at us? Here, have some cake."

"No thanks, I've got to go."

"But you can't go without your mail."

"No. Where is it?"

"Let's see now. Where did I put it?" she laughed. "You'll have time for a piece of cake while I remember."

"If you can't think of it just now," he said lightly, getting to his feet, "Gottlieb or I will be in again. Just hand it over to Slim."

"Wait a minute. Now I remember."

"Well then, please go and get it."

"Come on, let's take a look." She linked her arm through his.

Just then his quick eye noticed something under a little decorated Christmas tree on a table in the hall. It was most certainly a large bundle of mail tied with binder twine, and practically concealed under a layer of green tissue paper. Possibly a breeze had disturbed the paper upon his arrival. He walked along with Ada Pearl through the archway into the hall, stopping short by the tree,

"Well, what d'you know!" he exclaimed ironically, seizing the bundle. "If it wasn't here all the time!"

Ada Pearl loosed her arm and stood before him, contrite.

"Oh Reuben," she murmured, casting aside her pretences, and speaking sincerely. "It was only a little joke to get you to stay a bit longer. We've always been such good friends. The other guys around here are so dull and boring. They haven't any manners or education. They make me feel so lonely. And besides, you and I, well, we always understood each other."

"It's nice you remember it like that," he said courteously. "But I must go. Good night, Ada Pearl. And thanks for the coffee."

"You don't seem to realise, I don't invite just any Tom, Dick, or Harry over here like this," she said angrily.

"Thanks for the compliment, then."

She simply could not reach him. As always, his calm indifference enraged her. Blocking the doorway, she spoke swiftly, her voice charged with venom.

"How come you think you're so high and mighty, with the kind of mother you've got!"

She had her reward, for she had pierced his armour at last. His face flinched as if she had lashed at it with a whip. His lips tightened, Dropping the mail, he seized her arms, and she welcomed his hard strength, laughing as he pulled her to the couch, letting herself down limply beside him. With one movement, he threw her body face down across his thighs, her chin dangling near the floor, her feet kicking wildly.

"Reuben!" she sputtered, struggling and giggling helplessly.

Without a word, he pulled up her skirt, exposing her plump buttocks in their frilly silk panties. Avoiding her flailing heels, he administered a few sharp smacks with his hand, and then flung her from him.

"You bastard!" panted Ada Pearl.

Calmly, Reuben went back into the hall and picked up the bundle of mail again. Looking back at her, he said quietly,

Honey in the Rock 87

"G'night." Closing the door behind him with a gentle click, he plunged down the lighted steps, out into the starry evening.

When he slipped into the beer parlour a few minutes later, he found Joe and Gottlieb drinking together.

"You sure as heck didn't stay long," Gottlieb grinned.

"No," Joe went on. "We seen you sneaking along the road to Ada Pearl's. She figured you'd be in on train day. And she's all by her lonesome out there, and here you're back so quick like she set the dog on you."

"What's the news in the telegram?" Gottlieb asked as Reuben sat down with them.

"Just Merry Christmas from Auntie Vere."

"Just Merry Christmas, eh?" sneered Joe. "No, don't give him nothing," he said to the beer slinger. "He's too young. He ain't twenty-one yet. I should throw him out."

"Are you ready?" Reuben asked.

"Yeah, in just a minute," Gottlieb returned.

"What's your hurry?" Joe asked. "Has your Ma got one of the Leniuk girls out there working for her?"

"It's Leota," Gottlieb laughed, digging Joe in the ribs. "You know, the hell cat that's your favourite."

"Keep your hands off my girl," Joe growled. "I'll be showing her who's boss one of these days. I'd be scared stiff about her there with Reube, except he's too young for a razor, even."

"What you looking so sour about?" Gottlieb asked Reuben. "Can't take a bit of kidding?"

"He wouldn't kid nobody!" roared Joe. "Baby carriages are too expensive! Anyways, Leota, she's dead from the neck down. Except with me. Boy, she's a hell cat when she's with me. What d'you think of her, Reube?"

"She's—she's a decent girl. A beautiful and decent girl," Reuben ground out.

Gottlieb did not like the tension in the atmosphere, or Reuben's white set face and angry out-thrust of chin. Something of the loyalty that bound the Leniuk family so close, existed also in Gottlieb.

"Easy, easy," he muttered. "Leota's a cousin, sort of. Dad and Uncle Jonas would be sore if they knew us guys was talking her over in the beer parlour."

"Hell, we didn't mean no harm, did we, Reube?" said Joe good-naturedly. "You started it."

"Did you get the mail, Reuben?" Gottlieb asked, hastily getting up to leave. "Maybe we better go. Don't forget Ma's groceries."

"Getting colder," Reuben remarked casually as they strode along. "Going to freeze up again."

"What was wrong with you back there with Joe?" Gottlieb inquired, tightening the cinches on Patches. "What you so sour for?"

"Just born that way," said Reuben, mounting his horse.

With a brisk clatter of trotting hoofs, they soon left the little town behind them. Few clouds now trammelled the starry sky which still held some light in the west, deepening over its wide arc to navy blue in the east. On every side of the rutted trail, the snow-covered prairie fell away in waves, darkly white in the starlight.

"What happened with you and Ada Pearl?" Gottlieb asked.

"Nothing. I just got the mail and the telegram."

"You could of stayed a bit," said Gottlieb, turning towards him curiously. "She doesn't have smallpox."

"My dinner's waiting at home."

"You know, Reube, you got to get to know about life. No good listening to the folks. Cripes, there they sit out on the farm all their life, going to church and all that stuff. They don't know what goes on, they sure don't. Let me take you out and show you a good time . . . Don't get me wrong. I got my own ideas of what's right. I never hurt nobody. Never take a girl for the first time. That's my rule. No married women. No kid stuff."

"Why you don't get married?" Reuben asked idly. "Why you don't marry Sair and settle down?"

"Think I'm going to marry without money? Then you go on relief and raise a crop, all right. A crop of kids. And you can't feed them. That's just plain stupid. Get wise to yourself, kid," said Gottlieb patronisingly. "You can tie yourself up to some dame if you like, but you won't find me sticking my neck in the noose."

"Poor Sair."

"I never hurt Sair. She's as pure as the day she was born."

"Seeing her tonight?"

"Yeah, going to the pictures in town."

"Horseback?"

"We're taking Basil's team and sled. Whites are away; went to see their folks. Sair's running the place on her own."

Just then Reuben's horse shied at a large rock at the side of the road. Her hind feet slithered on some ice, but he kept his seat, speaking calmly to her "Come on, Darkie girl."

She continued to jump sideways, nervous and trembling, while Patches plodded on without a quiver.

"Needs a taste of the whip, that one," Gottlieb commented, looking back at them. "That's what I said to Dad the other day. I'd fix her."

Reuben managed to get Darkie to stand while he soothed her with his hands and his voice.

"We never laid the whip on her hide yet, Dad nor I. It would ruin her just as she's coming along so nice."

"Look at that," said Gottlieb. "Still jumping around like she's crazy."

"Never mind. It's this talk about a whip makes her jump. I'll sing her a lullaby when I'm alone with her."

"Well, here's the cut-off." Gottlieb turned his horse. "See you at the Christmas party. Think it over, what I said," he added, urging Patches to a canter.

3

Alone, Reuben sang Dan's song, which calmed and steadied Darkie. Her small sure-footed hoofs and slender black legs kept at a good pace, for she knew she was headed homewards. The prairie wind blew in gusts now, lifting the horse's mane and tail, crisping the snow, and bringing mournful sounds to the loneliness. On the top of a rise, Reuben could see the various lights of the district. Over there, small, like a star, would be Leniuk's. And nearer, the light of his own home.

"'Oh it's lamplighting time in the valley,'" he sang, spontaneous as the wind itself. And Darkie picked her way with more care, descending the hill before the last long level stretch of trail.

Leota was sitting comfortably in Florrie's rocking chair by

the kitchen stove, knitting the German way with flying fingers. She had washed her hair in preparation for the Christmas party, and it hung in a dark silken mass on her back, tied with a ribbon on the nape of her neck. When Reuben came in, she got up at once.

"Getting a bit nippy, isn't it?" she called cheerily, opening the oven.

"Wouldn't be surprised if she goes below zero again tonight," said Reuben, flinging down his things. Then noiselessly, he came up behind her at the stove. "Oh Leota!" he cried, hugging her and putting his cold cheek against her warm one. "You're so good to come home to "

"Reuben, stop it!" she protested. "I'll drop the plate and all your dinner. Look out now, I'll kick!"

"Dangerous woman," he teased, releasing her at once, but surreptitiously undoing her apron strings as he turned to the wash basin. "Cripes. Even hot water in the basin for me. You know, Leota, you're going to spoil that husband of yours."

"What husband?" she demanded, setting a place for him at the table. "What are they talking now at the beer parlour?"

"Nothing. I just meant, when you do decide to get married."

She set the plate of steaming food before him; sausages, sauerkraut and noodles. Then, bringing the lamp over to the kitchen table, she sat companionably nearby with her knitting.

"What are you making this time?" he asked, attacking his food with relish.

"This is a sweater for Mrs. White's baby that's coming next month."

"You ought to get paid for it."

"I do. Fifty cents for each thing I make, and she buys the wool. It's lots easier than scrubbing floors, and I can do it when I get the time."

"You should be knitting for your own babies."

"Reuben!"

"Well, don't you want to get married, settle down, have a family?"

Leota sighed. "Yes, I do. But I just don't like the ones that like me."

"You'll meet the right one some day." He shoved his plate to one side. "Come on, Girl, put that knitting away," he said.

"Mrs. White can wait. Have a nice piece of apple cake with me. No, you sit still. I'll get it."

"May as well," she answered, her face glowing.

She had never before been waited upon by a man. It gave her a sense of completeness, making her feel one with all other women who had known such grace. When they had finished the dessert, he would not hear of her going on with the knitting.

"A game of crib, that's what we'll have," he declared, taking the lamp to the little table by the love seat. "Two out of three wins the rubber."

Some undefinable feeling charged the air between them. In her heart, Leota knew what it meant, but she refused to examine the meaning, only waited, torn between anticipation and panic, her heart-beats sharp and painful. She could not concentrate on the game, nor did she get good cards to encourage her.

"You're going to skunk me," she said ruefully as Reuben's pegs raced ahead of hers under his competent square brown hands. She felt his arm lightly encircle her waist as she began to deal. His thick stubby lashes made odd shadows on his cheek.

"You'll catch up," he comforted her.

"Who was in town?" she asked.

"Oh, the usual bunch ... Joe ..."

"I bet he told you about the Hallowe'en dance," said Leota, laying down the pack for Reuben to turn up the top card. "Did you know I bit him?"

"Good!" said Reuben, flicking over the card.

"Kicked him in the shins, too," she confessed.

"Glad to hear it!"

She looked up at him inquiringly.

"What does that beer-swilling—hog—know about making love to a girl like you!" said Reuben indignantly. She thought she even detected a note of jealousy in his tone.

Although Leota was half expecting a kiss, she was not really prepared for one. She had no experience to guide her, either to nip it in the bud, or to bring it to flower. It came suddenly. Had Reuben been shy and boyish with her, she might have brushed him off lightly and then mothered him afterwards. But he wasn't like that. He kissed her hungrily and long. For all his gentleness, his arms tightened about her like steel bands.

The shock of such physical contact with him all but shattered Leota. When it was over, she turned blindly, with whitened face, to the little table, and leaned against it. He was not unaffected either, but she did not see that. Beneath his finger tips, he felt the uncontrollable galloping of her heart. He watched her anxiously, wondering for a moment if she might faint. But Leota had her own pride. She made an enormous effort to pull herself together, clasping her hands tightly to still their shaking.

"Was I so—repulsive—Leota?" he asked at last. "Did I seem just like Joe to you?"

"No," Leota answered weakly. "You're not like Joe. But I just—I wasn't thinking—Oh Reuben, why did you do it? It was always so nice with you. Now it won't ever be the same."

"Life doesn't stay the same, Leota."

"Anyways," she burst out, "what if Florrie and Jud came through that door right then. What would Florrie think of me?"

"Ma?" smiled Reuben.

"Yes. She'd think I was leading you on, right here in her own kitchen. She'd think I was a—a—cradle snatcher."

"My folks wouldn't," said Reuben. "If Ma and Dad walked in on us like that, know what they'd think? There's Reuben kissing Leota. Isn't he the lucky dog! That's what they'd think."

"But they wouldn't. Not with me. I'm old enough to be your gramma."

"Listen, Leota, if Gram was alive, she'd be eighty-five. Ma's sixty-two already, so you've got a long ways to go."

The conversation had helped to calm Leota. Colour had returned to her cheeks and lips. Now she was able to say with quiet directness, "But just the same, I don't want nobody like you kissing me just for fun. I don't want Joe mauling me neither. My sisters think I'm funny. Naomi says there's something wrong with me, maybe."

His arm slid round her again.

"There's nothing wrong with you. You're my dream girl. I dream about you all the time. With other girls I always figure, they're never knee high to Leota."

"You know how to talk nice," she said bitterly. "What about Ada Pearl? You write letters to her even."

Instantly she got the impression that she had somehow wounded him, so that in spite of all her own floundering, her heart went out to him.

"No, no," she murmured in confusion. "I shouldn't say that. It's not my business."

"I'll tell you just the same, so you'll know from me," said Reuben. "You see, I took her out to the dances in high school. She was my girl friend. But then, she got so awful possessive I quit her. I don't know why she's interested in me. There's lots of other guys around her all the time. She wrote to me and asked me if I was coming home this Christmas, so I just wrote back and said I wasn't."

"It's not my business," Leota repeated.

"Still mad at me?" he asked teasingly, giving her an affectionate hug. She stiffened.

"No, you mustn't, Reuben."

"How can I help it with you? A girl with hair like black silk, eyes like stars, lips like velvet, teeth like pearls . . ."

Even Leota had to laugh at this outrageous list of her charms. As he passed a hand lingeringly over her shining dark hair, he saw the pulse fluttering in her throat. He took her into his arms again, his face against her hair, moved by the sight of her innocence. In the end, she relaxed, resting her head on his shoulder with a strange feeling of home and peace. For without knowing it, Leota hungered for affection. The strongest of ties united all the members of her family, but they did not kiss. They rarely even touched each other. They seldom wept, and then only in secret. Leota was conscious now of a wonderful but terrifying loosening of bounds within herself.

He's sweet, she thought recklessly. And it's nice, like this with his arms around me. Then with a pang, she reminded herself, only he's so young. Just a kid. Only he never seems like a kid.

"Reuben," she said aloud, "why we don't go on with our game?"

"Sure. Why we don't?" he answered gaily.

Her next hand was full of sevens and eights, and the crib had a double run.

"Even steven!" cried Reuben, putting her peg level with his own. "Who said you'd get skunked?"

"My luck's changed," smiled Leota, her colour brilliant, her heart beating unevenly.

"What about a kiss for the loser?" teased Reuben.

She turned towards him and put her arms about his shoulders. It was rather like jumping off a precipice, but she did not hesitate. They held each other close. In a multitude of tender kisses, she gave him all her sweetness that had never been spent on anyone before. Outside, the wind moaned about the house, with a matching flicker in the lamp which set their joined shadows rocking silently on the kitchen wall. At length, like a small darting tongue of flame, desire leaped up in them both. With his cheek on hers, Reuben said,

"Why we don't go on with our game? It's even steven."

"Why we don't?" she said lightly, her heart aflutter. "It's anybody's game now."

"Leota, don't let anyone fool you," he said steadily, keeping her for a moment longer within the circle of his arm. "There's nothing wrong with you. You're warm and sweet. You're lovely!"

Picking up the cards, he began to shuffle and deal. Watching his hands, Leota thought, My God, what's wrong with me? I feel like I been sliced clean in half.

"I think I hear the folks coming," he said regretfully.

Tramping towards the house, Jud had stopped short. "Glory be," he muttered.

Plodding blindly on, Florrie fell into the snow behind him.

"Good grief, man! Right on my bad hand. And I bet I sprung a run in my silk stockings too!"

"I just seen something I shouldn't of," he said, helping her up.

"What?"

"Reuben kissing Leota. Frost come off that window today. You can see in pretty good with the lamp lit."

"I like a nice bit of honest love going on," chuckled Florrie. "But what'll we do? We better not walk in on them like that."

"I'll go back to the barn and holler, and you holler back,"

Jud suggested. "You tell them I'm fixing that gate Patches broke down."

Laughing to herself, Florrie waited, and when they had shouted back and forth a bit, she went on to the house. Reuben opened the door for her.

"Did you fall down?" he asked, solicitously brushing the snow off her coat. "What next?"

"Slipped on a patch of ice," she said heartily. "It's freezing up again. Getting pretty cold."

"Like a hot drink?" Leota asked from the stove.

"You bet. Just the thing."

"Dad need any help?" Reuben asked.

"No, he's just tightening up that gate Patches broke. He'll be right in."

Setting out cups, keeping up a bright chatter, Leota thought again, in wonder, I feel sliced clean in half. Florrie sat beside her, noting the girl's hectic colour and starry eyes. Her heart was touched. She yearned to mother her.

"Got your hair washed, eh?" she said approvingly. "Shines like a silver dollar!"

4

When Gottlieb rode Patches through Basil White's gate into the barnyard, he saw the light streaming from the kitchen window, and Sarah moving quickly about inside. As always, when he went to visit her, he experienced a warm feeling of homecoming. Wherever Sarah went, there would be good cooking smells, and order, clean clothes starched and ironed, the house scrubbed, everything shining with wax and polish. Yet she did not make a man afraid to set his foot on the floor; for her housekeeping had hospitality in it, and warmth and understanding.

Tying his horse in a stall, Gottlieb went up to the house, entering without bothering to knock.

"Well, look who's here!" said Sarah sarcastically, though he could see that she was glad he had come. "Only half an hour late. That's early for you."

"Got a cup of coffee, Sair?"

"Oh sure."

Flinging down his hat and gloves, and unbuttoning his coat, he sat at the kitchen table, smiling across at her.

"How's everything?"

"Everything's all right, I guess. I got the chores done. Even harnessed up the team to save time."

"Good girl. When will Whites be back?"

"Day after tomorrow. No more peace and quiet for me then."

Bringing two cups of coffee to the table, she sat down with him.

"What's on at the show tonight?" she asked.

"Tom Mix. It's called *Forbidden Valley*."

"Forbidden, eh? Jonas should see that."

"Oh, well, you're free, white, and over twenty-one. You don't need to sit there under his thumb."

"I'll say not."

With her shoulder brushing Gottlieb's, she thought again of Jonas's words, "If he don't mean marriage this time, you bust up with him!" She had thought of those words so many times in the last weeks, always with resentment and hatred in her heart against her step-father. She could not bring herself to tell Gottlieb the reason for his ostracism. I couldn't bust up with Gottlieb, she thought, loving the lean dark face beside her, any more than I could cut off my right hand. Even if I wanted to. I been Gottlieb's intended all my life, just about.

They had these moments of closeness, as though they were almost part of each other. He felt it too. He was so sure of her that his peace of mind stayed undisturbed by their frequent quarrels. She was the rock and anchor in his life, though he knew it not.

"Well, I'm ready," Sarah announced. "The cutter's just over beside the shed."

"I'll hitch up then."

"When I come, I'll bring the quilts."

Giving her a swift kiss, he went out. Oh, I wish it was always nice like this, Sarah thought as she put on her warm things. Then I wouldn't mind Mrs. White and all the kids. Just so I could see Gottlieb!

Basil White's team of bays made good time on the road to town, the cutter flying lightly along.

"We'll be early for the nine o'clock show," Gottlieb told her. "What d'you want to do for a half hour?"

"I didn't see Pro yet since she got married. I'd like to visit with her."

"O.K., I'll drop you off at Zimm's."

"Won't you come too?"

"Hell, no. It's different for you. You're her sister. I'd just feel out of place in the newlyweds' nest."

"Well, I don't need to go," said Sarah, feeling as she so often did with Gottlieb, that he was slipping through her fingers.

"Sure you want to visit with her. You go ahead, and I'll meet you at the hall five minutes to nine."

He drew up at the store which poured light and bustle into the street; for it would remain open every evening now until Christmas.

"All right then," she agreed reluctantly. "I do want to see Pro."

"Sure you do," he said kindly. "You go ahead. Five to nine at the hall." He steadied her arm as she got out.

At five minutes to nine, Sarah arrived at the door of the hall and glanced inside. Gottlieb was not among the few who sat on the hard benches. She walked quickly off into the darkness where she could watch until he arrived at the lighted doorway. Gradually a steady strickle of people came along the walk in twos and threes, paying at the ticket box, and disappearing inside. But Gottlieb did not come. She waited calmly at first, but with a progressive sinking of her spirits. Nine o'clock came and went. Impatiently she walked back to the end of the street, hoping to meet him; but the last stragglers passed her hurriedly, leaving her waiting alone. The day had been a mild one, but now a cold wind nipped her fingers and cheeks. Too proud to return to Prolet, she decided to go into the hall, hoping that Gottlieb would join her before the show was over.

The lights had already gone off, and the picture had started. She paid her twenty-five cents, taking a seat at the end of a bench near the back where she could see the entrance to the building. For some time, she paid no attention to the film, watching only for Gottlieb; but still he did not come. The ancient Western unfolded on the screen, with its moments of fear, suspense, anger, and love. Now Sarah watched it with dull eyes. In *The Forbidden Valley*, girls were married off by their fathers; they had no freedom to choose. Yet the heroine had a secret lover whom she stole out at night to see. Like me, thought Sarah. And here people pay money to see a thing like that. They should come around the Leniuk place, they'd see how Jonas keeps us down. In her bitterness, she chose to vent her anger upon Jonas rather than upon Gottlieb. Just the same, Prolet got married, the voice of her common sense spoke loudly to her. Nathan came and asked for her, and Jonas let them be. And she married a man who wasn't even a Christian.

And Prolet was happy all right. Humming around the little apartment, cooking the meal after a long day in the store, keeping it hot for *him*, knowing he would always be there. And when Nathan came in to have his supper, leaving someone else to take over for a bit in the store, he and Prolet didn't exclude Sarah. They drew her into their warm circle, making her feel loved and wanted. Sarah had realised, sitting with them, what a lonely man Nathan had been before his marriage. Now he appreciated everything about Prolet. Her cooking. Her ideas for the store. Her gay clothes and cheerful wit. He cherished her. And she had blossomed like a flower in the sun. Sarah could not begrudge Prolet such happiness, and she had left Zimmerman's in a gay, uplifted state. Only to sit on a hard bench alone, waiting, waiting, for the man *she* loved to come. And he did not.

"Do girls—outside—marry men they hate and fear?" the girl in the film asked her secret lover, the moonlight shining on her blowing curls, her face turned up to him, yearning and innocent.

"Oh no!" Her lover took her gently into his arms. He was supposed to be part Indian, dressed in a beaded buckskin coat and moccasins. He had black hair and an Indian face with pensive lines lengthwise upon the cheeks. "They generally marry someone they love!"

At that point, her black-bearded father looked over the stockade and saw them, saw also the pure white star of a horse who stood poised on the edge of a precipice, snorting a warning to his master. But Sarah could bear no more of it. Nothing on the screen could compare with her own disappointment, suspense, and misery. As quickly and quietly as she could, she got out of the hall, turning rapidly down the street, not knowing where to go, wanting only to get away before the lights went up and neighbours saw her sitting there alone.

Desolately, she wondered where Gottlieb had gone. She found her feet turning in the direction of the hotel. When she came up to it, it looked dark and deserted except for a dull light burning in the waiting-room. Weariness caught up with her, for she had wakened at six that morning, doing the work of a man and a woman both throughout the day. And she was used to going to bed at nine. When she thought of the drive still ahead, she grew angry. I'm going up and look around, she decided. I can always say I was just going to the 'Ladies'.

Through the transoms, she could hear the normal life of the hotel. The quiet snoring of some weary traveller. Men having a game of poker. An angry retort. A triumphant laugh. As she neared a turn in the corridor, she heard voices, a woman's high pitched laugh, the easy intimate conversation of men. The timbre of one of those voices she recognised at once; she would know it in a thousand for Gottlieb's even though she could not catch the words. As she rounded the corner, she saw light coming in a stream from the door of Room 9, which stood slightly ajar. Hastily, she tried to retreat, but from inside the room someone had caught a movement of hers, and sprang out.

"Up kinda late, ain't you?" It was Joe. "Come on in and join the party."

"Oh, I didn't mean—" She broke off, confused.

"Come on, you're perfectly welcome." He took her arm. "Look who's here," he said, drawing her inside. "You sure got your wires twisted this time, Gottlieb."

In the scarred battered room with its bent iron bedstead, sagging mattress and patched spread, Gottlieb sat on a ragged wicker chair with Ada Pearl on his knee. Small glasses and a bottle of sherry stood on the bedside table under the light of a boudoir lamp with a faded pink shade. Ada Pearl held a glass daintily in her hand with little finger crooked.

"Jesus!" said Gottlieb, aghast. "Tom Mix! Oh Sarah, I forgot!"

"Yes. So I notice." Sarah's face was expressionless.

A thin dark girl with a large painted mouth had the rocking chair behind the door.

"This is Lil," said Joe. "She works here now."

"Honest, Sair, it just went clean out of my mind," Gottlieb explained. "See, I came over here and had a drink with the boys. And then Ada Pearl, she comes with a telephone message for Joe's mother, didn't she, Joe? And of course Mrs. Weiman's at a shopping trip in Calgary, so then we got talking to Ada Pearl and Lil here. Then pretty soon Joe says, 'How's about a nice quiet little party up in Room 9? I got some real nice sherry, Spanish stuff.' Didn't you, Joe? My God I am sorry. Did you see the show through?"

Ada Pearl's laugh tinkled, her hand stroking Gottlieb's hair. Sarah saw the lipstick on his cheek and on the collar of his shirt.

"Come on, sit down," Joe invited, motioning to the bed.

"Have a drink," said Lil. "Got another glass, Joe?"

"No thanks," said Sarah proudly.

"Of course the Brethren always make it sound as if we were getting the D.D.T.'s," said Ada Pearl coldly. "You just don't understand that people can have a nice quiet little party with real good friends without getting drunk."

Without answering, Sarah took the proffered seat on the bed, while Joe sat on a straight-backed chair that creaked under his weight. As she watched Gottlieb with the girl on his knee, Lil laughing, and all of them wondering how Gottlieb could possibly have forgotten Tom Mix, she thought how dreary their idea of a party was, especially after the hospitality of Prolet's and Nathan's little home, which shone for her like a lighted lantern on the prairie. The thought of their gentleness with each other cut her to the heart now. She had had dreams of herself and Gottlieb establishing just such a marriage. And now she faced the truth squarely for the first time: it could never be.

"I'm awful sorry, honest, Sair," said Gottlieb penitently.

Ada Pearl continued to stroke his hair.

"Oh he's real hard to hold on to, isn't he? Doesn't want to be tied down. Just like Patches. You know Patches?" she asked Sarah condescendingly.

"All my life just about."

"Well then, you know what I mean."

All my life, just about, Sarah thought, I been Gottlieb's intended. I figure I could no more part with him than I can cut off my right hand. But suddenly, she wanted to be free of Gottlieb. She wanted to be the kind of woman she knew she could be on her own. Kind, patient, loving. Gottlieb was poison in her system, destroying her. But I can't, I can't give him up, she thought silently, desperately.

And then, like thunder, Jud's voice roared in her ears:

"If thy right hand offend thee, Brother, Sister, cut it off!"

"Hell, I didn't know he had a date with you," said Joe mildly. "If I'd of known that—"

"Look, Sair," said Gottlieb, getting up and setting Ada Pearl on her feet. "I'll go over to the livery barn and hitch up right away. I'll bring the cutter round. Just stay here and keep warm. I won't be two shakes." Putting a hand under Sarah's chin, he tried to lift her drooping head, but she shied away angrily. The fragrance of Ada Pearl's perfume lingered on his hands.

Outside a car roared along the road to the hotel.

"That must be the salesman that wired ahead for a room," said Joe, listening. "He's sure pulling in late. Lil, make with the duster in Room 4. Quick now!"

"I won't be two shakes," Gottlieb repeated, following the others out.

"Oh, don't go," said Ada Pearl smiling, as Sarah got up too.

"I'd just as soon wait downstairs," said Sarah coldly.

"Well, I'm awfully sorry about your show and everything."

It was a rare satisfaction for Ada Pearl to have this moment of triumph over one of the Leniuk girls after her failure with Reuben. Sarah stood at the door, looking back at her a moment.

"You're the one I'm sorry for," she said suddenly, straightening to her tallest and most imposing.

"What do you mean?"

"It's too bad," said Sarah, looking her up and down, "that you can't get a man of your own instead of borrowing other people's. Even writing to young Reuben to see if you might have a chance with him still. You must be hard up!" The dimples in her cheeks came and went with bitter amusement.

"Be seeing you!" Waving a glove, she went swiftly, before the other girl had a chance to answer.

True to his word, Gottlieb quickly appeared with the cutter and team, full of apology and courtesy, to which Sarah answered with cold silence.

"Well, I said I'm sorry," he said finally, as the horses pranced homewards. "What else can a man do?"

"You could turn up at the hall at five to nine so I don't have to sit there on a bench alone."

"It wasn't killing you to sit on a bench alone."

"It was too, killing me!" she cried out. "You been killing me for years!"

"It was an accident," said Gottlieb impatiently. "Just an accident."

"How would Jud and Florrie like it, seeing you like that with Ada Pearl on your knee and her lipstick all over you? After what Mrs. Fox done to Florrie?"

"Why bring Florrie into it? Look what she done herself!"

The instant he had said those words, Gottlieb regretted them, for he loved Florrie dearly. He always remembered her face as he had seen it hovering over him in his delirium when she had nursed him through measles when he was twelve. He remembered how she had sat up with him long nights when he had cut his foot hideously with the axe the winter he was fifteen. Now he hated Sarah for making him say such a thing.

"Well, it's more fun with Ada Pearl than with you, the way you sit there grousing at me all the time."

"You can have her," Sarah returned. "Don't come around to me no more. If I never see you again it'll be too soon."

"Oh sure. I heard that plenty times before. Plenty times."

"If you can't drive without turning the cutter over, let me do it."

"Go ahead! It's drifted along here, that's all."

She took the lines into her own strong hands. As if he could bear her company no longer, Gottlieb sat at the back of the sleigh, lighting a cigarette under the shelter of his jacket. They did not speak to each other for the remainder of the journey. When Sarah had driven up to White's barn, she jumped down, preparing to look after the horses, but Gottlieb came after her, putting his arm around her.

"Look, Sair, Ada Pearl don't mean a thing to me. She could never stand knee high to you, Sair. She don't mean a thing to me."

"If she don't mean a thing to you, why you have her sitting on your knee, putting lipstick all over you?"

"Oh, it's just for fun. She sits on any guy's knee just about. She don't take things serious like you." He took her into his arms. "Come on, Sair. Be a good pal."

Though all the magic of his charm drew her, she turned away, feeling as if she were tearing herself into pieces.

"You don't need to worry about Ada Pearl," he assured her. "I even felt disgusted the way she asked you, 'D'you know Patches?' Just like she knew him better."

"Please don't come around no more," said Sarah distantly.

"You're tired," he said kindly. "I'll put the team in."

He kissed her, but she stood stiff and wooden.

"Good-bye, Gottlieb," she said.

In the past, though he had never in his life known her to weep, she had slammed the door on him; she had left him, shouting and raging; but she had never parted with him in quite so calm a way after a quarrel. It made him uneasy.

"It's the Christmas party tomorrow night," he called as she went down the path to the house. But she closed the door very gently without answering.

Chapter Seven

I

"It really looks like a Christmas concert, don't it, Mr. Root?" said Billy White, grinning widely as he gazed with wonder about the unfamiliar classroom.

"Doesn't it, doesn't it," Dan corrected automatically. "Yes, it really does look as if the day has arrived." He glanced at his watch. Nearly half past three. "I think we should run over that last carol once more, boys and girls," he said patiently. "We want the whole thing to be just perfect. Take your places, will you please?"

Up on the rough board stage at the front, the bigger pupils again pulled aside the green curtains, and the entire class, clad in assorted costumes, formed themselves into a choir. At the little portable organ which the Leniuks had lent for the occasion, Fenna struck a chord. Dan lifted his hands for quiet, then dropped them and began to direct the singing of *Joy to the World*. How well they do it, he thought with a thrill of pleasure.

"All right, that will do," he told them. "I must say it sounds grand. Do it like that tonight, won't you? Well, go home now and don't forget to come back." General laughter. "Now let's see you get off the stage without falling off."

When they had filed down in an orderly manner, setting gold crowns, shepherds' staffs, and other properties carefully to one side, they put on their coats to depart bursting with suppressed excitement. Dan straightened the curtains and the improvised benches where the audience would sit. At one side of the room stood the Christmas tree in all its glory, decorated with paper chains and coloured balloons. Paper chains too, decorated the room and festooned the windows. At the foot of the tree lay bulky packages done up in red and green tissue paper, an inexpensive gift for each child in the district, from the youngest baby to the oldest pupil still at school. Dan had bought these with money donated by the school board. All that remained to be done now was to put the candy into the bags.

"Oh. I'll help you with that!" cried Fenna, jumping up from the organ as the others headed for home. "I don't have to hurry because I'm going over to White's for supper with Sarah, and it's just a step."

"I thought I'd measure them out with this mug," Dan explained in a business like way. "A mug of candies for each bag. If there are any left—" He shrugged.

"You can eat them yourself," Fenna giggled. "I won't tell. But if there aren't enough, Mr. Root?"

"Surely to God there'll be enough!"

They worked quickly and systematically at the teacher's desk. When all the bags were filled, they shamelessly ate up the few remnants.

"Just a minute," said Dan. "Let's have music while we work."

He had brought his radio in to the school to let the children hear some good Christmas music. "It will be Waltz Time on CBRM." He turned the dial. "There it is. Nice, hm?"

"Oh yes, lovely. There's my favourite song, *You're the Only Star in My Blue Heaven*!" Fenna began humming with the music, adding a richness to it as she moved gracefully from desk to tree carrying bags of candy. "Makes you feel like dancing," she said, sliding into dance steps behind the benches.

"Yes, doesn't it!" Dan agreed. Elated by his high spirits over the concert and a growing self-confidence, he placed his arm around her waist and took her hand to dance.

Since there was very little room to turn among the chairs and benches, they danced out into the dimness of the cloakroom. The song ended. While the announcer told in solemn tones the advantages of Miracle Toothpaste, Dan leaned against the wall, still in position for dancing. And his reason deserted him. His feelings, so long leashed and forbidden, rushed to take possession of him. His lips felt the fire of her cheek. Suddenly they were in each other's arms. He kissed her lips and her shining hair while her hands caressed the back of his head.

"Mr. Root," she gasped.

An icy hand gripped his heart. Mr. Root. He became conscious of the enormity of his actions, making love to a young girl whose father trusted him, kissing a pupil of his school, leaping that barrier which always lies between teacher and student, a barrier which is never set aside lightly. He put his hands on her shoulders.

"Come into the schoolroom," he whispered.

They sat down opposite each other on two benches. Dan took Fenna's hands in his own. In the fading light he could scarcely see her face.

"Please forgive me, Fenna. I—it was wrong of me."

"There's nothing wrong," she assured him, her voice singing with joy. At its note, that cold hand squeezed his heart again.

"It was wrong." he repeated. "I don't know what came over me. You and I are just two ships that pass in the night," he said sadly.

"Why?" she asked, stricken.

"Fenna, look, I'm a teacher. I don't know anything else but teaching, and I'm on the lowest rung of the ladder. I make forty dollars a month, and I don't own anything but what I can carry in my two hands. I've got to get some education if I'm ever going to get anywhere. It will be years before . . ."

"My father has four sections of land."

"I couldn't farm if I were starving. I'm only a teacher."

"Forty dollars a month is more than any of the men around here can earn. Even Gottlieb only makes twenty, and that's awful good, and he's the best worker in the district."

"It's good if you've got some land as well. And I've got to tide myself over the summer, too. I don't get paid in the summer."

"I sound like I'm throwing myself at you." Fenna bowed her head and a tear fell on his hand.

"I'll never forget you," he said, feeling as if he were speaking, insincerely, lines from a poor play.

"I'll remember you too, when I'm married to Philip."

"What are you talking about?"

"He came and asked my father last night. He wants me to marry him."

"What did your father say?"

"He's pleased. I told Philip I'd say tonight yes or no." She lifted her head, her face a pale blur.

"But Fenna, why?"

"You just don't know my father!" the girl burst out. She got up and stood at the window. "It's worse for me. He won't let me go out to work even. Just stay home year after year. I can go to some of the dances, that's all. And school. Only this year he didn't want me to come because the teacher was a man and he says I'm getting too old."

"It seems he was right."

"But I begged him; I even cried till he let me. I'd just die staying home doing chores all the time. Sometimes a person's just got to do something desperate, to change things . . ."

"You don't need to marry Philip."

"Yes, I do need to. Look at my sisters. Only Pro is married. Look at Sarah. *Twenty-six* and still piling up her hope chest. Look at Leota. *Twenty-five* and not even a boy-friend in sight. Naomi too. I just can't go on and on like that, not even allowed to go out working!" Fenna pulled her coat on savagely. "No, I'll marry Philip and make the best of it. Who else will come and ask Jonas for me? I got to go now or Sarah will be wondering."

"Don't do it, Fenna. Don't marry him," Dan pleaded. "I know I'm no one to give advice, but I'm sure you won't be happy with him. You'll be out of the frying pan into the fire."

"I'll be all right," Fenna muttered sullenly. "He's good-looking, and a preacher . . ."

"But those aren't reasons for marrying a man."

"Good-bye, Mr. Root," she said tragically. "Have fun, getting your education!"

"Fenna!" He strode after her, flinging his weight against the door so that she could not open it. "Please forgive me!"

"All right," she said levelly. "It just—happened. And I've been in love with Philip a long time, Mr. Root."

"I see. Will you dance with me sometime tonight?"

"Yes. Good-bye for now, Mr. Root."

2

"You was an awful long time over there," Sarah greeted Fenna shrewishly, opening the door for her younger sister. "The other kids went by ages ago."

"I was helping with the candy bags." Fenna's voice came faintly from the sitting-room where she removed her coat.

Sarah slammed a flat-iron down on the roaring stove, shoved in a hairpin that dripped from her braided bun, for her hair was freshly washed and slippery.

"You got to watch your reputation," she said sharply, carrying away a mound of ironed clothes. "No use getting yourself talked about with the teacher."

Fenna came into the warm lighted kitchen. "Nobody can talk about me and the teacher. I'm going to marry Philip."

"What did you say?"

"He came last night to see Father and ask him," said Fenna, colour staining her face, a faint smile on her lips. "So I'm going to marry him after New Year's."

Sarah threw herself into a chair, staring at her sister.

"What did Jonas say?"

"He's real pleased, if you want to know. Told me I could get married after New Year's, if I want."

Slowly Fenna became aware of Sarah's heavy eyes and drawn expression. "What was Herman doing here right now?" she asked. "I saw his truck just going away when I came in."

"He brought me my parcel, the things I ordered from the catalogue," Sarah answered. "I forgot it last night, so I waved the dishtowel at him when he went past this afternoon."

Fenna forced a laugh. "What would Gottlieb say to that?"

Sarah stood up, with a strong hand pulling the kettle over the heat to boil.

"I'll tell you now, once for all. Gottlieb and me had a bust-up. It's all over with him and I."

"But you're not going to stay home tonight, are you?"

"I'm going with Herman." Sarah paused. Even through her own suffering, she sensed something wrong with Fenna. As always, her innate motherliness asserted itself. "You want to come with us?" she asked. "Or is Philip picking you up?"

"I'll go with you and Herm. Philip figured I'd be coming with the folks."

"Men are awful," said Sarah, crashing some dishes down onto the kitchen table.

"Got much to do, Sair? I'll help."

"The cows to milk. You'd get yourself all dirty."

"There must be some overalls around," said Fenna desperately.

Sarah flicked an eagle eye at her. "Behind the back door, then, if you really want to. There's some of Billy's old boots there would fit you. That old leather jacket of his too." Her tone was kinder now as she held herself in check.

"Did you get some nice things from the catalogue?" Fenna asked, moving the large parcel from the chair so that she could sit down to buckle the boots.

"I didn't look yet," Sarah answered, tearing aside the wrappings. "I ordered a new dress for the party. This must be it." She shook out a brilliant garment and held it against herself. "How do you like it? I wanted red, but Gottlieb always says royal blue . . ." She flung the dress across the room. "I'll send it back!"

"No, no, Sarah. Royal is nice on you," said Fenna, picking up the dress again. "It's real pretty."

"There's supposed to be a petticoat with lace along the bottom," said Sarah rummaging among the papers. "Here! See, the lace shows when you dance. Just sometimes, when your dress swings."

"It's real nice," murmured Fenna, trying to gather strength from Sarah's warm tempestuous presence in whom love and jealousy struggled.

"I have to press them," said Sarah. "I'll press your green dress, too, if you like, with the chores done . . ."

3

"Boy oh boy! What a pretty blouse!" Florrie exclaimed as Leota emerged from the spare bedroom dressed for the Christmas party. "Pink. Just your colour. Matches your cheeks. And puffed sleeves really look smart. You didn't get that out of no catalogue."

"No, I made it," said Leota shyly.

"Black stitching on pink, and that little black velvet bow at the throat. Boy! You've got a nice full skirt there to swing when you dance, too. Give her a swing, Leota. Let's see how it looks."

Leota obligingly pirouetted, her skirt flying out showing a flash of white lace threaded through with pink ribbon on her slip. Entering the kitchen just then, Reuben whistled admiringly. He wore his only dark suit with a white shirt and a tie.

"All you good-lookers make me feel like an old bag," said Florrie, peering at herself in the mirror. "I shouldn't of went to that beauty parlour in Hosanna. Thought I'd get me another twist in the old wig for the party. But I dunno, seems like I better go to the Fiji Islands after what she done to me." With a stiff brush, she tried in vain to flatten the short pieces of frizzled reddish-grey hair. "Say, where's Jud? He's got to get me into my girdle. I can't get into it with this bum hand of mine all tied up."

"Oh, I'll help you, Florrie," Leota offered, shocked at the mention of Jud in such a delicate connection.

"No, no," laughed Florrie good-naturedly. "You're all dressed up now."

"You wouldn't be strong enough, Leota," said Reuben. "You've got no idea what an operation it is, getting Ma into her girdle."

"Shut up, you!" Florrie brandished the hair brush. "I wouldn't ask him except for a special occasion like this. I got to look my best on the dance floor for Jud's sake. I don't want him to be ashamed of the old lady."

"Ready, everybody?" Jud thundered, appearing in his Sunday suit, his face red and shining without its usual stubble of whiskers.

"Course I'm not ready!" cried Florrie. "What about my girdle man?"

"Glory be, your girdle! Well, come on, woman. What're we waiting for?"

"We was waiting on you," answered Florrie, leading the way to her bedroom, while Jud followed, winking broadly at the young people as he closed the door.

Embarrassed, Leota reached for her coat. She had stayed out of Reuben's way all day, and now she felt shy.

"You look lovely," he said, getting the coat from its hook for her. "How many dances will you give me tonight?"

"Oh, please don't ask me more than three times," Leota pleaded. "You know how they'll talk about us."

"I'll never get it on, woman!" they heard Jud shout from the bedroom.

"Can I help?" Reuben asked at the door.

"Better get me a crow bar!" Jud roared on the other side. "Whoops!"

"Hey, I can't breathe!" Florrie stuttered through torrents of laughter.

"What about a camera?" Reuben suggested.

Muffled grunts of prodigious effort came from the room, punctuated with helpless giggles.

"Yippee!" Jud yelled in sudden triumph. "Never mind the crow bar, Reube! She's in! She'll do!"

Jud tramped out of the bedroom, heaving himself into his coat.

"Everybody set now? Seems like we'll never get to the party with these women and their girdles!"

"Speak for yourself," snorted Reuben, fastening the buckles of his sheepskin coat.

"Talk about women holding things up!" shouted Florrie, appearing ready in her coat and overshoes, a splash of rouge on each cheek, and a fancy clasp in her hair. "You'll go on talking till the cows come home. Come on, let's get going!" She wound a long woollen fringed scarf about her head. "Got the hot bricks in the sleigh?" she asked. "Got your Santa suit?"

"You bet. Everything's ready. Don't get your shirt tail tied in a knot," soothed Jud, lighting the lantern. "Come on, Reube, you take one and I'll grab the other. These women!" Seizing Florrie by the arm, he swept her out of the house. Reuben blew out the lamp.

"Come on, Girl!" And he supported Leota down the slippery path to the barn, following the bobbing lantern ahead.

4

Light poured from the schoolhouse windows into the darkness; trucks roared down the road towards it, and teams and sleds drove into the yard. Excited voices of children called and shouted, while adult laughter and talk flowed in and out of the door. The men unhitched, while Leota and Florrie made their way to the building, each carrying a cardboard carton of food.

"Oh there's Mama and Jonas with Naomi!" Leota exclaimed, as still another team of horses drove through the gate.

"Isn't that Nate's old car parked over there?" asked Florrie.

"Good! Pro will be here."

"Everybody and their dog will be here by the looks of things," observed Florrie. "One thing, though, the Ulna bunch won't be coming. Ulna's concert's the same night, so thank the Lord for small mercies, we won't have Joe and them roaring around."

Putting their boxes in the teacherage, they went into the crowded schoolroom, where Mr. Root, spick and span in a well tailored suit, darted about, escorting the children, as they arrived, to the stage where they were hidden by the bulging curtains which shimmied with the breathless giggles and whispers behind them. Many people had already seated themselves on the benches, while others stood chatting in little groups. Prolet detached herself from a crowd and came to meet Leota.

"Why Pro!" Florrie exclaimed. "You're just as cute as a bug's ear!"

"Nice new glasses!" cried Leota.

"My eyelashes are all growing in again, too."

"Take off the hat and let's see your hair," Florrie begged.

Deftly removing a pearl hat-pin, Prolet took off the little black velvet beret.

"There," she said. "How do you like it?"

Her close-cropped hair lay in neat little curls, covering her round head, and framing her piquant little face with its turned-up nose and pointed chin.

"They showed me at the beauty parlour how to do it, so I can keep it this way myself."

"I like the hat, too," breathed Leota.

"Smart as a whip," Florrie agreed. "And you're a pair of happy love-birds, I can see that."

"Yes, I'm happy. Just terribly happy," said Prolet tremulously. "Well, I'll see you later. My old man's holding me the best seat on the bench. Oh, there's Mama and Naomi!"

"And here comes Sarah and Fenna," said Florrie.

Mr. Root dived through the crowd to the door.

"Would you please come right up to the platform, Fenna," he said crisply. "I'm giving them all their last minute instructions."

Without a word, Fenna followed him, leaving the other Leniuks knotted together. Florrie pushed her way forward to find seats for herself and her menfolk.

"There's nobody here yet," Sarah declared sullenly, her eyes darting about the crowded room.

"Gottlieb will come later, on horseback," Leota assured her.

"Oh *him*!" scoffed Sarah. "Herm's with me tonight. You're looking awful nice," she told Leota. "Got your blouse sewed real pretty. And it's done you good up at Zwick's. But it's always fun at Zwick's," she added with a catch in her voice.

"I like your new outfit, Sair," exclaimed Naomi. She looked charming herself with her dark hair curling on her shoulders, her flame coloured dress aswirl.

"It'll do," Sarah returned. "Mama, you should sit down if you're going to get a decent place," she suggested.

For a moment the curtains parted, revealing a flashing glance of Fenna, her shining hair tied back with a knot of ribbon, her colour like a rose above the green dress. Amid a buzz of talk, she stepped down gracefully to take her place at the organ.

"Did you see Philip back there?" Naomi whispered behind her hand to Leota. "Did you know that silly kid says she's going to *marry* him?"

Stunned, Leota asked, "Does Jonas know?"

"Yes. He says she can. After New Year's."

At the organ, Fenna struck a chord. The audience rose, stood to attention, and sang *O Canada*. Then everyone settled back expectantly, and the curtains slowly drew apart. Under the harsh lighting of the gas lamps on the stage, the little programme unfolded. The cowboy songs. The Christmas story acted out with its usual accompaniment of angels and shepherds. Recitations. A folk-dance. Carols. Then, like schooled soldiers, the children moved to precise positions, facing the audience, the whole class ranged on the stage so that all could be seen. At Fenna's signal, happily, smiling and triumphant, they gave forth with *Joy to the World!* Without a snag, the curtains closed, and the concert was over.

"Never had a nicer one than that," Florrie declared, whacking her good hand on her knee during the applause.

"Just let me get out," muttered Jud, rising to his feet. "I got to hurry and get into my Santa suit."

"That was a damn good concert," said Herman. "Went like a whiz. Zip, zip, zip. No waiting around getting tired of sitting."

"They sure can sing," Sarah declared. "It sure was nice."

One of the large windows at the side opened with a screech. Through its dark void came a rush of icy wind, bringing stinging needles of blown snow. A jingle of sleigh bells passed close by, and then a voice thunderous and oddly familiar.

"Is this the place? O.K. folks, I'm coming!"

And into the room tumbled a large scarlet-clad figure with white cotton whiskers. Herman closed the window while Santa gave his jovial laugh. The curtains swung apart, showing the children all seated on the stage floor, wildly excited, waiting for their gifts. Santa wasted no time, calling out their names, and distributing parcels and candy bags. Then, backing out of the door, he waved and shouted, "Goodbye until next year!"

5

While women sat on the sidelines or talked in little groups, the men quickly set to work, shoving the benches out of the way, and demolishing the improvised stage to make room for dancing.

"What's this about young Fenna, Naomi?" Sarah demanded watching Philip and Fenna sit down together across the room.

"He wants to marry her," Naomi returned flippantly.

"Did he come into the sitting-room like Nate did?" asked Sarah. "Did he propose right in front of everybody?"

"No, he got Jonas alone."

"What does Mama think of it?" Sarah asked, watching her mother's weather-beaten face bent affectionately towards Prolet and Nathan.

"I don't know." Naomi's eyes had strayed to the open door where Gottlieb stood framed, ruddy, handsome, and smiling.

Sarah saw him too, but she looked away. He had come on horseback, and his unbuttoned leather jacket showed the red and black plaid workshirt underneath.

"Here's your boy-friend, Sair!" whispered Naomi.

"I may as well tell you it's all over with Gottlieb and I," Sarah muttered. "We had a real bust-up last night."

"You'll get over it," said Naomi good-naturedly.

"Not this time. This is different, you'll see."

Three young men with instruments pushed past Gottlieb and began tuning up in one corner. Dan, meanwhile, helped small pupils recover lost mitts and overshoes, giving and receiving warm handclasps and Christmas greetings from those who were going home early.

"Would you call the dances, Mr. Zwick?" he asked nervously as Jud reappeared looking his normal self again.

"Sure. Now don't worry about a little thing. Just have a good time. Give the girls a whirl. What's it going to be, boys? A waltz, eh? O.K. folks, a waltz. *When your hair has turned to silver*."

Scratchily at first, but with gathering sweetness, the fiddles swung into the music, the banjo giving a rhythmic undertone.

"Maybe we'd better dance, Prolet," Nathan suggested. "We've got to go early, so we'd better dance while we can."

Some of the young men clapped and stamped, shouting, "Newlyweds! Newlyweds!" But Prolet and Nathan, the only couple on the floor, took no notice, moving in their own charmed circle, oblivious to all else but each other.

"Come on, Sair," said Herman.

Sarah stood up, smiling, showing a dimpled cheek, watching Gottlieb out of the corner of her eye. Soon dancers crowded the floor. Turning to talk to Leota and bring her up to date on all the news at home after their long separation, Naomi suddenly felt her wrist seized in a strong clasp.

"Coming?" asked Gottlieb, smiling down at her. He had

taken off his jacket, and his plaid shirt stood out gaily among the best Sunday suits. Flushing, Naomi danced off with him.

"Will you have this one with me, Leota?" Dan asked shyly. "I'm afraid I'm not much of a dancer," he added apologetically.

"Don't worry," she soothed as they started off. "Just let yourself go."

Philip sat alone, with a fixed smile, never taking his eyes off Fenna as she danced sedately with Reuben.

"We have to go now," said Prolet when the waltz was over. She hurried to say goodbye to the various members of her family. "Sorry we have to go so soon, but it's our busy time, you know."

"That was the best concert I ever saw," Nathan complimented Dan. "Just perfect."

Reuben got his mother for the next dance, while Jud came for Leota. Gottlieb stood at the sidelines with Naomi, talking to her in low tones, his smile intimate and flattering. Sarah and Herman continued together, while Fenna sat down again at Philip's side. A two-step came from the fiddles, lively and enticing.

With a "Yippee!" and "Let's go!" Florrie kicked up her heels.

On Jud's powerful arm, Leota felt as if she were flying.

"Here we go, Sair!" shouted Herman.

His was the type of dancing which the girls termed "old-fashioned." His elbows stood out from his sides, and his right hand pumped up and down. But with a truly musical ear, a light foot in spite of its size, and a capacity for moving economically in a small space, he sailed gracefully about the floor without crashing into anyone. Sarah enjoyed dancing with him, for she loved a good partner. Her eyes held a smile, her deep dimples came and went. As they twirled, her full brilliant skirt swung, now and then showing a flutter of white lace above her stout calves. When the music paused, and the dancers circled the floor, clapping and calling, "More! More!" Sarah deliberately marched Herman up against Gottlieb and stood there, glancing boldly around, laughing, and waving to her sisters. It was cruelly done, for Herman stood fully six foot four, and beside him Gottlieb looked simply insignificant.

"Let's change partners," Jud grinned as the fiddles wailed into a slow dreamy waltz. "I want this one with my old woman." And he took Florrie off, leaving Leota with Reuben.

They danced well together. Both knew, however, that the women sitting around on the sidelines gossiping or helping with the lunch, would note the conduct of every unmarried girl; they would draw their own conclusions, and the information they gathered that evening would serve as material for their tongues to work on for many lonely months to come. Leota tried to clear her face of all expression, while Reuben looked anywhere but down on his partner. They did not even talk.

As the waltz began, Gottlieb, without a glance in Sarah's direction, swept Naomi into his arms, holding her closely as they danced, his eyes half closed, his lips at her ear whispering nonsense, while she played up to him, laughing and flirting. Avid eyes followed the conspicuous pair, the plaid shirt and the vivid dress. With his arms crossed on his breast, Philip sat alone, watching Fenna dancing, dancing, going from the arms of one young man to the other as they tagged each other, fighting to get a chance with her. She glowed now, lightfootedly showing fancy steps, her bright hair sliding and shining.

"Take your partners for a square dance!" Jud announced next, while the musicians tightened their strings.

"This is ours," said Reuben firmly to Leota.

With Jud booming forth the calls, they spun through the movements of the Rattlesnake Whip, the shouts and the stamping feet shaking the whole building. Dizzily they sank down on the benches to rest, only to be called up again for a second session.

"I'll be waiting for you outside right now," Reuben said to Leota as he swung her madly for the last time.

There was no time to argue, and she sat down for a few minutes after he had gone. Well she knew how the gossips of the district liked to discuss the couples who went "out" together during a dance, but recklessly she made up her mind to take the risk. In the crowded intermission, she slipped away, snatching her coat as she went through the cloakroom where the older men stood haranguing about politics. She could hear the voice of Jonas above the others. The air felt wonderfully fresh after the schoolroom, but cold too. Her feet in their thin slippers sank into the snow as she skirted the outbuildings keeping clear of the light streaming from the windows.

"Good girl," said Reuben when she appeared in the gloom beside the sleigh in the cold light of the winter stars.

"Goodbye, goodbye little darling," voices sang, accompanied by the fiddles and banjo, and the rhythm of the dancers' feet.

"It's the supper dance," said Leota.

"Nice how the music comes out into the night," Reuben remarked.

Leota's teeth began to chatter with the cold.

"You sound like you're frozen."

Before Leota knew what he was about, he wrapped her round with the two front halves of his open sheepskin jacket, and clasped her to him.

"When you go home tonight, I'm going to miss you something awful," he told her.

"Reuben, I got to get back. Jonas saw me come out . . ."

"My dream girl."

"Someone's going by," Leota whispered, hearing the scrunch of heavy footsteps in the snow.

"Herman," Reuben breathed. "But he won't tell."

"I better go."

"Why is there always someone coming when I want to talk to you?"

They kissed, clinging together for a long moment.

Deliciously warmed and slightly giddy, Leota broke away, retracing her steps to the school alone. Within, she hurried to sit beside her mother, for there was much to speak of after her long absence from home. Herman came in a moment later. He never looked in Leota's direction, but went to find Sarah for the rest of the supper dance. Leota talked hurriedly, hardly knowing what she said. When the music stopped, she brought her mother some lunch. Presently, when the good food had vanished, washed down with many cups of coffee, the musicians struck up the after-supper waltz. Jonas, who had stayed with his friends in the cloakroom all this time, now threaded his way inside.

"You ready to go soon, Mama?" he asked Kazmiri.

"Yes," she smiled. "When you want."

He nodded, going outside to hitch up his horses. Other people also prepared to leave, thus thinning out the crowd. When Jonas returned, having got the team ready, his eye fell immediately upon Naomi dancing cheek to cheek with Gottlieb. All unconscious, they waltzed dreamily around the room.

"Naomi!" Jonas growled as they swept near. "We go now!"

Naomi came back to reality with a jolt, and shrugging her shoulders, went in search of her coat. Cramming a huge fur hat on to his big head, Jonas waited balefully for his womenfolk by the door. After a few quick farewells, Kazmiri and Leota joined him, and then Naomi, seething rebellion and defiance.

"Make yourself cheap," Jonas rumbled as they walked to the sleigh. "Skin your face in front of everybody. This I won't have!"

Cracking the whip over the horses' heads, he drove off.

6

Dan thought with relief that the whole thing would soon be over. Exhausted now, he longed to fall into bed. He yearned for the coming holiday with its solitude and peace. But still the party went on. And Fenna had promised him a dance. At last, during a waltz, he was able to draw her away from her latest partner. Unsophisticated, he did not realise that he would be watched, that his heart showed in his eyes.

"Have you told Philip yet?" he asked.

"Yes. I told him. But I said I wanted my last fling. A preacher's wife can't dance, you know."

"Jud and Florrie dance."

"Oh *them*! They're not real preacher and preacher's wife."

"Fenna, don't do it. Don't do it!" he pleaded. "Look at all the young men coming around you. I had to fight my way to get a dance with you. You've got nothing to worry about."

"You don't understand."

"Some day one of them will have the courage to face Jonas. Someone nice you'll really fall in love with."

"That's just what's happened now," she insisted.

"Mr. Root," Herman interrupted them. "Where's the

hammer? We're trying to open the window. It's so hot in here and the window is stuck."

"In the top drawer of my desk on the right," Dan answered. "Shall I come?"

"I'll get it."

As they danced past him, Philip saw how Dan shrugged off the other men who tried to cut in with Fenna. He saw Dan's face so close to hers. All evening he had watched his fiancée in the arms of one man or another. But he sensed something different with Dan. He began to think of all the hours Fenna had spent with him, practising for the concert. When the dance was prolonged at the insistence of some of the couples, Philip had worked himself into a towering rage. Sullenly he sat down on the desk to wait. Herman came by, searching in a drawer for the hammer.

"Here it is!" he said to Jud, and went off leaving the drawer open.

Just inside lay a text book and a sheaf of notes. Idly, spitefully, Philip took out the book and the notes, glancing at Dan from time to time.

"Oh Fenna! Fenna!"

Dan felt caught in a nightmare with the sweetness of the music playing on his taut nerves. Suddenly, he stiffened, coming to a standstill. Philip had opened the door in the big stove, his face now reflecting the firelight. In his hand he held something. Papers? A book? Incredibly he threw it into the stove, which answered with a great roar as the flames caught the paper, lighting up Philip's face.

"Filth! That's what you study!" shouted Philip, catching sight of Dan's look. "The fire's the place for that!"

Like lightning, Dan darted to the stove and opened the door. In a tremendous blaze lying upon the coals, he saw his notes shrivel, the Chaucer text, with its title still plain on the burning cover, crackling in the fire.

"You have no right! My book! My notes!"

Dan's eyes now reflected the blaze. Wild with indignation he rushed upon Philip, fists flying. Everyone stopped dancing, gathering around, while the music died away. Thin and underfed, exhausted in mind and body, the teacher was no match for Philip who defended himself with competence, seizing Dan in a hard wrestler's grip. With snapping of stitches and tearing of cloth, Dan wrenched himself free.

"Mind the stove!" Reuben shouted as they came dangerously close. "Watch out!" He gave Dan a great shove from behind. With the impetus of the push, Dan lunged forward; his feet somehow tangled with Philip's. They teetered. And then Philip fell, striking his head sharply on the coal bucket as he went down.

In mock bravado, Dan raised his am, showing a rent in his suitcoat at the shoulder.

"One - two - three - four - five - six - seven - eight - nine - ten! The winner!" he yelled, bowing to everyone. "Goodnight, ladies and gentlemen! Merry Christmas! Happy New Year!" Backing away to the door, he stumbled out, his legs tottering under him.

Chapter Eight

I

STUNNED for a moment, Philip heard the count continuing up to ten. He raised himself onto his elbow, but stars swam in the blackness. Angrily he made another effort, getting clumsily to his feet as Dan departed.

"I seen you," said Herman, closing the stove door with a clang. He stood with clenched fists, towering above everyone. "You burned the teacher's books. If you done that to my music, I'd bust every bone in your body!"

"It was filth," Philip choked. "We can't have that in the Lily of the Valley School, with innocent children here, and young girls, too." Brushing off his black clothes, he rubbed a bruised elbow, felt the back of his head.

"Who knows if it was filth," Reuben demanded, "now that you've gone and burnt it?"

Out of their stupefied silence, the crowd now began arguing, their voices loud.

"The teacher didn't trip him. Reuben pushed the teacher."

"Why you didn't keep out of the fight, Reube? Let them fight fair?"

"Just kept them from knocking down the stove and setting the school on fire, that's all."

"He can get the police on you for burning his books..."

"It was filth, just filth. No, I can't tell you what it was, in front of decent women..."

With a devilish grin, Gottlieb leaned against the door jamb.

"What did I tell you about the Teacher and the Preacher!" he muttered to Reuben.

Crimson with shame for Philip, Fenna stood where Dan had left her.

Why do they have to spoil everything! she thought. And all over an old book. And though she belonged to Philip now, and by knocking him into the dust Dan had insulted her, yet her heart had been in her mouth when she had seen the teacher getting the worst of the battle.

Disgusted, Sarah looked on while Jud and Herman harangued Philip who straightened his white dog collar and brushed the wood chips out of his hair.

"You just can't go and burn a person's books," Jud argued reasonably.

"Can't you? Well, I done it already. And that fellow should be fired, I'm telling you."

"It's a shame," Florrie murmured, while a scratching discord on the fiddles interrupted the general hubbub.

"Come on, folks!" Jud boomed. "Let's have the Home-Sweet-Home waltz."

Putting out the flaring gas lamps with their hard brilliant light, he brought in two coal-oil lanterns to give a romantic dimness to the schoolroom as the few people left danced to the strains of, *The West, a nest, and you, dear.* Under their feet they scuffed up torn Christmas decorations, dust, crusts of bread and half eaten bits of cake. The Christmas tree, denuded of its gifts, leaned askew, bereft of most of its bright balloons which had exploded during the party.

Sarah, waltzing with Herman, felt a terrible emptiness, Gottlieb had gone outside with some of the men, taking no notice of her last dance with another partner. And then, Herman had not asked her to marry him. At every party she could remember since her teens, at some time during the evening while they danced together, he would say cheerfully, "When are you going to marry me, Sair?" But not tonight. He never really meant it, she thought sorrowfully. Now he sees I really split up with Gottlieb, he just won't ask me.

When it was all over, as she pulled her coat down from a hook, she found herself beside Fenna.

"Why you didn't go home with the folks?" Sarah asked sharp and reproving.

"Who d'you think you're talking to?" Fenna flipped her hair out from under her coat collar. "You don't go home with the folks when you're engaged."

"To that—mug!" Sarah whispered fiercely, all her former jealousy of her sister rising again. "Look at him, burning the teacher's books and getting into a fight. You're just throwing yourself away on him."

"Get yourself engaged first before you start criticising," Fenna answered coldly, her eyes full of dangerous sparkling light.

Hurt and raging, Sarah thumped heavily away, her feet in their high-heeled shoes hurting unbearably. Since Herman and Jud stood deep in conversation, she busied herself helping Florrie gather the cake pans and the empty cups.

"Seems a shame leaving all this for poor Mr. Root to clean up," Florrie remarked.

But Sarah, collecting coffee dregs into a cup, had no answer.

She sure casts a shadow, thought Florrie. Well, it was too bad of Gottlieb flirting with Naomi all evening.

"I'll run you home, Sair," said Herman at last, coming to her side in coat and boots.

"It's just a step across the way," she replied sulkily. Nevertheless, she felt pleased that he had offered. Gottlieb wouldn't have. She made an effort and smiled at him. "I'm ready. Let's go."

In the cloakroom, Philip buttoned his long black coat, still arguing.

"And you!" he shouted as Reuben came through carrying a carton. "Why you don't mind your business when I was fighting with the teacher?"

"Want to burn down the schoolhouse?" asked Reuben, cheerfully continuing on his way.

Fenna wove through the figures of men getting into their heavy outdoor clothes.

"I'm ready, Philip," she whispered when she had come to his side.

"What d'you mean, you're ready?" he asked, glaring down at her.

In the lamplight, she could see a streak of soot across his cheek; but in spite of his dishevelment and his outrage, he still looked handsome, his face flushed, his fine features animated with anger. She shrank a little at his tone, so loud before other people.

"Ready to go home," she answered very low.

"Where's Jonas?"

"He went ages ago."

"You should have went home with your folks," he scolded her. "My car kept stalling all the way over here. I never should bother bringing it."

With downcast eyes, she waited until the cloakroom had emptied.

"Philip," she said desperately, "they went. They figured now we're . . . engaged . . . they thought you'd . . ."

"D'you want I should take you on horseback, maybe? In that dress?"

"It makes no difference," she said wearily. "I just want to get home now."

"I'll ask Herm to take you in his truck."

"You will not! Anyways, they went too. Listen, Philip, you could walk me home. I walk it every day to school, and it's not all that far. It would be fun."

"In those clothes?" He looked down at her thin stockings and the pretty silk scarf on her head.

She turned away from him, not knowing what to do. She could not go to White's to get her warm school clothes, for that would mean facing Sarah after the nasty things she had just said to her eldest sister.

"Well, come on," said Philip ungraciously. "I'll try to get the car going. But on a cold night like this . . . and the drifts . . . You'll find yourself pushing yet."

When the door had closed upon them, Jud looked into the cloakroom just to make sure that Philip had gone before calling Florrie over to the stove.

"Ready to go?" she asked, sweeping some rubbish to one side.

"Not just yet. Look, Florrie. Herman and me been talking, and we figure we better buy new books for Dan. Herm's going to Calgary and he says he'll get whatever it is got burnt if we get the name from the teacher."

"Well, I should hope so," said Florrie. "Why didn't Herm go over to get the name of the book from the teacher himself?"

"He wanted to take Sarah home. You know how it is."

"Herman and Sarah. Say, d'you suppose Gottlieb and her..."

Jud shrugged and sighed.

"I'll go over to the teacherage," Florrie offered, putting the broom against the wall. "I'll tell Mr. Root to write the name of his book on a piece of paper."

As she stepped outside into the bitter cold, pulling the fur collar of her coat about her face, Florrie saw Philip's car still standing by the gate. In the clear winter night, it roared and groaned, its wheels spinning. A couple of men, bent almost double, pushed and heaved at it, swearing and shouting. Then the engine died. After it had coughed a few times, it roared again, and this time the men succeeded in pushing the car into the rutted road where it bumped ahead towards Leniuk's.

Looks like somebody will have fun getting home tonight, Florrie thought, turning in the direction of the teacherage where a dim light still showed through the kitchen window.

2

Dan sat by the stove in the battered old armchair. Taking off his suitcoat to examine the damage, he had put on a sweater, laying the coat tenderly on the kitchen table, in despair at the sight of the gaping tear. For some time he had not moved, holding his aching head in his hands. But suddenly he became conscious of a low knocking at the door.

Damn them! he thought. Let them knock!

The door opened a few inches.

"Dan, you in bed yet?"

Recognising Florrie's voice, he started up.

"It's just me," she said, coming quickly out of the cold.

"Did you come to tell me I'm fired?" he asked.

"Nothing like that!" laughed Florrie.

"Won't you sit down?"

"I'll only be a minute. I know you must be just like dead."

"Why no, I'm full of vigour. Real he-man stuff. Ran a Christmas concert and dance, and won a free-for-all fight..."

"The whole district should apologise to you," declared Florrie. "After your lovely concert and all that hard work... Jud and Herm had a talk in there, and they want to replace your

Honey in the Rock

books or whatever it was Philip threw into the fire. Herm is going to Calgary, so if you just write it down on a piece of paper, we'll see you get it."

Dan looked back at her, his mouth twisting.

" It's awfully good of you. But you see, it's more complicated than that. He burned my text where I'd been making all my notes. And my essay. It was nearly finished, and it's due."

" We didn't know nothing about that," sighed Florrie. " And it's done now. Wouldn't it help, to have a new book?"

" Oh yes, of course. It's an expensive text," he added anxiously. " And as you say, it's done now. I'll just have to work like mad to do it over again."

" I'm awful sorry about all this."

" Well, Chaucer does call a spade a spade," said Dan with a wry laugh. " But what a crazy fight! If it hadn't been for Reuben, I'd have been knocked cold for more than the count of ten."

" I can't think what Philip done it for," Florrie pondered. " What came over him all of a sudden?"

Dan clenched his hands. " I was dancing with Fenna."

" So was every man there, through the evening."

" Yes, I know. But maybe it looked different to him when he saw me with her."

" Different?"

" You know. More intimate than the others."

" You mean, Philip figures there's something between you and Fenna?"

" Yes, maybe he thinks so."

" There's been some talk about you and Fenna around the district. Maybe he heard about it."

" Talk about Fenna and me?" asked Dan, turning white.

" Oh, that's nothing. If there's nothing to talk about, folks dream up something."

" But surely I didn't give anyone anything to talk about!"

" Of course you didn't. But talk gets around anyways."

" What are they saying?" asked Dan in agony.

" Oh, just that the teacher's in love with Fenna. But so are all the rest of the guys. She's a cute trick."

" Oh God!" Dan groaned, passing his hand over his eyes.

"Listen, Dan, when you haven't done nothing wrong, you don't need to worry. Why should you?"

"But you see I ... I did ..."

"Bet my bottom dollar you never even kissed her!"

"You lose your dollar."

"Good for you then!"

"But it wasn't good. It was wrong of me, and I can't forgive myself."

"What's a kiss?" Florrie asked.

"Nothing to one person, perhaps. But world-shaking to another," said Dan from the depths of his limited but intensely-felt experience.

"Well, she's got herself engaged to Philip now."

"Yes, but she's not in love with him. She's in love with me!"

"But if she's in love with you, why does she get engaged to Philip?"

"Because I told her I could never marry her. I can't afford to fall in love and get married at this stage of the game."

"You could ask her to wait," Florrie suggested. "She's not eighteen."

"I can't ask her to wait," said Dan heavily. "I don't know if I'm really in love with her or not. Perhaps I am ..."

"Nobody's pushing her into marrying Philip."

"No, but her father won't even let her go out working. He must be an impossible person to live with."

"Old Jonas? No, he's not so bad. He's got his reasons."

"What reasons?"

"Well, just look at it, Dan. See how the boys come around Fenna at a dance? Just like flies round the jam. Maybe he's right not to let her go out working. Could she handle things that might come up? Maybe Jonas is right to get her married off to a decent man who can take care of her."

"I don't know anything about women, Florrie. But it seems to me now you mention it, that Fenna has something unusual about her. This attractiveness to men. With most girls it isn't so obvious. But she just ... shines with it. I should think it isn't an easy gift to possess."

"Hm," said Florrie thoughtfully. "Sometimes you see a homely girl get the better deal."

"I can see what you mean when you say perhaps Jonas wants to protect her. But I don't think you can protect anyone that completely," said Dan, groping his way into a new realm of ideas. "Anyhow, I'm convinced she'd never be wanton . . . You know what I mean. She isn't fast and loose. She'd be too proud for that. All right then, look at all the boys around her. She doesn't give herself to any of them. Who really knows Fenna?" asked Dan heavily. "I think perhaps I do," he added. "Philip will crush her. Florrie, if it were Gottlieb or Reuben who wanted to marry her, I wouldn't worry. But Philip!"

"I dunno," mused Florrie. "Can a person crush Fenna so easy? She always struck me as a catty little thing. Mind you, I'm fond of her. But she wouldn't be my favourite of the Leniuk girls. Never figured there was much to her. She's awful cute, though."

"She's sweet," said Dan dreamily. "Sensitive and proud. Easily cast down. She's got a shy humour. All kinds of possibilities. The girls don't like her very much, and I think she's lonely. And it can't be easy to be your father's choice out of five girls."

"He don't spoil her."

"No. He loves her so dearly he's afraid to be kind. If she's catty, it's in self-defence."

"Ask her to wait for you!"

"I can't. I might change. I don't trust myself."

"Then you don't love her, really."

"What is love, Florrie?"

"You ask me that? You know what they say about me? A fallen woman? A newspaper wife?"

"That's why I'm asking you. Who would know better?"

It came to her how heart-breakingly thin he was, how blazing with life, how quivering with nerves. She took a deep breath.

"I learned about love the hard way," she said. "I wasn't twenty like you. I was over forty."

Dan looked up into the rugged face, the kind eyes with their shrewd laughing lines, the impossible hair standing on end.

"See, my folks died when I was your age," Florrie continued. "There was ten of us, and I was the oldest and Viv and Vere, the twins, they was the youngest, just two. So I raised the family. It took me twenty years before I got Viv and Vere married off in a double wedding. I never figured . . . I never figured how lonely I'd be with them all off my hands . . . So the first guy that was nice to me . . . I was cooking in the hotel then . . . I figured this was it. And after all I said to my sisters *and* my brothers, I got myself in a fix." Florrie laughed, wiping her eyes. " It was just being lonely, Dan, that's all. I didn't want him; he didn't want me. So when I seen Jud's ad in the *Prairie Messenger,* I told the kids I was going to try my luck some place else for a change, with them all married and gone.

" I met Jud at Hosanna in the old Chinese restaurant, and soon as I seen them eyes and that broken nose, I figured this was the guy for me. But I says to him, ' Look, I've got a baby coming. That's why I'm here. To get away from my folks.' And Jud, he says, ' God moves in mysterious ways. We need you Gottlieb and me, we need you. If it wasn't for that baby, you wouldn't be here!' And he says, ' God won't punish you all the rest of your life for one mistake!'

" That's love for you, Dan. That's love. And what woman wouldn't love a guy like that!" She put a plump arm about Dan's thin shoulders. " So here I am now, with my face wrinkled up like a prune laughing at Jud's jokes all this time!"

He smiled brilliantly. " I love you, Florrie," he said.

" Listen to him!" she shouted with laughter. " Sixty-two years old, and a good-looker like this says he loves me!"

She was about to tell him that she was not sure that Fenna would be one to help her man up again when life had kicked him in the teeth, as happens to all men occasionally, when a loud thump came at the door, and Jud entered, eyes twinkling, face ruddy with the cold.

" We're all hitched up, Reube and me, ready to go, Florrie. Done enough yarning out there for a year. Did you get the name of the book for Herm?"

" The book? Oh yeah, the book! Write it down, Dan."

He hesitated. " I don't know what to say. You see, if they don't have it at one place, then it might be found secondhand, or perhaps somewhere else."

" Go along with Herm," Florrie suggested. " Take a little trip to Calgary. Do you good. Visit your mother."

"I'm—not really welcome there. I had planned just to stay here and work."

"All alone?" asked Florrie, buttoning her coat and tying her scarf over her head. "Oh no, Dan! You come on over at our place for the holiday. I'll feed you up and get some meat on your bones. Leota's gone now, so there's the extra room. Look, you take this trip to Calgary with Herm and drop in on your mother, and then come back to our place. I know mothers. They always want to see their sons. You take her a little something. I got a nice batch of German cookies Leota made. Little coloured candies sprinkled on top. You take those to her."

Well, I don't know how to thank you." Dan picked up his suitcoat from the table. "Better put this away. It's a wreck."

"Let's have a look at it," Florrie demanded. "Say, it's mostly the stitches. That's awful good stuff. Looks like the kind we used to get before the war. There's years of wear in that suit yet."

"It was my father's," said Dan stiffly. "It's the one decent thing I own. Or it *was*, I should say."

"We'll take it along." Florrie folded it over her arm. "This hand will be out of bandages soon, and I'll have a go at it."

Stuffing his pyjamas into a knapsack, Dan paused.

"I ought to stay and clean up the school in the couple of hours left of the night..."

"Forget it!" boomed Jud. "Florrie and I will clean up after dinner tomorrow, today I mean."

"But with that hand..."

"Well," said Florrie merrily, "I won't be able to wash up the cups. I'll leave that to Jud. But you should see me! I'm still a heller at the end of a broom!"

3

"It's going all right now," said Fenna as Philip's car clattered along. Wrapped in a thick khaki quilt, she shivered as her breath steamed in the icy air. Even through the quilt the cold of the leather seat penetrated to the bone.

"There's no telling," said Philip sullenly, keeping his eye on the road. "You should have went with your folks. I didn't see Jonas go."

"Of course he figured you'd take me," she answered, her voice high against the din.

"You was having too good a time, that's all," Philip shouted back. "Dancing cheek to cheek with the teacher."

"I did not!" Her voice sounded unnecessarily loud as the engine died again, and the car came to a stop on the dark lonely windblown road.

"Now!" Philip growled. "Here we are again!"

Clambering out with a flashlight in his hand, he opened the bonnet of the car, came back for a wrench, to make noises in the engine meaningless to Fenna. Then seating himself behind the wheel, he tried once more. A gentle wheezing was the only response. Discouraged, he crouched there, silent and angry.

"I did not dance cheek to cheek with Mr. Root," protested Fenna. "You're saying what isn't true."

"Listen! Are we engaged or aren't we?"

"That's what I want to know!"

"Did you see me looking at any other girl?"

"Well, but you don't dance. I only wanted to have my last fling. You said all right to that."

"Just to have a few dances, all right. But flirting!"

"I wasn't flirting!"

"Are you my girl, or aren't you?" he asked quietly, his tone almost tender.

"You know I am," she answered, warming towards him. But, she thought, why doesn't he take me in his arms? Oh, if only he would!

"That's all I want to know," said Philip, fruitlessly trying to start the engine again.

"I wish you would kiss me, Philip." She spoke despondently into the silence.

A roar of the engine answered her.

"You wouldn't want me to stop now, would you?" Philip cried as they moved forward, quickly picking up speed.

Yes, I would, Fenna thought fiercely. Never mind the car. Stop now and kiss me!

They hurtled on, slowing down at last at Leniuk's gate.

"Can you get out while I still keep moving?" Philip asked her. "If I stop I'll never get going again. Quick now!"

Unwrapping herself from the quilt, she saw Philip bend towards her, his eye still on the road as he kept the car slowly moving. Their heads bumped. He gave her the briefest of kisses somewhere above her left eye.

"Jump now!" he cried.

She staggered out into the drifts. The car gathered speed, made a large turn at the gate and rattled off. Chilled and lonely, Fenna struggled with the barbed wire and the posts, her hands aching with the cold.

I'm engaged, she thought, crawling numbly towards the house. He kissed me, and I could hardly feel it.

And remembering the warmth of Dan's embrace, the touch of his hands and his lips, she wept bitterly, the hot tears burning her freezing face.

Chapter Nine

1

IN THE rattletrap ancient truck, Sarah and Herman bounced along over the frozen ruts and treacherously hidden ice, soon covering the short distance to Whites' gate. Here, Herman stopped and switched off the lights. In the bitter cold of the cab, Sarah fumbled with the door handle.

"I'll just come in with you and see you get your lamp lit and fires going," he said authoritatively in the darkness.

"I'm all alone, you know," she laughed nervously.

"All the more reason."

He gave the door handle the wrench it needed, and they stepped out. Floundering in the snow in her uncomfortable shoes, Sarah led the way to the back door.

"Got a match?" she asked him in the dark kitchen.

Producing one, he lit it expertly on his thumbnail, and brought its flame to the wick of the coal-oil lamp. In its wan light, he stoked the kitchen stove, took hot coals on a shovel to the sitting-room heater. Sarah sank down on the woodbox, taking off her overshoes and tight pumps with a sigh of relief.

"Not a bad place they've got here," said Herman, "but don't it get lonely with everybody away?"

"I can sure do without the kids. Yelling round me all day. Treating me good as dirt. And *she* never says nothing to them."

"Well, have some peace and quiet while you can."

"Darn right I will."

A comforting warmth soon began to pervade the kitchen. Sarah rose, stocking-footed, to remove her coat.

"Come into the sitting-room," she suggested, picking up the lamp. "May as well. Nobody here to stop you."

"Snug place. Heats up fast," Herman remarked as they

seated themselves on the comfortable sofa. "But it'll be cold up in the loft to go to bed."

"Oh I don't sleep in no loft," said Sarah. "I sleep right here. This thing makes into a bed, nights. She's got no separate room for a hired girl. But I don't care. I like it better this way. See, I got my box here with all my things and I can watch no kids getting into it."

"What box?"

"Here."

Sarah removed a throw made of many knitted coloured squares sewn together, to reveal a large wooden chest.

"See. I made it to put my things in."

"You made it? No kidding? Hammer and nails?"

"I made it. Hammer and nails, and hinges and varnish too." She glowed with pride. "I wanted something to put my things in."

Herman passed an admiring hand over it.

"I didn't know how to make it so it would lock, so I just fixed that hook to keep it shut," she explained.

"Well, you made a darn good job of it."

"My *hop*e chest," said Sarah harshly.

"What's in it?" Herman asked.

"You wouldn't be interested."

"Sure I would."

Sarah undid the catch. Gottlieb never asked to see my things, she thought in bitter revelation. Lovingly she laid back the lid which stayed upright, being held in place by a piece of leather. The box was lined with padded silk in brilliant stripes. Within, her work lay in beautiful orderly piles.

"This here now, is a bedspread." It was crocheted in white cotton. Sarah laid it on the darkness of the floor. "It's called the snowflake pattern. Every piece is a snowflake, and every piece is different, just the way snowflakes are." She folded it deftly and laid it aside. "These here are my pillow-slips." She piled them up to show the embroidered edges. "I got lots of towels too." She pointed out the tatted edges and the flowers she had worked into the most ordinary of towels to bring touches of beauty to her future home.

Sarah delved further into her box.

"Then there's my wool quilts."

One at a time she brought them forth, giving Herman one end to hold while she held the other and stretched out each, to show the full loveliness of her patterns, the butterfly, the double ring, and the fan. Rugs lay at the bottom of the box. One was made of old silk stockings dyed in bright colours and then braided. Another was hooked, discarded woollen garments having been dyed and snipped up to make the wools to hook into the canvas. The last she had made on a loom, dyeing her own wool to make the special shades in it.

Herman admired everything, feeling the quality of her materials with his sensitive finger tips. Her gloom quite shaken off, Sarah's natural animation and cheerfulness returned.

"Well, that's all, I guess," she said at last, at once beginning the job of returning her treasures to their places.

"They're beautiful, Sarah. All beautiful." He handed her a pile of towels. "Wish you could see my place. I do a bit of woodwork now and again."

"I'd love to," she said, carefully replacing the towels and lowering the lid of the box.

"Let's go now!" Herman got to his feet. "Let's make a night of it, Sair."

"May as well," she returned. "Nobody here to tell me what I can't do. Wait till I get on my old shoes!"

The truck seemed colder than ever, but Sarah, full of reckless adventure, scarcely noticed. This is fun, she thought. I never had fun like this with Gottlieb. I should of bust up with him ages ago. In the icy wind, Herman bent to crank the truck; in a moment the engine roared to life. He leaped to his seat with a slam of the door, turning strongly into the churned-up road.

"Still a light on at the teacherage," he remarked. "My God but that Dan Root put up a fight. You'd never think he could, so thin."

"Good for him!" Sarah shouted above the roar of the truck.

"A person can't go around burning other people's books," said Herman fiercely.

"Fenna's engaged to Philip."

"I know."

They drove on for some time without speaking while Herman concentrated on the idiosyncrasies of the road. Once he said, "Hope we don't get stuck. Long cold walk back." They swung down a valley and turned up a hill. "This is the worst," he muttered, shifting gears, and grinding steadily ahead. "Nearly there now . . . Well, guess we made it!"

Sarah had never been inside his house before, and she passed through the gate with a thrill of anticipation. She noted the little screened-in summer veranda facing eastwards where one could sit in the shade of a hot evening and catch the breeze. The house lay near a shelter belt, and several of its windows looked into trees. Herman took her through the front entrance which opened into a small vestibule, and then led her into the sitting-room.

"It's warm and cosy," Sarah exclaimed.

In the familiar darkness, Herman found a lamp and lighted it.

"This Rex heater is the thing. Keeps the heat in all night." He looked about with obvious pride. "How do you like it? There's this room, two rooms through there, and the kitchen."

"It's awful nice, Herm," said Sarah, thinking how she would love to lay her colourful rugs on the bare floor, make pretty curtains for the windows, and slip covers for the old couch and armchair. The piano, too, could be polished until it gleamed. "I love it," she declared.

He bent to drop a shy kiss on her cheek. To his astonishment, she turned her head swiftly and gave him her lips.

"You're nice, Herm," she said softly, caressing his arms lingeringly with her strong hands. "You can kiss me again if you like."

He did not need a second invitation. Then she pulled away from him with a laugh, and began to examine the pieces of music on the piano.

"I only play by ear," she told him. "I wish I could read the music notes."

She stole a glance at him. His highly coloured face had become very red, his expression that of a man who asks no quarter in his self-inflicted pain. Turning back to him, she laid her head against his shoulder in a gesture touchingly feminine in so big a woman.

"You always say no to me," said Herman gruffly. "But it don't hurt to try, try, try again. Will you marry me, Sair?"

"Yes," she answered, hiding her face, her ear against his loudly pounding heart.

"Don't fool with me, Sair. I'll hold you to it."

"I'm not fooling." She lifted her head, facing him proudly. "I said I'd marry you, and I mean it."

"When?" His tone held a hint of sarcasm. Her gaze did not waver.

"Any time you like."

Herman glanced at his watch.

"It's three o'clock in the morning, pretty near. I'm going to Calgary today, and I'll get the licence. Will you marry me on Christmas Eve?"

"Yes," said Sarah.

He stood looking at her, still unbelieving. She smiled courageously, showing her dimples and fine teeth, but he noticed that the smile did not reach her eyes.

"Of course I been Gottlieb's intended so long," she said steadily. "But that's all over now."

Abruptly he took her arm, clasping her hand in both his own.

"Come into the kitchen and look around," he suggested. "See how you like it." He picked up the lamp, leading the way. "See, here's the sink with the pump in it so you won't never have to carry water. I just finished building these cupboards around it. That's why there's no paint yet."

Sarah looked eagerly about her, exclaiming joyfully over the compact convenient room, so thoughtfully arranged.

"What's this?" she asked, running a finger tip over some intricate design carved by the handle of a cupboard door.

"Just S for Sarah," said Herman casually.

"S for Sarah?"

She took a closer look. Lovingly carved into the wood by each handle was a flower design about the letter S.

"I just stuck it in there, thinking about you, evenings, with the chores done. Never did hope you'd really marry me, but you couldn't stop me thinking about you."

He shrugged, then took out a knife to make some infinitesimal correction in one of the flowers. She turned away with bowed head.

"I said I'd marry you, Herm. But I can't. I just can't."

He sheathed the knife slowly. "Why not?"

"I'm just not—just not good enough."

"What d'you mean, not good enough?" he demanded. "Why Sair, you're like a queen to me."

She clenched her hands.

"You should have somebody just mad about you, like I was about Gottlieb. And I'm—I'm—not!" she choked out. Then, to her horror, a loud hard sob shook her, and then another.

"Sair, girl," said Herman tenderly, taking her into his strong arms, "never mind about being mad about me."

"Oh but you just don't know," Sarah wept, tears gushing forth. "I flirted with you cheap as brass so you'd ask me to marry you. It's all over with Gottlieb and me, after I been his intended so long. And I just can't go on working for Mrs. White all my life. I want my own home and my own babies!"

"Think I'd go carving S for Sarah if I didn't want to marry you?"

"But you won't want to now," sobbed Sarah.

"Told you I'd hold you to it," Herman said sternly.

But Sarah was thinking that Gottlieb had never spent his evenings planning a kitchen convenient for a woman, and carving S for Sarah. She had never enjoyed the luxury of crying on Gottlieb's shoulder. Now she wept as she had never wept, for all the lonely evenings she had spent wondering what woman Gottlieb was with; and the many times he had said good-night, letting her go, often without so much as a kiss, to find her own way through tight barbed wire gates into whatever house she worked at; and for his callousness towards her, and for breaking her heart. Knowing all this, Herman let her weep, swaying gently with her in his arms.

"I'm always such a mess when I cry," said Sarah finally, moving to the pump with averted face. She gasped at the icy coldness of the water as she bathed her eyes. Herman silently handed her a ragged towel.

"Do you really want to marry me, Sair?" he asked. Heartwrung by her desolate appearance, he put his big arm unobtrusively around her, looking considerately away from her red eyes. "You're the only girl for me," he declared.

His rock-like calm had a soothing effect upon Sarah. She

rejoiced now that she had never laughed at him behind his back, nor allowed her sisters to do so.

"We're good friends," she said thoughtfully. "I do like you, Herm. And I respect you."

From his silence, she thought she knew that pain with a knifelike edge had turned in his heart. Like . . . Respect . . . His feeling for her was love of enormous proportions, she saw that clearly now. And the burning tears smarted her swollen eyes again.

"Don't, Sair," he murmured.

"Anyways, Herm," she wept, turning her face away from him, "I don't love Gottlieb no more. There's nobody else but you."

"We'd be happy," said Herman confidently.

"Yes." Sarah steadied her voice. "I think we would."

"I said Christmas Eve to get married," Herman went on, "but if you want to wait a bit . . ."

"No," said Sarah decisively. "Let's not wait. It isn't like we didn't know each other."

"Getting on for four o'clock," said Herman. "Look, I'll run you over to Whites' and give you a hand with the milking, and then come back here to do up my chores before I go."

He lowered the wick of the lamp.

"You know I'll have to ask Jonas for permission to marry you," he said quietly.

In spite of her swollen eyes, Sarah rounded on him with her old temper and arrogance and spirit, the qualities in her which he found the most attractive in the world.

"What d'you mean?" she flared. "Have to ask Jonas for permission! I'm free, white, and over twenty-one!"

"Sure. But Jonas would figure you didn't get much of a man if I couldn't stand up and ask for you."

"He'd put you through the meat grinder."

"I don't think so," said Herman mildly. "Let's go over to Whites' now and do the chores, and then go and see Jonas."

"You mean . . . you'd really ask him! Stand up in front of them all at home, and ask him?"

"Yes," said Herman. "You're worth that much to me at least. More, even."

"Never will I forget you did this," she said humbly.

Honey in the Rock

Blowing out the lamp, Herman gave her a hard hug in the darkness.

"You'd better marry me," she said with another flash of spirit. "I just about spent the night with you."

"Make an honest woman of you yet!" he teased.

Laughing, they wandered out of the house hand in hand, their feet crunching the hard snow. In the dark sky with no sign in it yet of dawn, the stars shone paler, colder. The wind had a keener edge. Sarah walked towards the truck with a curious lift of the heart. Herman was tall. She could hold up her head beside him instead of trying to conceal her height as she had always done with Gottlieb. The thought of Gottlieb still brought a dull pain. Odd and heart-breaking memories of him clung to her mind. The turn of his head. His hands on the steering wheel of the truck. His intimate smile. His deft way of lighting a cigarette. The flash of green eyes in a dark face. Little details, such as one remembers about someone who has died. But it's all over between Gottlieb and me, she thought. All over.

When they drove into Leniuk's farmyard, it was half past six, and breakfast time in the house. At the stove, Leota was frying bacon and eggs, while Naomi and Jonas washed themselves after milking, and Kazmiri dished out the porridge. Fenna still slept.

"Sounds like Herm's truck!" Naomi exclaimed, scratching at the frost on the window to see who had driven in. "Sarah's with him!" she called. "Put two more plates on the table, Leota."

The men boomed good mornings as heavy feet clumped up the steps. The kitchen was suddenly very full while Herman and Sarah warmed their hands and everyone talked at once.

"Merry Christmas!" shouted Herman to Kazmiri, waving his glasses in the air to clear them of steam.

"Staying for breakfast?" Naomi asked.

"Thanks, but I have to do my chores and get away to Calgary."

"You got to eat some place," she drawled. "May as well be here."

"I just come to ask Jonas something."

Everyone quieted at once.

"What is it, Herman?" Jonas asked civilly.

"I want to ask you to give me the honour to have Sarah for my wife. You, and the respected Mrs. Leniuk." He took Sarah's arm. "If it would please you, Jonas."

Caught completely off guard, Jonas groped for words.

"Why, why . . . You and Sarah?" He looked at them standing side by side, and suddenly his rather charming ugly smile lighted up his dark face. He nodded his big head slowly. "It pleases me, Herman. Pleases me very much. Very much." He held out his hand; Herman took it warmly. "And you too, Mama?" Jonas asked, turning to his wife, a suspicious moisture in his eyes.

Kazmiri's deep gaze took in everything. The traces of weeping on Sarah's face. Herman's complete confidence, and the obvious pleasure of Jonas. She stretched out her hands.

"You are a very welcome son. I am so glad. So glad."

"Three Leniuk girls in a row!" shouted Naomi. "Knocked flat like hens in a hailstorm!"

"Good for you, Sarah," said Leota tremulously. "You'll have such a nice husband."

"Breakfast everybody! Breakfast!" Naomi cried. "Come and get it or we'll throw it away."

"Come, sit down," said Jonas to the newly engaged couple, his great hand and arm gathering them in. "It is such happiness."

"You'll have to excuse us if we eat and run," Herman apologised.

"Whites are coming back today," Sarah put in. "I have to get some baking done up before they come."

"We figure on getting married on Christmas Eve," said Herman. "Quiet like. In the church at Ulna."

"No wedding feast?" asked Mama in disappointment.

"Oh come on, Sarah. Don't do Mama out of a wedding," cried Naomi. "Let us make a feast here for you after the ceremony."

"Well then, just a little party. We want it all quiet. Just the family."

"Very nice," said Mama, pleased and smiling.

"And very kind too," said Herman graciously.

Fenna now appeared at the curtained doorway to the loft,

her hair unbrushed, a dressing-gown thrown on over her pyjamas.

"What's all the row?" she asked crossly, yawning and rubbing her eyes. "A person just can't sleep."

Biting into a huge piece of toast, Naomi turned to her.

"We've got a wedding on our hands!"

"Not till after New Year's."

"Oh yours is old stuff," said Naomi, flapping the toast in Fenna's direction. "Here's Sarah and Herman engaged."

"Sarah and Herm."

"Yeah. Come and tell them congratulations."

"Fenna!" Jonas roared. "Get yourself dressed and decent!"

"Naomi, mind your tongue," cautioned Mama as her youngest daughter vanished. "No need to spoil things for Fenna."

Sarah, finishing her breakfast, declared that they must go.

"I'll give the truck some water and start her up," said Herman, throwing on his things. "Come out in a few minutes, Sair. No use standing around in the cold."

Kazmiri beckoned Sarah alone into the sitting-room.

"Do you love him?" she inquired anxiously. "You've been crying... And it was always Gottlieb with you."

"Oh *love*," sneered Sarah.

"It's important," her mother persisted.

"Why you want to know if I love him?" cried the tormented Sarah. "What about you... You married Jonas and you didn't love him."

"I loved..." Kazmiri put a hand to her head as if her daughter had struck her. "I loved four other people. I wanted you all to have a chance..."

"Oh Mama!" Writhing with shame, Sarah turned away to the window, breathing on it to clear a space in the frost to look through. "Mama, I'm sorry!" she burst out. "I was Gottlieb's intended so long, I didn't see how I could marry somebody else. But that's all over now. And Herman is good. Like gold. I'll be a good wife," she said, tying a scarf, peasant fashion, over her head. "I'm not going to eat my heart for Gottlieb the rest of my days."

"Be kinder, Sarah," her mother pleaded. "Be kinder."

"I'll try," whispered Sarah meekly. "He's ready now . . ." Mother and daughter looked at each other. "I hope you're glad, Mama."

"I'm glad. So glad."

2

As Herman drove the truck off the highway on to the uncertain road leading back to the Lily of the Valley district, Dan could hardly believe that the trip to Calgary could have been so successful. They had been gone the better part of two days. With the excitement of Herman's engagement, his stopping at the Whites' to ask Billy to do the chores in his absence, his second stop at Zwick's to inquire if Florrie needed anything from the big city, at both places announcing his coming wedding, he had not been able to make the early start he had planned. It had also taken a long time to reach the highway before they could make any speed, so that they had not reached Calgary until late afternoon, when Herman had immediately suggested they should visit Dan's mother first thing.

Grinding along the snowy road with its now familiar landmarks, Dan smiled at the memory of that visit. The heavy truck stopping before the respectable looking house . . . Himself with Herman towering over him stepping out to knock on the door . . . Big Bill opening it, offering supper and a shake down in the sitting-room for the night for both of them . . . obviously admiring the tough practical Herman, even to the crashing chords of Chopin Herman had awakened on the piano. Dan savoured bits of the conversation.

"How's this runt doing out there, teaching in your school?" Derision in Big Bill's tone. And the quiet sincerity in Herman's answer,

"Best teacher we ever had!"

When he could get her alone in the kitchen while Herman and her husband talked about Social Credit and found themselves in perfect agreement, Dan had given his mother the parcel of little German cakes.

"A present from Mrs. Zwick!"

"Why Dan!"

How her face had lighted up. And Dan thought now what

it had done to his self-respect and morale to be able to return home in this way, confident, asking for nothing, and with something to give.

Early next morning, while Herman had gone off on his own business, Dan had searched the bookshops for a copy of Chaucer, and down in the east end of the city, he had found one. It was old, but in good condition, containing many pencilled notes written clearly in a scholarly hand. He was thrilled by some of the remarks in the margins. He felt no longer alone in his study of Chaucer, for a kindly older student looked over his shoulder, humorously discussing the poetry with him. He had the book stuffed into the ever overloaded pocket of his greatcoat, and took pleasure in feeling the bulk of it, hard against him.

Herman also seemed pleased with the trip, singing and whistling to himself as they journeyed homewards.

"I'm going by Leniuk's first," he told Dan. "I must see Sarah right away," he smiled. "Jonas, too." The sun was sinking slowly in a blaze of cerise, purple, and gold, as they drove into Leniuk's yard. "I'll just be a minute!" Herman jumped nimbly from the cab. "Come in, won't you?"

Dan climbed down. The buildings stood out starkly against the glowing sunset, and in its golden light he saw Fenna coming from the barn to the house, her hair blowing back, the sun lighting her face. She wore old clothes and carried an empty pail, for she was about the chores, but to him she looked beautiful. As she came near, she saw him, stared as though at an apparition, and gave a cry of astonishment. The bucket dropped with a clatter.

"Fenna!"

He put his hands lightly on her shoulders.

"I've been thinking since the Christmas party," he said in a rush. "About our situation, and how we're in love with each other. Wait for me, Fenna," he pleaded. "Give me three or four years. You'd only be twenty-one or two then. I'd have something to offer, and we could be married. Please wait for me, Fenna!"

She stared, dumbfounded. Added to the shock of seeing him here in the yard, was this completely unexpected proposal of marriage. To wait . . . three or four years! She thought him mad. But she saw the gentleness and sanity in his look, recalling with part of her mind that Philip's eyes sometimes held the glitter of the fanatic. This was no madness on Dan's part. It was honest, real, naked feeling.

But she said flatly, " I promised Philip."

" You're not in love with him."

" Of course I am, Mr. Root."

" I love you, and you love me."

" Oh no, Mr. Root. It's always been Philip with me."

Dan had only two small clues to go on. The lilt of joy in her voice when he had asked her to forgive him after he had kissed her in the cloakroom, and the tear that had fallen on his hand. Yet he was certain that she loved him.

" Postpone the wedding," he begged. " Give yourself time to think. Those years would pass very quickly, Fenna. You could finish school and train to be a teacher as you once thought. You don't know your own possibilities."

" But it's all arranged. I'd be letting everyone down."

" It's the woman's privilege to change her mind, you know."

" I'm not changing, Mr. Root."

He moved a little away from her, his head bare, his coat unbuttoned, his scarf blowing free in the wind.

" Go and get warm up at the house," she suggested anxiously. " I still got chores to do."

" No . . . I'll walk over to Zwick's . . . Keep out of your way . . . Guess I made a big mistake . . . Sorry."

" At least fix your scarf in this cold wind," she said, distressed, solicitously winding it round his neck and doing up the buttons of his coat.

Neither was aware that both Leota and Naomi had now appeared on the path towards the house, and that they could not avoid coming past the truck with waist deep drifts of snow on either side. The buildings were outlined more blackly still against the sky now, which was losing its colourful glow. On the clear air, a dog's bark could be heard a mile away, and voices carried like bells.

" Fenna! Wait for me! " cried Dan, suddenly taking her into his arms.

" It's the teacher," whispered Naomi. " He's *kissing* her! "

" Get past them quick," Leota urged. " Pretend not to see."

"Mr. Root!" Fenna gasped. "Father might come out, any minute."

"I wish he would," Dan answered clearly into the twilight, as the sisters passed within touching distance. "Where is he? My intentions are perfectly honourable. I want to speak to him, if you will consider marrying me."

"I'm—I'm honoured," said Fenna with a strange touch of dignity and compassion new to her. "But I've given my word to Philip. Goodnight, Mr. Root."

"Don't you think," he called after her as she joined the others, "don't you think you'd be happier waiting three or four years for me than going to *Tibet*?" With this last parting fling, he pulled his coat collar up about his ears and set off with long strides down the snowy prairie trail.

"What's it all about?" giggled Naomi as Fenna caught up with them.

"He was just asking me to wait three or four years to marry him!"

Their voices followed Dan like mocking laughter. He distinctly heard the words "three or four years."

"We didn't see you struggle when he was kissing you," chortled Naomi as they stood together, talking in low tones, watching Dan's figure outlined darkly on the whiteness, looking smaller and more lonely every minute. Even so, "he was kissing you," followed him like a hiss; but he would have been surprised if he had heard exactly what Leota answered.

"You little fool, Fenna," she whispered. "Go after him. Tell him you'll wait. He'd be worth waiting for."

"And you let him kiss you," said Naomi.

"He just grabbed me," Fenna explained primly.

"But you didn't scream and struggle," hummed Naomi.

"It's written all over both of you that it's the real thing," said Leota trembling. "You're nice with Mr. Root. Even doing up his scarf."

"Oh, he doesn't take care of himself. He was going to walk clear over to Zwick's with his coat undone and his scarf coming off, that's all. And it's got moth holes in it even!"

"Knit him a new one," tittered Naomi, cracking her gum.

"Who's going to wait four years?" Fenna demanded. "How do I know if he'd be true?"

"He would," declared Naomi cheerfully. "He's the type . . . Oh Fenna, think of the hope chest you could pile up. Enough things for the rest of your life . . ."

"What did he mean about going to Tibet?" Leota asked, dazed. "That's a country someplace around India, isn't it?"

Fenna moved impatiently.

"Oh sure. But he talks like that. In poetry, sort of. Sometimes it's hard to know what he's talking about."

"When he says, ' Fenna, wait for me! ' that's not hard," said Naomi.

"Oh, go after him, Fen, before it's too late," pleaded Leota.

Fenna actually hesitated.

"I gave my word to Philip."

"He's out of sight," mourned Leota.

"Don't tell up at the house," Fenna begged as lamplight appeared in the window.

"Course not!" Naomi opened the door as Herman came out. "Your passenger got tired waiting and walked on," she told him. "Better watch out for him and pick him up. His scarf's got moth holes in it."

"Why he didn't come in and get warm?" wondered Herman, peering into the gathering gloom.

"Oh, he's shy," Naomi grinned. "Too many women here for him."

"Well, I'll be taking one off your hands soon," shouted Herman joyfully, bending to crank the truck.

The girls went in. Naomi and Leota made teasing remarks to Sarah, who, blushing and flustered, spilt some soup on the floor. At the kitchen table sat Philip, solid, calm, and self-possessed, a smile on his well carved lips.

"I didn't know you came," said Fenna stupidly, still distracted by Dan's behaviour.

"Oh these lovers!" groaned Naomi, pouring out soup. "A person trips over them all over the place! "

Setting hot steaming cups on the table in front of Philip and Fenna, she put the rest on a tray and bore it off to the sitting-room where her sisters followed her.

Well, after all, he's here to court me, Fenna thought. They should leave us alone sometimes.

"I just wanted to ask if you'd come out to Hosanna and

stay awhile in the Christmas holidays," said Philip as Fenna sat down beside him. " My mother and two sisters want to get acquainted, you know."

" Yes, of course," Fenna answered with a sinking sensation.

" Well, what's wrong?" he asked.

Her hair gleaming in the lamplight, her cheeks like roses, she sat drinking the hot soup, looking up innocently at him, her heart full of guilt at having just come from the arms of another man.

" D'you really think we're right to marry, Philip?"

" Of course we're right," he said confidently. " I've prayed about it, and I know. Besides, we both come from Russian-German families, we're both from the Church of the Brethren in Christ; you can sing and play the organ and teach Sabbath school, and I'm a preacher. We make a perfect pair."

He did not speak of love. And yet she was curiously lulled by his reasonableness which made Dan's importunate proposal seem foolish and wild by comparison.

" Well, how about the visit to my folks?" he insisted.

She smiled at him, quieted and sure.

" Of course I'll come. Tell them thanks from me."

Chapter Ten

I

STANDING at the window of Mrs. Jebson's little sitting-room in Hosanna, Fenna watched the darkness coming down. She heard the wind whistle around the small frame house with its draughty floors, and shivered, wondering how she and Philip would get back to the Lily of the Valley District for New Year's Day, or if they would get there at all. They had come in Philip's car, but they would not be able to get through the drifts in it to return. The thought made her spirits droop. Never having been away from home before, she had not been prepared for the homesickness that nearly overwhelmed her, even in five short days. The sight of this cold room, in spite of its lace curtains and modern chesterfield, and the grating in the floor where the heat came up from below, made her long for the big roaring heater at home, for the creaking chairs and the hand-braided rugs. And there would be the New Year's dance at the school tonight. Only she could never dance again.

"Please let me help," she begged, going into the kitchen where Philip's sister Jean was busy making sandwiches. Sister Betty was lying down with one of her headaches which always seemed to come on just when there was extra work to be done, and Mrs. Jebson, a semi-invalid, usually rested throughout the afternoon.

"I'm finished," said Jean, wrapping up the fragile delicacies in a damp tea towel. "And I made the cake this morning, and the cookies, so there should be enough food." She worked swiftly with the bent appearance of one rushed and under pressure.

Any of her own sisters could have done that much preparation of food as quickly and nicely, Fenna thought, and still have been smiling and easy.

"I hope the people will come tonight in the cold," she said doubtfully. "After all your trouble."

"They'll come. They'll want to see the girl Philip is going to marry."

Jean swept the kitchen table free of crumbs, straightening her thin shoulders wearily as she washed out the dish cloth at the sink. She and Betty taught school in Hosanna, supporting their widowed mother and this small home. When Philip had felt the call to preach, they had secretly resented it. By his own efforts, Philip had put himself through Bible School, renting out the home farm which consequently always lay in a tangle of Russian thistle, neglected, burnt out and blown out, a source of indignation to his sisters. And now when he might have helped a little towards carrying their heavy burden, he was about to marry this immature child, the daughter of a Bolshevik woman, a newspaper wife. Jean could not pretend to be pleased.

"I could help get supper, couldn't I?" asked Fenna.

"It's all ready. Soup in that big pot on the stove. I'd better set the table. You wouldn't know where the things are, or how to put them. We do things different here from the farm, you know."

Resignedly, Fenna sat down while Jean spread a snowy cloth on the dining-room table, found immaculate serviettes, and even hastily wiped over the spoons with a cloth dampened with silver polish. Both girls jumped at the opening of the front door and the stamp of feet as Philip came in, Fenna with intense relief, and Jean with irritation at not being ready.

"Put those boots on the newspaper, Philip," she called. "Don't get snow over everything after all my work."

With the guilty feeling that she was leaving Jean to work like a slave, Fenna escaped to the sitting-room.

"Supper ready?" Philip asked, carelessly stamping snow about, flinging his boots in the direction of the folded newspaper put down to receive them.

"Just about."

Fenna tried to absorb some comfort from his presence. He shrugged off his coat, rubbing his hands to warm them. She searched his face, to find relief from the terrible loneliness she had known since he had gone out after lunch.

"Do you think we'll make it home tomorrow?" she asked pitifully.

"The car sure won't make it; you know that. But I met Bronson just now, and he says Gottlieb has the day off tomorrow and he'll come by for us with the team."

"Oh good for Gottlieb!" cried Fenna with exquisite joy.

"Well, I like that!" Jean stood in the doorway, arms akimbo. "Do you have to be so glad to go home after all the trouble we went to?"

"I'm sorry, Jean," said Fenna, contrite.

"It would have been a good chance for you to get to know Mother."

"Well, I promised Mama I'd be home tomorrow. And she has the wedding dress to make. She'll need me to get the right fit."

"Wedding dress! You mean you're going to be all rigged up like something out of the catalogue? In January?"

Prolet had worn her brown suit to be married in, with a gamin little hat; and Sarah her new dress, the royal blue, because Herman liked it. But Fenna had different ideas.

"A person only gets married once," she said coolly, wanting to wound. "If ever," she added.

"Philip, it's suppertime." Jean turned away to call her mother and sister.

"You must try to get on with Jean better," said Philip, very low. "After all, Jean and Betty and Mother will be part of your family."

He spoke quietly, but she could see that he was very displeased. He had a certain look of cold anger which she was coming to recognise.

"Come to supper now," he said, turning away from her.

The little dining-room off the kitchen had a festive air with candles on the table and Christmas decorations hanging in the archway. The soup smoked in the bowls, while bread buns still hot from the oven kept warm in a spotless napkin. Jean had indeed gone to a lot of trouble. Ashamed, Fenna could not look up as Betty and Mrs. Jebson took their places at the table.

"Have a good day, dear?" Mrs. Jebson quavered as Philip ended the long grace. She was a little woman, pale and grey-haired, her eyes red and wrinkled as though she wept continually.

"Not bad."

"Eat up your soup while it's hot, Mother," said Jean briskly. "I don't see why you and Fenna have to go tomorrow, Philip," she went on. "It's New Year's day, and we wanted you here."

Betty bent her delicate features over the soup, her brow still knotted with the pain of her headache.

"Oh well, it's only a week to the wedding. Then they'll be back again," she said, trying to bring peace to the situation.

Fenna picked up her spoon and set it down again.

"But we won't be back," she said in consternation. "We'll be getting married at the Lily of the Valley Church, and then have the wedding supper up at home. Of course you're all invited to come."

"Don't be silly, Fenna," said Jean sharply. "You can't expect Mother to make a trip like that in January, with weather like this. Besides, all Philip's friends are here around Hosanna. Naturally you'll be coming to Hosanna to get married. It's a much bigger and nicer church, and it's only Philip's due."

Helplessly Fenna looked across the table at Philip.

"I agree with Jean," he told her.

"But my folks—"

"It's different when you marry a preacher," said Jean. "A lot of people would be hurt at being left out, and that wouldn't do Philip's career any good. Down in the Hosanna church basement there's a kitchen and plenty of room for a reception."

Fenna said nothing, trying to eat though her appetite had now deserted her. Memories of Sarah's wedding supper thronged her mind. Was it only a week ago? It seemed like a century. Just the family, but what happiness! Prolet and Nathan stuffed into the same chair together. Sarah and Herman pouring out the innocent apple cider at either end of the kitchen table which groaned under the Russian-German food. The wedding cake. The Christmas cookies. Braided bread with poppy seeds. Apple cake. As well as all the savouries. Nathan suddenly singing with abandon some wild Yiddish song, followed by a tender Russian lullaby especially for Mama.

154   *Honey in the Rock*

The girls harmonising on Mr. Root's song. The thought brought a lump to Fenna's throat. Then the hymns while the nuts were passed around, and the oranges. The burning peels in the heater making a wonderful odour. Jonas pleased and smiling, joining in with the hymns in his deep bass. The joyous singing in the Low German:

> The wings of the morning
>   He'll give unto me
> Though I lie down in hell
>   Oh still there He'll be!
> The wings of the morning! The wings of the dove!
> The wings of the morning! The wings of His love!

But Fenna's wedding supper was to be in the church basement, with strangers. Her sisters would never let themselves go like that outside of their home, Fenna knew. They would sit stiffly trying not to make any mistakes, for her sake. She looked around at the Jebson faces, all of them singularly alike. Only Philip had the curly hair, the deeper colour of eyes, the ruddier skin. Suddenly she felt it was all wrong that she was to become one of them. She did not belong among them. Panic rose within her. She did not want to marry Philip. I just can't marry him, she said to herself, for the first time framing in definite thought the uneasy disquietude she had often felt.

But the wedding day had already been announced. The expensive material for the wedding dress had been brought for Mama to work on. How could she draw back? What would everyone say? But I can't marry him; I just can't, she thought desperately, eating a few tasteless mouthfuls in utter silence.

"I'll help with the dishes," she said when supper was over. "Please let me do it."

"Of course not." Jean began gathering up the china with infinite care. "You take Mother into the sitting-room and wait for the guests. I'll do these. This is very fine china and breaks easily. I don't want the set spoiled."

Sitting in the best chair opposite Mrs. Jebson, Fenna became even more frantic.

"After you and Philip are married," said Betty holding her

drooping head in a cold damp hand, "Mother will be able to come and stay with you for a visit. You'll like that, won't you, Mother?"

"If they have a little service for me like this sometimes," Mrs. Jebson agreed plaintively. "You see, Fenna, I can't get out, so we have some people in like this at home, and a bit of a service. It's all I live for." She shivered in a draught. "Get me my sweater, Betty. Oh you with your headache! Fenna will get it. The grey one at the foot of my bed, Fenna. And while you're up, Fenna, get me my pills. Not the pink ones, the white ones. In that little box on my bedside table. And a glass of water too, please."

By the time Mrs. Jebson had taken her pill and put on her sweater, the first guests knocked at the door. Jean came, hurriedly drying her hands. Quickly the room filled up with people, men and women, about a dozen of them, all strangers to Fenna and older than she. They shook hands with her, and sat down talking with great animation, constantly eyeing her. Then Philip, with authority, announced the first hymn.

The service went on, but Fenna did not hear a word of it. Her heart beat like fluttering wings bruising themselves against prison bars. They would be dancing now at the Lily of the Valley School, she thought, the fiddles piercing the winter night with poignant sweetness, the harness bells jingling as the sleds drove into the schoolyard. Suddenly the thought of the school Christmas tree, and the darkened cloakroom, and Dan's arms and lips, swept over her. And again, his proposal in the cold wintery sunset by Herman's truck. Maybe I do love Mr. Root after all, she thought miserably, yet terribly aware of his youth and imaturity. Maybe in a couple of years I'd be sure. To wait for him, even at home, at this point seemed a heavenly escape.

The artistic little sandwiches came around on lovely plates. Fenna roused herself, trying to make conversation with Philip's friends. She was aware of Jean's high-pitched voice rattling on. She stirred her coffee, accepted a piece of cake which she could not possibly eat. There was only one thing to do. She must tell Philip that she could not marry him. Tonight. The guests were but a blur of faces to her; she could not remember one name. She could not think of a single sensible remark. They'll think

I'm plain stupid, she thought. All the better. They'll think it's best when they heard we had a bust up.

Mrs. Jebson said at last that she was tired and must get to bed. That broke up the party, and soon all got ready to go, gathering up coats and boots, bracing themselves to face the cold. There were only two bedrooms, one for Mrs. Jebson and the other shared by the two daughters. But since Fenna's arrival, Betty had slept with her mother, while Fenna shared with Jean, and Philip slept on the chesterfield in the sitting-room.

"You can get Mother to bed, Betty," said Jean wearily, as she shut the door on the last guest. "I've still got all these cups and things to wash. Fenna, you may as well go to bed too. Then Philip can make down the chesterfield to sleep on. The sheets are in this drawer, Philip." Expecting to be obeyed, she went into the kitchen, bearing away the last of the cups.

"I got to talk to you, Philip," Fenna whispered desperately. She could hear the querulous voice of Mrs. Jebson in the back bedroom, and Betty answering her, nearly in tears. Dishes clattered in the dishpan.

"What's up?" he asked.

Now that they were alone for a moment, he was gentle, taking her hands into his firm cool grasp. He had a kind of magnetic quality that drew people to his church, that encouraged the sinner to repent, that made the weakling do his bidding and be strong. He was flushed with the success of his sermon. His curly hair, usually so carefully brushed, had become attractively rumpled. And he was looking at the girl he desired. She found that she could not say what she had planned to say. Confused, she felt she had been wrong after all. Of course I'll marry him, she thought. It's all arranged, and I'm crazy about him.

"I wanted to be married at home," she whispered with trembling lips. "I wanted the wedding supper at the house, like Sarah did."

"I know," he answered, holding her hands. "But you see, Mother and Jean and Betty, they have so little to make them happy. Couldn't you let them have this great pleasure? I'm their only brother, the only one most likely, that will get married in our family."

"Really, Fenna!" Jean stood in the doorway watching them, drying a dish, turning it over and over, her pale face flecked with redness.

Philip dropped Fenna's hands.

"She was just saying, Jean, that of course she wants to give you the pleasure of planning the wedding supper, even though her folks was expecting it out at the Lily of the Valley."

"Well, I should hope so. It's only your due, Philip."

Fenna went slowly into Jean's bedroom, reassured by the thought that she would never have to be like Jean or Betty, getting old and cranky, unloved and unwanted, without a hope of ever getting married.

Chapter Eleven

I

"Leota, can I borrow your pink blouse for the dance tonight?" Naomi cried, whirling into the kitchen after milking.

Leota had just put a pile of dirty dishes into the dishpan. From the basement come the singing hum of the separator where Jonas worked with a steady hand. Dressed in the heavy clothes of a man for chores, Naomi still looked beautiful, her dark hair rich and lustrous, curling damply on her forehead.

"You can take it then," said Leota in hushed tones. "But what about Jonas? Does he know?"

"Sure," said Naomi carelessly, kicking her boots down the stairs. "I'm going with Reuben. Reuben asked him at church, so everything's as pure as the holy angels." She hung up her windbreaker on a peg by the door.

"Reuben!" said Leota, feeling her knees go weak. "I didn't know you was interested in Reuben!" A curious stiffness had come into her lips, and her mouth seemed to be full of sawdust. Afraid of betraying herself, she added with a forced little laugh, "You know you always said he was so slow he would— he would stop in his tracks if he went any slower."

"Yeah, I know. But a person could change their mind. Thanks for the blouse. I'll try not to split the seams. Why you don't put on some weight? Then your clothes would fit me better!" She lifted the curtain that covered the stairway to the loft, and disappeared with a chuckle.

Leota stood motionless for a moment. Then tears rushed forth into the dishpan. With a gasp, she controlled herself, wiped her face on her apron, and made motions of going on with the dishes. The downstairs door slammed. Shouts between Reuben and Jonas came up to her, and a low murmur of men's talk. Reuben was here, in the house. To her consternation, she felt sick and weak as though suddenly stricken with illness. The tears kept coming, struggle as she would against them. Finally she heard the men tramping up to the kitchen. The door opened, and Jonas set down the milk and the cream on their shelf for her to deal with. Reuben shut the door and took off his coat while Jonas washed his hands.

"It's going to be a cold night," Jonas said. "See you wrap up warm in the sleigh."

"I've got hot bricks and robes," Reuben replied.

"Don't bring her home too late now."

"We can see the New Year in, can't we, Uncle?"

"All right, all right."

Jonas clumped into the sitting-room, and the curtain fell behind him. Mama raked the fire in there, talking cheerily. Leota was left alone with Reuben. At once he saw the wetness on her lashes and thought he knew the cause.

"Leota," he whispered, "I only came to take Naomi for Gottlieb. They're gone on each other since the Christmas party."

"Why he didn't come himself to get her?" muttered Leota angrily.

"He figured Jonas wouldn't let her come with him, after seeing them dancing cheek to cheek."

"Let him come and do his own courting!"

Leota clattered and flung the dishes about with nervous shaking hands.

"How else can I ever get to see you?" whispered Reuben, putting warm and comforting arms about her, kissing her reassuringly. For a brief moment, Leota yielded, realising for the first time how terribly she had missed his daily companionship, his humour and affection. But then the precariousness of the situation came to her; she glanced hastily at the curtained doorway, pulling herself free.

"Damn," said Reuben quietly, following her look.

Leota went back to the dishpan, while Reuben took up a towel, polishing the plates and whirling them into their appointed places in the cabinet. Leota found herself curiously free of her sudden malaise, as if a powerful drug had been administered, heady and strange in its influence. When Naomi clattered downstairs in her high heels, sweeping aside the curtain, looking radiant in the pink blouse and as ripe as a peach, Leota was able to say, almost gaily.

"Well, this one would make a good husband for you. See how quick he dries dishes!"

"Bet you wouldn't see Gottlieb doing them," laughed Naomi.

"Bet you would too," said Reuben. "Boy, when Ma says, 'Dishes, Gottlieb!' he jumps to it."

"Go on!"

"Sure. See, Ma didn't have girls, so she has to get her men to give a hand now and again."

This new view of Gottlieb made Naomi double up with mirth.

Kazmiri lifted the curtain to look in.

"Are you ready?" she asked. "Now don't be too late."

Naomi was sudenly demure and respectful, Reuben all deference to the older woman. At the dishpan, Leota wondered if they would ever go. Yet she found herself tensely waiting for a last look from Reuben as general good nights were spoken. She heard only, with a heart like stone, that he was going to White's tomorrow to see if he could catch a ride to Ulna on the following day with Basil, who had mentioned to someone that he would be driving in with his team.

"Then you are off to the north again?" asked Mama kindly, Jonas looking in too, and listening.

"Yes, this is my last fling."

"Oh, let's get started!" cried Naomi impatiently.

"Now don't be too late," Jonas rumbled again.

"No, we won't." Naomi led the way down the stairs, her last high laugh fading on the wind outside, and they were gone.

Yawning and bearlike, Jonas stretched his big arms high, declaring that he was too tired to keep awake.

"And then they go and dance, those young folk," he said. "Dance all night, I betcha." He himself wanted only his bed.

But Kazmiri settled herself by the sitting-room fire, her knitting in her lap. In the kitchen, Leota finished her chores, refusing to think, struggling only to look cheerful and normal, to be able to control her voice, and answer Mama's occasional remarks.

"I think I'll go on with my knitting too," she said when

she had finished. But torture was to begin again, this time from an unexpected source. Mother and daughter clicked their knitting needles and warmed cheeks and toes beside the glowing heater while Jonas's peaceful snores rose and fell rhythmically in the adjoining room.

"Leota, I wish you would get married," Mama suddenly remarked in the same even tone in which she had said a moment ago that the cold wind seemed to have dropped.

Leota looked up from her work, startled. Under the movements of her swift fingers, the shawl for Mrs. White's baby now lay in creamy folds on her lap. Her face, flushed by the heat of the fire, seemed younger than Naomi's, revealing herself vulnerable, untried, torn between sadness and wonder. Her gaze, bemused by dreams, quickly hardened.

"Me?" she echoed.

"Yes," Mama answered decisively. "Pro is gone, and Sarah. Even Fenna. Naomi won't stay for long . . . I wish she wouldn't be so wild."

"She's not all that wild."

In the lamplight, the older woman looked weary, and Leota noted with a pang the whitening strands in the grey hair, the tired lines in her mother's strong face.

"Oh," she exclaimed, glad to turn the conversation away from herself, "Naomi likes a good time, sure, but it's only fun. Jonas is too hard on her."

"I wish you girls would try to understand," said Mama wearily. "Jonas gives you a good home. He's never stingy with anything."

"I know, Mama, it's true. Only . . ."

"He wants to keep the wrong kind of men away, that's all. It's so you girls will be happy in the long run. And you see, it does work out. Prolet has a good marriage. And Sarah too. Herman is a good man for her."

"And Philip." Leota spoke guardedly. None of them knew what Mama really thought of Philip.

"Fenna's very young." The weathered hands slowed in the knitting. "But you can't say her man is the wrong kind, or that he got her into trouble, or anything like that."

"Oh no!"

"She's very young, but she's so set on Philip. Jonas has

given his permission, and Fenna has lots of sense. It will be all right."

Only you don't really think so, Leota thought, her heart shaken for Fenna, longing to tell about Dan's proposal, but bound by the promise to Fenna not to.

"And you too, Leota. You should be thinking of getting married."

"Oh Mama!" her daughter burst out.

"If it would mean you would have to leave this district when you get married, you mustn't stay for me, Leota. I left my mother too. I went. I had my time."

The girl stared in astonishment. She must be thinking of Sam Slade, down in the Sequinah Valley. But Mama had never liked Sam any more than Leota had. It was strange, too, how Mama seemed so full of such talk tonight, when she rarely intruded on the affairs of her daughters. But now she gazed back at Leota almost pleadingly, as though trying to reach her from a great distance.

"It would have to be someone just right for you, my daughter. Perhaps some man much older who would understand you."

Only I don't know a man older, thought Leota wildly. There's only Herm, and now Sarah's got him. And he was never interested in me.

"Or even," Mama went on steadily, "or even someone younger."

Leota felt the impact of those words like a blow over the heart.

"Whoever it would be," said Mama, expertly joining blue wool on to grey, "never mind what anyone thinks of it. Just so long as the man is right for you. You are that kind of a woman. Good farm and money won't matter too much. But the man will have to be just right." Mama sighed, lapsed into silence, spent.

Leota bent her head, resolutely counting stitches, trying not to think. But from her turbulent mind, terrifying questions presented themselves. What had Mama seen? That quick kiss in the kitchen? What had she guessed? Leota knew her mother to be shrewd and observant; but surely this affair with Reuben had been so secret as to raise no suspicions. But what else could it mean? Leave this district... Just right for you... Or even ... someone younger.

"Oh my, I am tired." Mama stifled a yawn, rolling up her knitting. "I think I'll be getting along." She rose, lighting a candle from the flame of the lamp, just a little light so as not to waken Jonas.

"I'll be getting along too," Leota said distantly.

"You take the lamp, then. Good night." Kazmiri gave her daughter a loving, beseeching look, but the girl kept her eyes on her work.

"Good night, Mama," she murmured.

Alone, Leota took the lamp, going swiftly to her room, the room she shared with Naomi, now mercifully deserted except for the untidy litter of Naomi's clothes. It was icy cold. She got to bed quickly, burying herself deep under the warm wool quilts. Stillness lay upon the house. From far off came the eerie yapping of coyotes, making the night seem all the more desolate.

Ever since she had returned home from Zwick's, Leota had re-lived again and again in imagination the happiness she had known there. But she had refused to examine her feelings and see where they were leading her. There had been Sarah's sudden wedding and the wedding supper to think of. And Fenna's engagement and the strange proposal from Mr. Root, and her departure to Hosanna to visit Philip's folks over the holiday. Life had been too full for thinking. Now she began to think and probe relentlessly.

I'm in love with Reuben, she thought, feeling her face grow hot with shame in the bitter dark. I'm a fool, a fool. Even Mama sees through me.

How had it all happened? she wondered. Maybe Reuben had felt sorry for her, pitying her for the sordid encounter with Joe. There was a sweetness in Reuben. He would want to comfort her, but he would not think she would be such a fool as to fall in love with him, a kid like himself. Vividly in her mind rose a memory of him as a mischievous imp of seven barely reaching her shoulder as she bent to scrub his black hands and dirty face one day when she was "keeping" him when Florrie and Jud went to town. You didn't fall in love with someone like that. But then there was that other memory of him, riding behind her saddle in the prairie darkness.

If he did ask me to marry him . . . But he won't, he won't. But if he did, her thoughts pursued mercilessly, what would I say? In all honesty, she knew what she would want to answer. Only I couldn't, she thought. What would everyone think of me with a kid like that? But Mama just said not to care what anyone thinks . . . At the same time, in her imagination, Leota could see little children around her, with the line of lip and nostril that Reuben had, children looking up at her with his clear gaze.

She did not know what time it was when Naomi stole in, flinging off clothes in every direction, and crawling into bed beside her, to fall asleep at once, while Leota still lay awake. Then she dozed, to be harshly awakened by the strident ringing of the alarm clock, feeling more exhausted than she could ever remember. Even the sight of her wrecked pink blouse, tossed under the bed, could not rouse her. She dragged about the work until Naomi, dancing around to some imaginary strains of music heard only by herself, noticed her sister's bruised eyelids, and with a crack of her chewing gum remarked, " Wrong time of the month for you?"

" Girls," said Mama, coming upon them in the kitchen, " we're all invited up to Zwick's today, and Gottlieb is bringing Fenna. But one of you will have to stay back for milking. Jonas always stays. He must have his holiday too."

" I'll stay," Leota volunteered quickly. She could not face Reuben again in the light of her new self-knowledge.

" But you feel tough," said Naomi, longing to go. " I went to the dance last night. It's your turn now," she offered generously.

" I'll stay by the fire and keep warm. I don't feel like the trip, not today."

Mama sighed. " You all right?" she asked.

" Yes. Just tired, a little."

" Well then, we have a quick lunch and go early."

When the sound of the sleigh bells had died away, and they were all gone, Leota sat alone in the kitchen with its spotless waxed linoleum, gleaming stove, and polished lamp chimneys. The fire, in warmth and continual tickings and mutterings, lent a kind of companionship; but the windows, frosted by the cold, gave back a grey nothingness to the room. She knew she would not weep, for the hot agony had abated. Now her heart ached dully, and the winter stretched endlessly ahead, cold and empty. She did not mind being alone, for to Leota, aloneness brought healing and strength. But oh, if she could have had him in just once, to the warm fire, she thought, and set out the cups and plates. The white cups with the blue and gold rim. And the braided bread with the poppy seeds. And coffee. If only they could have had a last intimate talk together. And a last kiss. Longing and desolation filled her heart.

The paralysis of her spirits weighed down her whole body into lifelessness. And yet, so tightly drawn were her feelings, like the strings on an instrument, that the sudden stamp of boots on the back doorstep set her heart rocking. She opened the door leading downwards to the basement just as a snowy figure entered below. Reuben took off fur hat and mitts, beating them against the wall to free them of snow. He glanced up and saw her.

" Everybody gone but you?" he asked.

She watched the snow melting on his face and hair, almost frightened by the relief and joy that rushed over her.

" They've all gone."

" I've just been over to Basil's to see about catching a ride tomorrow. Would it be all right if I come in, do you think?" he asked with a short laugh.

" Oh yes, come in," Leota answered, keeping her voice light.

As he bent to unfasten his high overshoes, he felt her tender kindness come down to him like a wave.

" I'll just put on the coffee pot. Bring your things in so they'll dry," she went on.

He came up the steps a moment later, hesitating to drop wet clothes down on such a clean floor.

" That's all right," she assured him, setting the coffee pot over the heat. " Snowing pretty thick, isn't it?"

" Cover up my tracks," said Reuben.

" Did you—will you get a ride with Basil tomorrow?" she asked politely.

" You bet. Eight o'clock in the morning . . . Leota, why you didn't come to our place?" he asked, drying his face and hair on the roller towel behind the door.

She did not look at him.

"Well, somebody's got to stay."

"Figured maybe you didn't want to see me."

She sensed something different about him. She had seldom known him angry, but he looked angry now with that stubborn outthrust of chin.

"Oh Reuben," she said without thinking, "right now I was just wishing I could see you."

In moccasined feet, he crossed the kitchen in a stride. Leota did not stop to consider all that she had pondered in the night. He was everything she had ever known in a man of chivalry, and gentleness, and very real companionship. She loved him as her own soul. She went into his arms feeling as though she belonged there.

"I had to see you," said Reuben at last, his arms still so tight about her she could hardly breathe. "Leota, I love you. I love you. Would you marry me? I can't go back up north without knowing if you'd say yes. I think about you every minute. I just have to know. Will you, Leota?"

She recognised his complete sincerity. And she saw that he too had become acquainted with doubt and with the fear of a rebuff to his pride. It had cost him something to come and ask her to marry him. Always before, she had felt that she alone was on the the defensive, while he had seemed so confident and in command of the situation. But now that he laid bare his heart, stripping himself of every defence, all that was tender in Leota, and womanly, and mature, rose to steady her. She said gently:

"When you're going to get married, you got to be sure."

"I'm sure!" he retorted impatiently. "Aren't you? Don't you care about me, Leota? I thought maybe you did."

"I do care," she said swiftly. She could not see him tortured, but nevertheless she stood her ground, refusing to be swept off her feet.

"Then why you don't say yes?"

"I never could think straight with my ribs being broke."

"Sorry." He relaxed his hold a trifle.

"Reuben, why we don't sit down and have a cup of coffee, and talk about things?"

He fell silent. The fire whirred and ticked, while the coffee began to perk, sending out an appetising fragrance.

"O.K.," he said shortly, "if that's the way you want it."

With quick deft movements, she put a cloth on a little table near the sitting-room heater, set out teaspoons, cups and plates, just as she had longed to do.

"You're treating me like company," he said in an offended tone.

"You are company." Leota's lashes fluttered. "My special company. Maybe you could carry in the coffee pot. Watch. It's hot."

"Will you let me sit beside you?" he asked, offhandedly.

She nodded, smiling, and set a chair for him.

"I never had special company before," she told him. "It's nice, with everybody out."

He was touched, understanding the loneliness her words implied. Sliding his arm around her, he sat himself so close that her shoulder must fit against his.

"Now, what things do you want us to talk about, Leota?" he asked, truculent in spite of himself.

She stirred her coffee.

"What would Florrie think?"

"Why, you're Ma's favourite!" Reuben exclaimed jubilantly. "She always said you're the pick of the bunch of the Leniuk girls!"

Leota shook her head.

"It's different, when somebody likes you, to suddenly say you're going to marry their son."

"Ma would be so glad!"

Leota turned herself to look at him, though the tears stood in her eyes.

"You got to think, Reuben," she declared vehemently. "I'm five years older than you!"

"I seem just like a kid to you?"

"No, honest, you never do," she said slowly. "But you see, I figure what happened is that I went up and lived at your place, and we saw each other every day and had a lot of fun, and now that's what makes you think you—you want to marry me."

Reuben laughed. "'This is so sudden', eh Leota? Well, you got me all wrong. This isn't sudden. I haven't changed my mind about you for four years."

"Four years?"

"Yes. When I was sixteen, I danced with you at the Christmas party. You wouldn't remember, but we had three dances. They changed my life," he said, half teasing.

"Reuben, do be serious."

"I am," he assured her. "I really saw you then, for the first time, after knowing you all my life. I was going round steady with Ada Pearl. Ma didn't like it, but she never said. It was my last year in high school in Ulna. I started out dating Ada Pearl just to show it didn't matter about all that gossip of Mrs. Fox when I was born. Well, Ada Pearl was good fun in those days," said Reuben defensively. "I liked her. But after that Christmas party I mentioned, well, I went back to Ulna after New Year's thinking about you. And when I saw her again, suddenly she just looked cheap to me. I quit her dead."

"Is that the truth?" Leota asked sceptically. "We did hear you'd quit her after Christmas that year."

"Oh I didn't stop speaking to her. But I stopped going to the dances and shows for the rest of the term. Told her I had to study and get through my exams. After you, she was just ... cheap. She always kept asking me what she'd done. But she hadn't done anything. After really seeing you, I just didn't want her."

He was for taking her into his arms again, but Leota held him off.

"No, no. Let me think straight," she begged. "There's other things, too."

"What, for instance?"

"There was some girl cousin up north you liked."

"Well, I took out other girls after high school, but none of them was ever knee high to you, Leota."

"You might change your mind," she said faintly.

"After four years of not changing, I don't figure I'll ever change now. Especially now," said Reuben brushing his cheek against her hair.

"But what makes you want to marry me?" she asked wonderingly.

"That's easy. I want a girl who can make jokes in the Low German so it'll seem like home. And I want a Saturday-keeper, even though up north they all keep Sunday. And somebody who can sing Dan's song, and make braided bread . . ."

"You talk just like Jonas."

"Maybe Jonas is not so dumb as some people think."

"That's what Mama says. Have a piece of braided bread," she offered, the dimple showing in her left cheek. "You know, the kind the girl you want will have to make."

They grinned at each other with their old comradeship.

"But I loved you first and thought up all the reasons afterwards," he told her. "I mentioned to Aunt Ruth there was a German girl at home I was interested in. That was when she was sort of pushing my cousin at me. I said I'd have to try to persuade you."

"I'd be scared stiff of all the relatives," Leota confessed.

"Why, they'd love you all to pieces. There'd be welcoming parties all over the place."

"I'd be scared of what they'd think of me."

"Cripes! You talk as if I was going to show them a painted-up wife with a bottle of hootch on her hip. But *you*, Leota, *you!*"

"You said that for four years—for four years you been sort of thinking about me. But you never told me . . ."

"Would you have listened to me when I was seventeen?" he demanded. "I didn't know what to do. Coming home every Christmas hoping you wouldn't be engaged to someone else . . . And then every time I tried to say something, somebody would be coming. And I thought maybe you just felt sorry for me."

"I didn't know what to think myself," she confessed shyly.

"What could I do?" asked Reuben. "Even now, I wouldn't go and ask my folks for permission to get married. It would look bad in the district, like there was some reason we couldn't wait. But I'll be twenty-one in March, and the farm will be my own. I was going to wait until spring to ask you. But last night . . . it seemed I was hurting you. How about it, Leota? You still didn't say one way or another."

She saw that she must answer now.

"If you—if you don't change your mind by spring," she said, her dark lashes downcast. "But don't tell everyone just yet," she pleaded. "Because if you do change your mind, you must tell me . . ."

"Never will I," murmured Reuben in the Low German.

"Never will I. Come to me in the spring, Leota. I'll write and tell you when I've got the house ready. We'll get married up north where nobody knows about me, and nobody knows about you."

They were very gay and happy. Reuben seated himself, lordly, in Jonas's big chair, pulling Leota down on to his knee. The few hours of winter daylight were almost spent. The room had become grey and shadowy, the fire glowing redly through the cracks in the top of the heater.

"I'll have to go on account of chores," said Reuben at last.

"Me, too." Leota jumped up guiltily. "If we sit here too long, Jonas might walk in on us."

"Would you mind?"

She considered for a moment.

"No, I wouldn't mind too much. But I want to wait until spring, Reuben, and then I'll tell him."

When Reuben was ready to go, she took his hand.

"God go with you," she said simply.

"And with you," he returned, deeply moved. For both of them felt at once that this inadvertent joining of hands and naming the name of God had placed a blessing on their pledge to one another, and given them assurance of its rightness.

The falling snow soon swallowed up Reuben's figure. But Leota, dreaming and smiling, her face aglow, unconsciously sang snatches of song as she got ready to do the evening chores. Outside, the big flakes touched her cheeks like kisses, and she blushed thinking so, spilling the chorus of "Honey in the Rock" at the astonished cows.

Chapter Twelve

1

GOTTLIEB sat in the beer parlour with Joe. He kept apart from the main crowd with their rumble of talk on the other side of the room. Pushing Patches hard, he had ridden far that day, and now he looked weary, beaten by the wind, and more than slightly drunk.

"You know something?" said Joe, leaning across to him. "You're drinking too much these days. If you don't watch out, you'll be getting yourself on the Indian list."

"I don't drink so much," protested Gottlieb sourly.

"You know something? You'll end up an old drunk. Look at the way you come in here Monday. Sweating . . . shivering . . . You'll lose your job and end up froze to death in a snowbank. If I wasn't your friend, I wouldn't say nothing. But Jees, Gottlieb!"

"'You waited too long to say you were sorry,'" sang some drunken voice from the corner. Gottlieb stared down at the table.

"'And now I feel sorry for you . . .'" the singing continued.

"Forget about Sarah, man," Joe urged. "There's just as good fish in the sea as ever came out of it! Get yourself another girl."

"This here's got nothing to do with Sarah," growled Gottlieb.

"No? Well, what's eating you then?"

"I just been to a wedding."

"Your own?"

"No. Fenna's. My little cousin Fenna's. The only real cousin I got. All them Leniuk girls, they're not my real cousins. Just Fenna. My mother was her father's sister. They say Fenna even looks like my mother . . ." Gottlieb took another drink.

"So you went to her wedding! She got married to the preacher, didn't she? Well, you said yourself that's what was gonna happen."

"Yeah. Well, I just went to the church part, not the supper. The wedding supper was a big do in the basement of the church in Hosanna. I didn't go to that, but I figured I could see her married even if Sarah was there. My own little cousin."

"Nobody kicked you out, did they?"

"No. I got a seat at the back so I could get away quick when it was over. I was by the aisle, so Fenna came right past me with Uncle Jonas." Gottlieb looked up bleakly at Joe. "They had slapped the kid in the face, both cheeks."

"You drink too much," Joe answered.

"No, I wasn't drinking. But I got eyes in my head. She passed so close as me to you. Hell, I know the marks of a hand on a person's face. Finger marks."

"Marriage," sighed Joe, shaking his head.

"Make anybody want a drink."

"Too bad the teacher didn't get her."

"Seems he asked her and she turned him down."

"Oh well, she'd know a guy like Mr. Root couldn't face old Jonas."

"That's where you're wrong," said Gottlieb excitedly. "He did go up there, and he would've asked Jonas for her, but Fenna told him Philip was the only guy for her."

"Who told you this?" Joe asked, astonished.

"Naomi."

Joe whistled.

"That teacher's sure got more guts than I ever gave him credit for."

"I can't figure out Uncle Jonas letting Fenna get married like that." Gottlieb passed a hand over his face. "Naomi and Jean Jebson got the bride ready. You know Jean? Philip's skinny sister, the one with the glasses. Uncle Jonas just took Fenna down the aisle when she was ready. But you'd think he'd see her face . . . I grabbed Naomi after, and I says, 'How come the kid got her face slapped?' And she says, 'Jean done that. Fenna lost her nerve and got hysterics, but Jean fixed her.' Then she told me, she says, 'You know what? Mr. Root proposed... Asked Fenna to wait a couple of years for him... But Fenna turned him down, the little fool! Even though he was right up there at the house, ready to speak to Jonas. And now she gets slapped in the face!'"

"Maybe it was just a touch of hysterics," Joe suggested amiably. "Maybe Fenna will settle down now. Have some kids, and be happy."

"Maybe," said Gottlieb sceptically. "But I hear tell the preacher's mother is going out there to live with them when the weather gets better. Just imagine, in that little house of his, with the newly-weds!"

A drunken quartet in the corner started up woozily again:

"'You waited too long to say you were sorry,
And now I feel sorry for you...'"

"I got to go," mumbled Gottlieb, taking another drink.

"You had plenty," said Joe. "My advice to you is, get yourself another girl. There's two Leniuks left. Hands off Leota; she's mine. There's still Naomi!"

"I want a girl that'll be true," replied Gottlieb, staring down at the table. "Naomi's not like Sair, you know that. All the guys know that. But, like you say, there's still Naomi. I'm not allowed up there at Leniuk's, but I get to see her, I sure do. On my days off, I always go by their place. Now and again I'm lucky if Jonas goes off with the team to the coal mine or something. I watch when he goes... But she's not Sair."

"Leota would be true."

"You know something?" Gottlieb lifted his heavy lids to look Joe in the face. "You don't have no more chance with Leota than a snowball in hell."

"I got just as good a chance as the next guy. I was figuring maybe next spring I could build a little place away from the hotel. Then I could say to Jonas, 'See, we'd have our own place. She wouldn't have to work like a hired girl with drunks around...' By Godda, if Mr. Root figures he can face old Jonas, well I can too!"

"Next spring, eh?" Gottlieb swallowed down a drink, toyed with his glass thoughtfully.

"Sure. I got to work fast though, the way the Leniuk girls

are popping off like hot-cakes . . . I better get out there and make hay." Joe grinned. " Give things a shove."

" Right up to Christmas I'd believe you," said Gottlieb, his head swaying unsteadily. " But now, things move so fast, it's all a person can do, hold their hat and hang on."

" You should of married Sair! Did you figure she'd wait forever?"

" I just wanted things . . . stay like they was."

" Think I could come to the Valentine party out there?"

" Sure. And I'll give you . . . personal invitation to come out to the Valentine party," said Gottlieb thickly. " Personal invitation. Get it? You'll see you got no more chance . . . than . . . snowball in hell."

2

Bitter winds blew over the prairie, bringing snow, piling up drifts, blocking the roads. The farm homes with their brave plumes of smoke, were like little oases on a desert of white. The Leniuk womenfolk had always loved this time of year in spite of the hardships of the outdoor chores. But with these done, and the fires built up, the curtains drawn against the cold, and the lamps lighted, they could work at their cross-stitch embroidery, or knit, or quilt. Now they welcomed the roaring fires in the cookstove baking the bread. It was a time of peace and cosiness. Except that the shadow of Fenna hung over them.

Walking through the swirling snow, the winds and the drifts, she came and went like a ghost. At first she appeared only every few days, but gradually her visits were almost daily. She would come in, chilled and silent, not knowing whether she was welcome or not, until the girls had helped her off with her snowy things and brought her in to the sitting-room stove. Then they would give her a hot drink and a special piece of apple cake or braided bread. Never had they been so tender and kind to her. Gradually she would relax, smile a little, and join in the conversation about sewing, or the farm, or the harmless gossip of the district.

Kazmiri became alarmed at the frequency of these visits.

" Is it too lonely, Fenna?" she once asked.

" There's not much to do," her daughter hedged, not meet-

Honey in the Rock

ing her gaze. "And then I'm used to the walk, going to school, and I want the exercise."

"It won't be lonely, when you have a baby," said her mother hopefully.

Her cheeks burning from the heat of the fire, Fenna did not answer to this.

"Philip's mother is coming to stay with us when the roads get better," she told them without emotion.

"Well, that will be company for you. You won't be so alone."

But when a Chinook wind came briefly from the mountains, bringing respite from the cold, reducing the drifts and making roads passable even by truck with a minimum of shovelling, and Mrs. Jebson arrived, Fenna's visits home became more frequent than ever.

"Can you just go and leave the old lady like that?" Naomi asked one evening as the supper hour drew near and Fenna slowly made ready to depart.

"It isn't so lonely now, is it?" her mother asked.

Fenna stood at the door, looking back at them. Mama with her head bent over a pair of socks she was knitting for Jonas. Naomi braiding a rug, and Leota putting a bright cross-stitch band on a towel. The heater giving out a cheerful warmth. The bright rugs on the shining floor. And the three of them.

"You can have . . . all this, any time you want it," she said strangely. "Don't you want me to come?" It was a cry of anguish.

Dropping her knitting, Kazmiri went quickly to her daughter.

"Yes," she said, taking Fenna's limp hand. "You come. Any time you feel you want us, then come. We are here."

"Maybe you'll have a baby," Naomi suggested cheerfully.

"I think I am," said Fenna. "I'm a week over my time."

"Oh good, Fenna!" cried Leota. "Aren't you glad? If it was me, I'd be tickled pink!"

"Listen to who's talking," laughed Naomi, cracking her gum. "I better tell old Joe." She glanced across at Leota hoping she wouldn't mind the joke which was only to cheer Fenna. But Leota, conscious of Reuben's latest letter rustling in her apron pocket, did not even hear her.

"It would be good, Fenna," said Mama, hope coming alive in her. "But maybe it's nothing yet."

"It is," said Fenna dully. "I never go over. And I know. I feel like I never felt before." She bowed her head. Her hair had lost its lustre, and the radiance that had been her chief beauty, was no more.

"Did you tell your husband?" Mama asked.

"No, no! I told him— I told him— He thinks I'm—"

"Fenna, always tell your troubles to your husband now," Mama advised.

"You don't want me!"

"Yes, yes, we do. But you are married. Your husband has the first right to a thing like this."

Fenna did not look up.

"I'll walk a piece with you," Naomi offered, putting away her handwork. "If you'll milk, Leota."

Jonas had gone to the mine for coal and had not yet returned.

"Sure, I'll milk," Leota agreed. "If you like this cross-stitch pattern, Fenna, I'll show you next time," she added.

"A bit of sewing would be good," nodded Mama as Naomi put on her coat.

"Baby clothes!" said Naomi, her eyes shining. "We'd all help. Imagine beating Sarah with the first grandchild!"

Even Fenna had to smile wanly as they set off.

"There's snow in that wind," Naomi warned as they hurried along in the gathering darkness. She kept looking about, expectantly. "I bet we get some bad weather again soon."

"It's never so bad I couldn't make it home," said Fenna. "But you don't want me. Mama doesn't want me."

"Of course we want you. We just figured with another woman there, it wouldn't be so lonely."

"I just got to get away from her, that's all."

"Tell her you got a baby coming, and you can't put up with her! Tell her she'd better get back to town!" cried Naomi, trying to put some of her own unquenchable spirit into Fenna.

The headlights of a truck appeared in the distance, and its roar filled the quiet of the evening.

"That's Gottlieb." Naomi felt a pleasurable thrill of excitement as he came nearer. "Say, why you don't catch a ride home with him?" She stood in the middle of the road, waving. The truck careened forward, slithered on some ice, and finally came to a shuddering standstill.

"Want to get yourself killed?" Gottlieb shouted, opening the door and leaning out. "My brakes ain't what they used to be."

"Whole truck ain't what it used to be," laughed Naomi. "But it'll take Fen home to her place, won't it?"

"Oh sure. Want a ride, Fenna?"

"If you guarantee not to kill her on the way."

"Can't guarantee nothing. But come on, Fenna," he said kindly. "Jump in."

"Be seeing you!" Naomi shouted as her sister climbed into the cab.

"See you at the Valentine party!" Gottlieb called back, leaning out again.

Naomi waved her hand, going off laughing into the darkness. Gottlieb roared the engine, and the truck leaped forward. The road, rough with hummocks of ice and hard snowy ruts cut by passing sleds, made their progress slow. Finally the truck stalled.

"She's boiling," said Gottlieb briefly. "I'll just wait a bit for her to cool down." Turning off the headlights, he rolled a cigarette before getting out to look at the engine. "Needs water," he told her.

"I better walk on," she said uneasily.

"Hold your horses. There's a creek someplace here, isn't there? But I guess it's froze solid."

"Naomi broke the ice for the cattle in the pasture, said Fenna suddenly. "It's quite close to here. I'll show you. D'you have a pail.

"Ready for anything," he answered, producing a battered jam tin.

"Just through the fence here."

Floundering through the uneven drifts of the field, they came at length to the creek where the water hole gleamed darkly in the grey-whiteness. The tin did not hold nearly enough.

"I'll stay on this side of the fence," Fenna suggested, "and put the water in. And then you go back for more."

Several trips finished the job, and once more they climbed into the cab.

"Here we go!" shouted Gottlieb gaily, switching on the lights.

Darkness had really come now, and sleet rattled on the windshield like handfuls of thrown sand. With a flourish, the truck stopped at the door of the manse just as Philip opened it.

"So long, Fenna!" said Gottlieb as she stepped out.

"Just a minute!" Holding the door of the cab open, Philip kept his wife from moving. "What was you two doing up there on the road just now? I seen the headlights coming, and then they went out."

"What did you say?" Gottlieb shouted, incredulous. He switched off the ignition. "Was you asking me what was we doing with the headlights off?" he asked quietly his eyes blazing.

"You heard me."

"We—we got water for the engine. It was boiling!" cried Fenna desperately.

"Water?" Philip sneered. "Where does a person get water on a night like this?"

"Out of the creek," Gottlieb answered levelly.

"Think I'm going to believe that? I know all about you and your reputation in town!"

With Philip and Fenna backing away from him, Gottlieb forced his way out of the cab, slamming the door behind him. He clenched his fists.

"We got water. Out of the water hole in the creek. See? That's all."

"Oh Gottlieb!" cried Fenna. "Please, just—just go!"

"What's all this shouting?" came a querulous woman's voice from inside.

"Gottlieb!" said Fenna faintly.

"All right, I'll go. But any time you want me to beat his brains in, just let me know. If he's got any brains to beat in!"

"Then I got out of there," Gottlieb told Joe at the beer parlour. "I figured if I stayed any longer, maybe I'd just be making it worse for her. So I beat it." He toyed with his glass.

"Poor kid. Bet he's thinking there'll be a Zwick baby coming now."

"Know something?" said Joe conversationally. "You had enough. Ada Pearl was asking for you. Said she didn't see you around lately."

"Not interested. I want a girl that's true. Then a guy like Philip gets a girl that's true, and look how he treats her. Like dirt."

"Well, there's the Valentine party coming up. At least you'll see Naomi then. Me, I'm still waiting to give things a shove with Leota that night."

3

"Where's Leota?" Joe asked Naomi when he finally arrived at the Valentine party after shovelling his way through drifted roads for hours.

"She's home," Naomi answered with an enigmatic smile.

"How'd you get here, then?"

"Oh, I come over with Herm and Sair in the cutter. It's awful handy, having married sisters." She waved to him, dancing off with Gottlieb, while Joe sank down moodily on a bench on the sidelines.

"Wouldn't you like me to help you make a butterfly quilt?" Sarah asked Fenna who sat alone in a dismal little heap near Joe. "It's a pretty pattern," she added, sitting beside her sister, "and I've got heaps of nice pieces." She looked happy, serene, smiling.

Out in the cloakroom, Philip talked politics with Jonas and Herman. At the front of the schoolroom, Dan Root sat chatting with some of the parents about the progress of their children. One of the pupils came along with plates of cake and sandwiches. At the sight of food, Fenna put her hand against her mouth, shaking her head.

"Why I didn't stay home!" she whispered to Sarah. "The smell of sandwiches . . . I wanted to stay home, but Philip made me come . . . It was his turn to look after the dance, and he says it wouldn't look right if I didn't come."

"But you should get out to a party sometimes," said Sarah. "D'you feel sick?" She looked anxiously at Fenna.

"It's the smell of that awful coffee..."

"That's because you're expecting," whispered Sarah excitedly. "Lucky you!"

Rubbing his hands, Philip came up to them.

"You're not eating, Fenna. What about a nice cup of coffee?"

"No, I just couldn't."

"That's the way it is, at first," said Sarah significantly. And then she happened to look up, and at that moment her eyes met Gottlieb's as he danced by with Naomi. "And I'll sure be interested to see this Zwick baby when it comes," she added loudly.

Neither Gottlieb nor Naomi heard her. But Fenna gave a cry. With a hand over her mouth, threading her way among the dancers, she ran swiftly out of the schoolhouse.

Philip stared at Sarah, his face tight and hard.

"Just where do you get your information?" he asked.

At once she knew how far-reaching would be the wrong that she had done. She saw the implacable quality of his anger.

"It isn't true!" she cried heatedly. "I said it to get back at Gottlieb when he was dancing past here."

"No smoke without fire," Joe commented sourly. Bitter at Leota's absence from the party, he sat moodily on the bench, an onlooker at the drama of the lives of others, getting enjoyment out of watching Philip's face. "I heard that before, about the Zwick baby. And as a matter of fact," he went on, grinning, "even the teacher has kissed your girl."

"Shut up, Joe!" hissed Sarah, getting quickly to her feet. "It's just lies, all lies!"

"Ask him then!" Joe challenged.

"All right, I will." She beckoned to Dan who came over at once, polite and unsuspecting. "Mr. Root," she said breathlessly, "Joe here is being just horrid and telling lies about Fenna, trying to give her a bad reputation. She was always a good kid. Joe's saying you—you kissed her. Tell them it isn't true."

Although Dan felt the schoolhouse shifting on its foundations while Philip faced him with glittering eyes, he kept calm.

"I asked her to marry me," he said courteously, looking steadily back at Philip. "I forced my attentions upon her, but she turned me down flat. She said you were the only man who mattered to her."

Listening, Joe grinned, admiring and thrilled, taking it all in to pass along at the beer parlour.

"I didn't think I had much of a chance," continued Dan. "But, nothing venture, nothing gain! I was wrong to think I had any chance at all. She was completely loyal to you. So, you're the lucky man." With Sarah aghast and Philip speechless, he went on, "I—I never had the chance to congratulate you before. Please accept my congratulations now."

"Oh Mr. Root," cried Billy White, rushing up to the tense little group. "It's time for the Valentine dance!"

"Right," said Dan, moving away.

He was calm, though pale, and his nerves did not betray him. He heard his own voice instructing the little orchestra about the special Valentine dance in which a large red cardboard heart would pass from hand to hand, while the music was to stop at short intervals to catch and eliminate whichever couple was holding the heart.

"Eliminate," he repeated, "that's the thing."

With a fixed smile, he asked Naomi to dance with him, joining in the idiocy of the game, laughingly handing on the big heart whenever it came their way. He did not care now if everyone in the district laughed at him, if what he had said would save Fenna from any further criticism. He held his head high, using pride as an armour against the gossip, telling himself again and again that time would heal his own pain.

Sarah hurried along the sidelines, out through the cloakroom to the snowy porch, Philip following quickly in her wake. In the darkness, they could see nothing of Fenna. From the window of the manse, a pale light shone without any vitality in it. Mrs. Jebson would be there, complaining and quarrelsome.

"Where did you hear about the Zwick baby?" Philip demanded.

"I didn't hear nothing. It was just something nasty between Gottlieb and me."

"Don't forget you're a married woman now."

With his cold hard look, Philip took his coat and left the building.

Sarah turned back into the cloakroom where she felt Herman's warm arm go round her.

"Like to dance?" he asked.

"Why do you care about me?" she asked Herman. "I'm a real bad woman."

Seeing Fenna so lonely at the party, she had wanted to comfort her. And what had happened to her good intentions? The sight of Gottlieb's dark alive face had given her a jolt, like being kicked in the stomach by a mule, Sarah thought, grieving, as she waltzed with Herman. She wished passionately she had never heard the joke Joe was spreading about the "Zwick baby," for it had shocked her, and now she herself had passed it on.

Smiling, Herman hummed the simple tune in her ear as they danced, tossing the red cardboard heart to the next couple, and sliding quickly out of the way.

Chapter Thirteen

I

EARLY March brought a sudden unexpected foretaste of spring. One evening the sky held an unmistakable sign, a golden arc of light against the western horizon, hemmed in with heavy purple cloud, the sign of the Chinook wind. In the night it came, with sharp rude slamming and banging at first, of loose shutters or any lightweight barrel and box left lying about, but with growing intensity whining and then roaring until buildings rocked and creaked on their foundations. The Leniuks awoke to find the frost melting off their windows, giving at last the long view over the countryside which they had missed for many weeks. A great piece of tin which Jonas had once nailed on to the leaking barn roof, had partially ripped loose. Every few minutes it whistled upwards into the air, to crash down again a moment later as the wind played about it. When Naomi set the windmill working to pump water for the stock, the blades whirled around like something gone mad, water came up with the strident clamour of the mill, gushing forth as from a bottomless river. The snow had sunk down, and here and there on the hills, the brown earth shouldered its way through the grey-whiteness.

"About time we had a warm break like this!" Naomi cried, coming in from the morning milking. "Feels good. No mitts. No hat."

Her hair had blown about; the wind had whipped rich colour into her cheeks. Outside work suits her, Leota thought, turning pancakes at the stove. It makes her look prettier, even.

"Maybe Fenna can come now it's warmer," Kazmiri suggested, seating herself at the breakfast table.

"The road will be mush, Mama," said Naomi slipping in beside her.

Leota brought a platter of bacon and eggs. " She didn't come for so long. Even now Mrs. Jebson's gone back to town."

" She doesn't feel so good always," said Mama.

Jonas came in from outside. While he silently hung up his things and washed his hands, the three women at the table tried to gauge his mood.

" Warm today," he said pleasantly.

" You could bring Fenna home, perhaps, Jonas?" Kazmiri asked gently. " Philip has to go to Hosanna to a wedding. She will be lonely all by herself without even Mrs. Jebson there."

" You could make it in the little sleigh," Naomi suggested casually.

Jonas passed a hand over his rough grizzled hair, helped himself to eggs, bacon, and pancakes.

" She didn't come for such a long time," his wife went on.

Jonas looked speculatively out of the window at the condition of the snow and the roads.

" Well I . . . maybe I could."

" For dinner-time, then?" asked Kazmiri, her face alight.

He nodded. " I could leave at eleven . . ."

" So nice then. We make a good dinner, Leota. And I have some baby clothes Fenna wore all those years ago. I must look at them again and see if some she could use."

" Mama's going to love being Gramma," Naomi laughed as she and Leota cleared away breakfast. " Good thing there's one of us who won't disappoint her."

Plans for the day went happily ahead, and promptly at eleven, Jonas set off with the team and small sleigh, the wind lashing the manes and tails of the horses as they turned slowly along the sodden road. The sun shone warmly down, water dripped in more and more rapidly falling drops, while each slope had streams rushing down it. Humming to herself, Naomi moved restlessly about the house which now felt stifling from the heat of the kitchen stove with its burden of cooking. Clad in a skirt and a cool pretty blouse, she kept making excuses to run outside. Taking pleasure in the balminess of the air, at the same time finding its sweetness almost intolerable, she looked constantly towards the road leading far off to Bronson's. All at once, Gottlieb, mounted on Patches, rode across the barnyard.

Watching him from the kitchen window, Naomi breathlessly

took stock of the situation. Mama and Leota were too deep in conversation in the sitting-room to have seen him. They had spread all the baby clothes out of Mama's trunk over the chairs, and stood about exclaiming, laughing, and discussing. Without donning sweater or boots, Naomi went swiftly outside, leaping lightly over the puddles on her way to the barn.

"Well, look who's here," she drawled, gaining the doorway as Gottlieb dismounted.

"What are you doing here? Looking for eggs?" he asked.

"You bet!" she cried, pulling his hair, for he too was hatless. "Come on, you egg. You're just right for the cake we're baking."

Roughly he broke her hold on his hair with his hard fingers.

"Well, Uncle Jonas went off to town at last, didn't he? He could of gone a bit earlier on my day off."

"He's just gone to get Fenna home, that's all. You better go. Getting bold as brass, coming right to the yard."

"Well, who's afraid of Kazmiri and Leota?"

Naomi leaned against the door jamb, the wind whipping her skirt about. She had not seen Gottlieb for some time, though they were always on the lookout for one another. He looked back at her, his rough dark curls blowing, his colour ruddy from exercise and good health. But Patches, where he stood, constantly received the drips from the overhanging roof. Impatiently, he shook his head, and without further ado, stepped determinedly into the barn, brushing past Naomi and escaping Gottlieb who idly held the reins.

"Sure makes himself at home," Naomi giggled. "Look at him, helping himself to hay." She darted off with a laugh. "Needs to be tied," she said from the depths of the horse stall where she quickly secured the reins to the manger.

"No woman will ever tie him if he don't want to be tied!" said Gottlieb, coming after her.

"Or man neither," Naomi returned, giving his hair another hard pull and diving under Patches' chin to escape.

"Just spoiling for a fight, you are," teased Gottlieb, appearing suddenly from under the belly of the horse. With a flash of bare legs, she had leapt the wall of the stanchion. He was around it in a second and seized her arm as she rushed out. But she was strong and wrenched herself free, her rich hair falling over her flushed face. Panting, they ran about the shadowy barn, now here, now there, Naomi leading the way with her infectious laughter in and out of the stalls. Patches, busy munching, raised a hind hoof whenever they came near him.

"Got you!" muttered Gottlieb, trapping her in a corner. But while he grasped empty air, she slunk past him, jumping for the ladder going up to the loft. He grabbed one of her feet. She kicked violently, pulling her bare foot out of the shoe. He threw it down, seizing her other foot. Through the leather, she could feel the warmth of his hand. Climbing higher, Naomi tried to stamp on his fingers, but only succeeded in losing her other shoe. With a shriek of laughter, she got up into the loft, pushing down his head and trying to loosen his fingers on the rungs as he came steadily upwards. Pelting him with handfuls of hay to blind him momentarily, she moved towards the opening above the manger where Patches was. But having gained the loft, he lunged at her, seizing a tail end of her blouse that dangled out. She spun round to free herself, and at once the blouse spat its six small buttons in a shower.

As she tried to pull her blouse together in front over an inadequate brassière, she lost the advantage of the fight. He should have been warned then by her expression of panic, but he did not notice. In the dimness of the loft, she saw the gleam of his eyes and his white teeth as they wrestled. This time she did not escape, and they went rolling over and over in the hay together.

She cried out once, "No, no! Gottlieb, please, *please*!"

But as soon as he had kissed her, she thought her very bones must melt. She ceased to resist, holding him in her arms, while the Chinook wind made weird music on a broken pane mended with paper in a high window of the loft, and relentlessly worried the loose tin on the roof, lifting it up and crashing it down.

2

Leota ran into the kitchen to rescue her pies from the oven. "They're just right," she called cheerily to her mother. After taking them out, she lifted the lid of a saucepan

Honey in the Rock

and stirred the beet soup. She had also prepared rice rolled in cabbage leaves, a favourite dish of Fenna's.

"I think they come now," said Kazmiri from the sitting-room window.

Looking out, Leota could see a dark speck far down the prairie road. She watched until she could definitely make out the horses and sleigh.

"It's them all right," she agreed. "Well, dinner's nearly ready."

Meanwhile, she wondered, nervously, about Naomi. Some time ago, now, she had seen Gottlieb flash past into the barnyard, while her mother bent over the trunk, not noticing. She considered whether she should slip out to the barn and see if he had gone, or at least warn Naomi that Jonas would soon arrive. For of course she's out there with him, Leota thought. And all hell will break loose if Jonas finds them together, alone. With the team and sleigh becoming larger on the horizon, Leota went outside, picking her way through the mud and slush, apron and dress fluttering.

From the barn door she saw Patches' black and white rump with its switching tail. Lifting his head from the manger, he eyed her suspiciously. Leota advanced a little way, glancing about at the cavern emptiness. Then, above the banshee whining of the wind, she thought she heard, coming from the loft, an astonished cry of pain, instantly stifled. Trembling, her hand pressed against her lips, she fled back to the house and leaned weakly against it. Jonas came on, ever closer. Shading her eyes, Leota looked out across the prairie. She could see the horses quite plainly now. But wasn't Fenna with him? She did not seem to be sitting up front. Was she lying there in the back of the sleigh? Or hadn't she come after all? Anyhow, Naomi must be warned. Slowly, anxiously watching Jonas, Leota went back to the barn.

3

Gottlieb lay with his face pressed against Naomi's bare shoulder. She gazed at him, thinking without regret, I'm his now. And then fiercely, And he's mine. Gottlieb lay against her shoulder, dark lashes pressed tight against flushed cheeks, looking for all the world like a little lost boy who had cried himself to sleep. Cradling his head in her arms, Naomi held him close to her breast, whispering in the Low German, " My darling ... My little one ... My dearest ..."

" Naomi! " Leota's voice suddenly cut in, urgent and hurried. " Naomi! "

Gottlieb's eyes flew open, alert, wary.

" It's Leota," Naomi breathed.

" Naomi! " The voice below had taken on an edge of despair.

" I'm coming! Right now."

Naomi got up, trying to pull her clothing together. The button on the waistband of her skirt dangled on a thread. She moved a large safety pin from the hem and made the waist secure, tucking in her blouse as best she could. Gottlieb seemed to be choking on something he wanted to say, but she held her finger to her lips. Then she slithered down to a manger below.

Leota stared as her sister appeared.

" What's wrong with you? " the younger girl demanded with bold brightness.

" Jonas is coming back. He's nearly here."

As she spoke, Leota's gaze went from the hay sticking out of her sister's hair, to the buttonless blouse, to the sagging hem of the skirt, to the bare feet. And snow still lying around, she thought wildly.

" Well, let him come."

Naomi took one of her shoes out of the manger, and strode into the next stall, swinging her hips as she went to retrieve the other one from where it lay defencelessly in a heap of manure, looking as though it had been hurled there.

" But Naomi! " Leota gasped. " What about Gottlieb? "

" Well, what about him? " Naomi asked carelessly, stuffing her feet into her shoes.

" Isn't he up in the loft? "

" Of course not."

" Then who is? "

" No one," Naomi asserted impatiently.

" No one? Then what," asked Leota, " is no one's black and white pinto horse doing here? And what will Jonas say when he sees it? "

Naomi had forgotten Patches. Now he loomed enormous in

the barn. He turned his big head right round to look at them, a ridiculous wisp of hay hanging from his lips. Naomi dissolved into helpless laughter at the sight of him. Even Leota had to giggle when he turned away in disgust to go on with his munching. But the close jingle of sleigh bells roused them both.

"Get up to the house and change! Quick!" cried Leota.

"What are you going to do?" Naomi asked, laughing hysterically.

"I'll do something. But run now, quick!"

Feeling like a complete fool, Gottlieb could hear them talking, their voices raised against the sound of the wind. He should have gone down when Naomi had, he thought. But at that time he had not been able to bring himself to face Leota. He wondered what it would be best to do now. Jonas, on his homeward journey, would have a complete view of the whole countryside, and could not miss seeing Gottlieb if he rode forth. The old man would want to know just what had been going on. There would be impossible questions. Vacillating, Gottlieb stayed where he was, hoping that Leota would find some way of dealing with his horse, especially as Jonas was driving right into the yard.

Leota did her best. Hastily opening the rear door of the barn, she led Patches outside, tying his reins to a post where he would be hidden by the whole bulk of the barn itself. Then, closing the door again, she found a battered old lard pail and began to look for eggs. She actually did find one in the manger where Patches had been feeding. Her idea was that when Jonas had gone up to the house, she could bring the horse back in again and leave the rest to Gottlieb.

Jonas came in with the team. She faced him quietly, holding the pail and one egg. He looked at her without speaking, taking the horses to their stalls. That was not unusual. Yet for some reason she could not understand, Leota felt a quickening of her heart beats, as if there was something strange in the air. The wind played a funny harp-like tune on the broken window of the loft, and it whistled under the flap of loose tin on the roof, lifting it, crashing it down. Just as Jonas came to hang some harness on a peg, a shadow darkened the entrance and Patches stood there, hesitating. He had merely untied the reins and walked around to the front doorway. Frozen, Leota watched him clump in, trying to find his place again. Without a word, Jonas took the reins and tied him in a stall.

Dragging a comb through her hair, Naomi watched the barn through the bedroom window. She had flown up the stairs without disturbing her mother who was rearranging the contents of her trunk. Shaking with excitement and nervousness, Naomi donned slacks and a short-sleeved pullover. Then she saw Patches ambling round to the front of the barn, mane and tail lifting in the wind. Fascinated, she stared, watching him disappear inside. In an agony of suspense, she waited to see what would happen next, and it was only then that she had time to wonder what had become of Fenna.

She didn't come, Naomi thought with a sudden stab of realisation. She couldn't of come right in behind me, and I never took my eyes off the window since. She experienced a feeling of anti-climax and disappointment, especially for her mother's sake. She looked intently at the sleigh. What's that thing loaded into the back of it? she wondered. Looks like a blanket . . . She had half a mind to rush out and see, and to speak to Mama. But she could not leave her vigil. She waited, tense and quivering. There'll be fireworks now, she thought. Luckily I'm not there. He'll think Leota's having a love affair!

An explosion could not have startled her more than did the appearance of Gottlieb on Patches. They shot out of the barn door like a bullet from a gun, Gottlieb riding with lowered head, the hooves of the big black and white horse kicking up mud and slush as he plunged forward on the gallop through the barnyard and down the road, never slackening his pace. Then nothingness. At last Jonas appeared, walking slowly towards the house, with Leota creeping after him at a distance.

"Naomi! Leota!" Mama called. "Is Fenna up there?"

Naomi tore down the stairs four at a time, landing at the bottom with a light grace.

"She isn't upstairs. Did she come then?"

"I don't know," Kazmiri answered uncertainly.

At the sound of footsteps, Naomi stood her ground, waiting to see what Jonas would say. He came in very quietly and stood inside the door, not noticing her at all. Automatically he moved aside to allow Leota to enter, but he did not seem to be aware of her either. He had eyes only for his wife, his face grey and drawn.

"Jonas," said Kazmiri distinctly. "What is it?"

She looked suddenly tired, old.

He came to her side and took her arm, a strange, unfamiliar thing for him to do. Then he led her, gently, courteously, into the sitting-room, letting the curtain drop behind them.

"Leota, what happened?" Naomi whispered, so unstrung she could scarcely stand.

"Upstairs," Leota muttered, her face as white as paper.

"Patches gave us away!" Naomi moaned, throwing herself on the bed. "I saw him go in. What did Jonas say?"

Leota wrung her hands; her lips moved but made no sound.

"Tell me," Naomi pleaded, agonised.

"It isn't you and Gottlieb," Leota managed at last, sinking down on the bed beside her sister. "It's Fenna."

"Fenna!"

Leota pointed a shaking finger to the window.

"She's out there in the sleigh. She's gone and hung herself."

"You're crazy!" cried Naomi, with a feeling of sickness enveloping her. "The baby clothes . . ." she said hysterically. "The nice dinner, and the table all set . . ."

Leota swallowed hard.

"Jonas told me. He said he found her in the barn. He cut her down and took her home in the sleigh."

The two clung together like drowning people.

"I was thinking about Mama and the baby clothes and everything," Leota continued, "and I says to Jonas, 'Should I go tell Mama?' And he says, 'No, I'll tell her, Leota.'"

They stared at one another, listening, but no sound came up to them save the whining of the wind about the house, and the rising of the piece of loose tin on the barn roof, and the crashing down of it.

"In the sleigh?" Naomi asked, trying to take it in.

"Yes."

"But tell me what happened. I saw Patches go into the barn . . ."

"Jonas was unharnessing the team. I was just standing there with an old pail and that one egg..."

"An egg? What for? To throw at him?"

"There was an egg in the manger..."

Naomi gave a laugh that was almost a sob.

"You was standing there with that egg..."

Leota shut her eyes desperately.

"Patches came in, and Jonas just tied him up."

"What did he say?"

"Nothing."

"Nothing? Well then, what happened?"

"Then he told me... about Fenna."

"But I saw Gottlieb come out of there like he was loco!"

"He was up in the loft, so he heard all about it. He came right down, Naomi, just like he didn't care what Jonas would think. His face was all wet with tears."

"He... cried?" Naomi asked, shocked.

Leota nodded: "He comes right up to Jonas, and he says, 'Should I go for the police?' And Jonas says, 'Get Jud. He'll know what to do.'"

"You mean he didn't ask Gottlieb what was he doing there?"

"No. It was so funny. He didn't ask about Patches or nothing. It was just like he was knocked cold."

Naomi stood up and walked restlessly about, her gaze straying unconsciously to the window, then shrinking away from it.

"But Leota, why would she go and do a thing like that? Oh damn that piece of tin!" she shouted as it lifted again in the wind and crashed down. "Damn the wind!" And suddenly she dropped down on to the bed, and buried her face in the pillow, her shoulders shaking.

Leota sat as still as stone, still shocked by the cry that was wrung from Jonas when he told her what had happened, and by the sight of Gottlieb's streaming face as he leapt from the loft, ready on the instant to do anything he could to help them, and by Jonas's thick words, "I will tell her, Leota."

4

By afternoon, the violence of the Chinook wind had spent itself. The vivid blue patches of spring sky disappeared, and icy sleet hissed against the ground. In the barnyard and on the cellar stairs and in the kitchen, men came and went. Huddled around the sitting-room fire, the Leniuk women could hear the deep voices, the slamming of doors, the scrape of heavy boots. They themselves were very quiet. Each had taken to her handwork and spoke little. Though the men helped themselves to hurried meals of the good food waiting in the kitchen, the women did not feel hungry. Anxiously Leota scanned her mother's face. Kazmiri had not crumpled under the blow. She looked so normal sitting there in her print cotton house dress and brown sweater, her thick wavy grey hair in its usual soft knot, her strong tanned face with its high cheekbones and fine lines still serene. But now and then her hands would drop to her lap, while her deep eyes gazed at vacancy.

It's the shock, Leota thought. She can't feel it yet.

Naomi hunched in her chair, her eyes heavy, her lips drooping.

The house quieted, and the voices of the men now came from outside. Leota went to the window just in time to see Jud driving off with the little sleigh. He had hitched his own team to it, and had taken the road to the church.

"They're all going now. What about a cup of coffee, Mama?" she asked in a voice that shook.

"No, I . . . Well yes, we should eat, maybe," said Kazmiri faintly. "Bring us something here by the fire then," she suggested, her tone grateful, kind. It hurt Leota so much that the tears filled her eyes. She wiped them away, going determinedly into the kitchen. Dark figures still moved about the barnyard. Gottlieb and Herman separating, going off in different directions on horseback. Jonas, his shoulders bowed, talking to Philip and the Ulna Mounted Policeman. Far down the road the little sleigh moving into the dimness. Snow had begun to fall, bringing down an early evening.

It fell all night, with a return of wintery weather, treacherous ice on the roads, and a cold blustery breeze. The girls and

Jonas moved in a daze about their chores and then went back into the sitting-room to be with Kazmiri. At the sound of shouting in the yard, Naomi got up hastily, feeling that she could endure the depression of the sitting-room no longer, praying that it might be Gottlieb.

"I'll go," she said.

It was not Gottlieb. Jud and Philip came up.

"Where's Jonas, Naomi?" Jud asked gruffly.

"Tell him to come in," Kazmiri called from the fireside, as she recognised Jud's voice.

Diffidently the two men entered the sitting-room, the heavy snow melting off their boots. Leota's heart contracted at the appearance of Philip. He was unshaven, his eyes sunk back in his head. They all drew strength from Jud with his stocky strong figure and ruddy face.

"It'll be tomorrow, we figure," he said steadily. "See, we'll dig most of today . . . It's froze solid . . ."

"Where do they dig it?" Philip demanded harshly. "They can't put her in the churchyard when she's taken her own life. She can't lie in hallowed ground."

"D'you think it would matter, Jonas," said Jud gently, "if we dig it just inside the churchyard?"

"In the field, outside the churchyard, that's where she belongs," Philip insisted with a wild look.

"Oh God," groaned Kazmiri. "Your religion . . . It's too hard for me!"

Silently Jud looked to Jonas for the final word.

Jonas rose, pressing his hand against his head as though it hurt unbearably.

"Don't dig it in the field," he said suddenly, his face clearing. "Dig it on the little hill there, other side the road. You know, Jud?"

A half smile came over the crooked features, Jud nodded.

"Come on, Philip."

"Sair's here," said Naomi from the doorway. "Herm's going on with you to help." she told Jud as he was leaving. "He says Pro will be coming this afternoon," she went on, going to her mother's side. "We'll all be with you, Mama."

Without a word, Kazmiri went on with her mending. She had a great mound of heavy woollen socks on the floor at her feet, socks belonging to Jonas. As she bent to this homely task, he did not seem to be able to bear the sight, and followed the men outside.

Chapter Fourteen

1

FLORRIE had laid out the body as decently as possible in the church, and she was waiting there until the carpenter from Ulna brought the coffin. Her breath hung in clouds in the bitter cold. The silence of the place had washed back and forth like the sea roaring in her ears; but now the crack of pick and the scrape of shovel came clearly and ghoulishly across to her. Well, she thought, looking over to the little hill, where the men worked, even if she don't lie in hallowed ground, it'll be a mighty pretty spot in summer with that bit of rosebush. She blew her nose loudly on a soiled handkerchief borrowed from Jud. Nicer than the churchyard, really, with all them old wooden crosses falling down . . . But poor Kazmiri. Why don't they think of the living?

She asked Jud about it that evening when they were snug and warm at home.

"Couldn't they of put her in the churchyard for Kazmiri's sake?"

"I asked Jonas," Jud admitted. "Philip wanted to put her in the field, but Jonas he says, 'No, put her on that little hill.'"

"His own child! But of course, I guess he figures he'd be damned in God's sight if he let them bury her in the churchyard."

"Well, it's put down like that in our church laws, but anyways, she won't be in the field with horses and cattle coming around," Jud comforted her.

"Who's going to give the sermon?" asked Gottlieb, who had accompanied them home for the night. He stood with his back to the stove, his face wind-chapped, his eyes red-rimmed.

"Me," answered Jud flatly. "Jonas says Kazmiri wants me

to say the words." He held his head in his hands. "Gonna be hard to know what to say. I only done it once before. That was for an old man gone to his proper rest."

"Can't very well say, 'I fought a good fight,' for her," said Gottlieb with twisted mouth.

"Maybe she did fight a good fight," said Jud thoughtfully. "We don't know. Maybe she did."

"Make it short," Florrie suggested. "Read a bit out of the Bible. Something nice."

"Good idea," he answered, groping for her hand.

Gottlieb stared at them as if he had never seen them before, old and tired as they were, supporting each other in their trouble.

"You'll do it nice, I know," said Florrie wiping her eyes. "Kazmiri couldn't of chosen anybody better." Silently she handed him the reading glasses and his worn Bible.

2

The church was filled to overflowing the next day.

"This is the time you'll all come to church," said Philip cynically as Dan arrived at the door. "Dozens of converts . . . overnight . . . like Paul!"

Dan wished he could say something comforting, but no words seemed adequate to the occasion.

"Why, here's even my sisters come out to my church!" cried Philip as an old car roared to a stop on the road. "Never come out here before. And Joe bringing them out too! Bet he never seen the inside of a church in all his life!"

Dan stamped the snow from his boots as Philip went out to the gate to escort his mother and sisters to the door.

"Mother should never have . . . wouldn't listen . . . shovelling for hours . . . decent of Joe . . . Terrible thing . . ." Jean's fretful voice rose and fell on the breeze

The people of the district stared only at Philip and his family and at Dan and Joe, finding places on the pews, while Jud gave out the first hymn: "What a Friend we have in Jesus." The chords of the organ under Sarah's strong hands, poured forth into the quiet. When the long song was done, Jud stood before them, and a hush fell.

"Friends, we come here for a sad occasion, to bury . . . to bury a young friend. I been trying to think what Jesus would be saying to us if he was here now . . . I . . . it's best just to read His words, friends. There's more comfort in what Jesus says than anything I or any man can think up." He opened the Bible, his hand reaching into his pocket for his reading glasses.

Good grief, thought Florrie. They're at home. We clean forgot about the glasses. She pressed a hand against her eyes.

But Jud did not need the glasses, really, for he knew the words by heart, the words he had chosen. He spoke first in the Low German, and then in English.

"'Take heed that ye despise not one of these little ones,'" he said, his gaze sweeping the congregation, the grief-stricken faces of the two families, those of close friends, the curious looks of others, and the innocent eyes of the children. "'For I say unto you, that in Heaven, their angels do always behold the face of my Father which is in Heaven.

"'For the Son of man is come to save that which was lost.

"'How think ye? If a man have an hundred sheep, and one of them be gone astray, doth he not leave the ninety and nine, and goeth into the mountains, and seeketh that which is gone astray?

"'And if so be that he find it, verily, I say unto you, he rejoiceth more of that sheep than of on the ninety and nine that went not astray.

"'Even so it is not the will of your Father which is in Heaven, that one of these little ones should perish . . .'"

"Let us pray," said Jud.

"Dear Father, we know that you found this lost sheep of ours already. You wouldn't wait a minute to go looking. Dear Father, we know that you look after all of us like a flock of sheep. And You gather up the lambs in Your arms, and carry them in Your bosom, and gently lead those that are with young. So we know that this young friend of ours will be tenderly cared for now she's gone from our sight. Amen."

He raised his head and picked up a hymn book.

"It'll be *Honey in the Rock*, friends. *Honey in the Rock.*"

While Sarah swung into the tune on the organ, Jud went on,

"Yes, friends, even in this tough experience, we got to find some sweetness. God will send comfort. For there's always honey in the rock."

Usually, at such a funeral, after the final hymn, the people filed by to view the remains, but this time, as soon as the singing ended, the pallbearers stepped up and carried the coffin outside to the little hill, the family following closely behind, outsiders coming at a respectful distance. While the coffin was being lowered into the earth, it was customary with the Brethren that someone should sing a hymn. The Leniuk sisters had felt it was fitting that they should perform this office, and they stood close together at one end of the grave, while family and close friends grouped themselves near.

"What'll it be, Sair?" Pro whispered, for they had been too dazed to make a decision.

"*Will there be any stars in my crown,*" Leota suggested, for they harmonised well on that hymn.

"No, no," Naomi whispered. "She never liked it."

Sarah stood up straight, facing the crowd, desperately holding herself under control. She announced loudly, "*In the wind blown along,* by the Leniuk sisters, in memory of Fenna."

"Not that! Not that!" muttered Philip in a low harsh tone.

"She'll have what she liked best, at the end," declared Sarah, and no one dared to contradict her.

"I had to," she wept to Herman afterwards. "I had to give her what she liked best. I feel like I killed her, talking about the Zwick baby..."

The four sweet voices burst into song, Sarah's clear soprano leading as the first shovelful of frozen clods fell upon the coffin.

" ' I am like the Russian thistle
In the wind blown along...' "

The bitter wind carried the singing in odd snatches to the silent crowd... The three Jebson women waited, pale, uncomprehending, and alien. Dan Root stood with bowed head, his face covered with his hands. Gottlieb and Herman worked doggedly with their shovels, while the girls sang on, Sarah faltering a little, gathering strength again, the others following.

> " ' Though I'm an outcast, still He's there
> Hand outstretched for to save;
> And I'm not too lost or lowly
> For His outstretched hand to save.' "

When it was over, Naomi and Gottlieb exchanged a long look. Her family would go into mourning now, they knew, and it would be many weeks before she could go to any social affair. Gottlieb must go back to Bronson's, to his job; and in no time the land would be ready for seeding. Yet he felt that something must be said. As the people dispersed, he managed to get to her side and say, " Be seeing you." She turned away in bitter disappointment.

" Would it comfort your mother, Leota, if Jud and me was to come over now? " asked Florrie.

" Yes. It would comfort us all," Leota assured her.

" I'll get supper on for you," Florrie suggested. " And Jud will do up the chores."

3

As the lines of sleds and teams proceeded on the way down the road to Leniuk's, Jonas led the way, followed by Jud and then by Herman. At the gate, Kazmiri got out stiffly, going up to the house alone. Reaching her bedroom, she took off her warm things, dropping them on the bed. Lifelessly, she sat down in a chair by the window, though she could see little through the flowery frost pattern on the glass. A few minutes later, Jonas came in to her.

" Jud's putting the team in," he explained.

She did not look up.

" Kazmiri," he ground out.

He so seldom used her name. She had been " Mama " all those years while the children clung around her. But now—

" Kazmiri," he said, sitting down beside her.

Her gaze shifted and fixed itself upon him. He put a great work-blackened gnarled hand on her shoulder, a hand so hardened by labour that callouses had entirely obliterated the natural lines in the palm. His face was ugly, contorted by the effort at self-control.

"God," he said, and choked on the word. "God don't care where she's laying."

"Your God," Kazmiri whispered, shaking him off, and gazing at the window again, "... too hard for me."

He sank back into the chair for a moment, defeated, distrustfully eyeing her face, outlined like stone against the window and the dismal grey of the sky outside.

"What do they know what's *hallowed* and what ain't!" he said with such fierceness that she roused herself to look at him again. "That young twirp ... Philip ... Why, we staked out our church land before he was even born."

When he saw that she turned away again, he seized her hand.

"Kazmiri," he pleaded, "listen! We staked it all out. The church land run clear to the edge of that little hill there: It was blessed, back in the old days. Only, when me and Jud went to put the road through to town, we let it run through the churchyard a piece, and cut off that little hill. See, it's a mile closer that way, and the church only lost that little hill. That was back in the old days, and folks don't remember. Most of those old folks died by now, or went away. Only me and Jud knows about the hill. That's why I says when they come here, I says, 'Don't dig it in the field. Dig it on the little hill there, the other side of the road.' It *is* hallowed ground, Kazmiri, like you wanted it."

"But you said you'd be ... damned if you didn't put her in the unhallowed ground."

"I know. But I couldn't ... I couldn't ..." He shook his head, staring down at the floor.

"Thank you for Fenna," she said, thinking herself enlightened.

He lifted his eyes to her face.

"It was for you, Kazmiri. For you. Maybe God don't mind where she's laying, and maybe he does, I don't know. But *you* mind, Kazmiri, so I put her in the land that was blessed ..."

"For me?" she gasped. "For me, Jonas? ... God won't damn you for this, Jonas," she began. "So kind ... so good to me ..." But she could not go on. And as she let the flood of her grief go, she felt a blessed relief, knowing him strong and with her in this darkest hour.

When Leota came up the back steps and into the kitchen, she heard her mother sobbing. The sound tore her heart, and she burst into unrestrained weeping. At the sight, her sisters lost what control they had managed to keep up. Florrie raked at the dying embers of the fire, threw on kindling, and tried to bring some warmth back into the kitchen. The men, coming from the barn, hesitated to enter the house, filled as it was with lamentation in the keening wind. But within those walls, life had struck the rock a fearful blow and revealed a hidden store of honey, long distilled and infinitely sweet.

4

With teams and sleds departing in every direction, Dan walked slowly back to the teacherage, the collar of his threadbare coat turned up against the cold, his head bent against the stinging wind. The words of his song, sung by those sweet fresh voices with slight lilting accents, caught by the wind or half-drowned by it, still echoed in his mind. He reached his own door at last, thankful for the loneliness, the silence, and privacy from curious eyes.

Inside, he saw that the coal bucket needed replenishing and the wood box stood empty. He filled the pail with coal, returning outside with the axe. While he chopped the wood, he thought about the funeral, comparing it sardonically with that of his father, the only other funeral he had ever attended. He remembered the long sermon, solemn and rather pompous, that the minister had preached, not a word of which he now recalled. But Dan felt that the few simple sentences Jud had spoken, and the Bible reading he had chosen, would remain with him always.

As he picked up an armload of wood, a car ground slowly along past the teacherage, Philip walking behind holding a shovel. The car came to an abrupt stop, and Joe got out. He and Philip began to dig in the drifts and ruts, stopping occasionally to shove and push, while Jean sat in the driver's seat. Dan flung the wood into the teacherage, and picking up his own shovel, went to help them. The three men struggled together, digging, pushing, digging again.

"If we can just get it past here," puffed Joe, "the rest of the way is pretty clear."

"Come home with us, Philip," pleaded Mrs. Jebson, opening a door of the car and leaning out while the men rested a moment. "Don't stay here all alone. Dear God, how can you bear it?"

Philip did not answer, but bent to dig again.

"Mother!" Jean burst out, staring straight ahead. "Close that door. You'll be in bed after all this. I told you not to come."

Mrs. Jebson slammed the door to. Though she and Betty were wrapped up in blankets, they were already chilled.

"I never stayed a day in bed when your father was alive," the older woman sobbed brokenly. "I raised three young ones and worked hard on the farm, and now I'm just told to behave myself. Can't even speak a word of comfort to my own son."

"He isn't listening!" snapped Jean, starting the motor again. "Never did listen to anybody."

"Here we go!" shouted Joe triumphantly, as the car moved on to a smooth part of the road. "We'll be O.K. now."

"Sure you'll be all right?" Dan asked anxiously as Jean moved over for Joe to get behind the wheel.

"Not too bad from here on," Joe assured him. "We'll make it all right."

Shouldering the shovel, Philip watched the car go off.

"They'll get through . . . Thanks, boy scout," he laughed desolately.

"Come along to my place for a while," Dan suggested. "Don't go back to an empty house."

"That's what they all say to me," Philip mocked. "'Come to my place. Don't stay all alone.' I burnt your books, Dan Root. Are you figuring you'll get your revenge now? Kick me while I'm down?"

"It was lucky about burning my books," said Dan quickly. "Because I went to Calgary to buy another text, and I made it up with my step-father. So I'll never hold it against you."

"Everything turns out for the best, don't it?" said Philip trudging wearily along the road.

Well, let him go, Dan thought. At least I tried.

But he could not let Philip go. Look what Fenna did when she was desperate, he reminded himself. He seized Philip's arm, dragging him through the schoolyard gate.

"In you go," he said firmly. "I need a fellow intellectual to talk to."

"I tell you I'll be poor company. I hate you and everybody."

"I know. But come in anyhow."

When they reached the door of the teacherage, Dan pushed Philip in ahead of him, and they both stumbled over the firewood at the entrance.

"I've done the chores," said Dan cheerfully. "Just have to build up the fire a bit. You sit down and keep your coat on until the place gets warm."

Drunk with exhaustion and mental chaos, Philip sank into the armchair, while Dan got a good fire roaring in the stove, swept up the bits of bark and coal dust from the floor, and opened the oven door to get more heat into the room.

"Now it's warming up. Let me take your coat," he suggested. "Why don't you take off your shoes and put your feet in the oven? I often sit like that in the evenings."

To his relief, Philip responded like a tired child.

"I always have some hot chocolate at this time of day. You'll have some with me, won't you?"

"Just don't bother about me, please," growled Philip.

Nevertheless, Dan poured two good-sized cups of milk into the top of a double boiler. He always kept an emergency ration of plain chocolate in the cupboard, using it sparingly. Now he took out two bars, cut them up into small pieces with a knife, and added them to the milk. Setting this mixture to heat over hot water, he sat down beside Philip.

"'When the light that is in thee be darkness, how great is that darkness,'" Philip suddenly intoned, as though giving out the text for a sermon.

"You have your faith," Dan ventured.

"My faith!" Philip laughed. "That's a good one! I'm just telling you my light is darkness! I'm so trained in my faith I can't speak without the scriptures coming through . . . But I'm telling you, I haven't got no faith left."

Dan rose to stir the hot chocolate.

"Everybody blames me," muttered Philip.

"Really?"

"Tell me I left her alone too much. But that's the life of a preacher on the prairie. My circuit to do every Sabbath. Meetings and weddings . . . She knew all about that before we got married."

"Yes, she must have."

"Then there was all that gossip about the Zwick baby. Gottlieb used to come sneaking round here. Made me wonder if it really was a Zwick baby that was coming."

"Gottlieb is only interested in Naomi," Dan declared. "They dance cheek to cheek at all the dances. If he has been sneaking around, it's to see Naomi."

"Well, anyways, our baby was called the Zwick baby from here clear out to Hosanna! . . . And then I got the letter from my Bible School. I'd been accepted to go out to India next fall. So I told her . . ."

"You mean you hadn't told her about India before?"

"A preacher might get a call at any time," Philip explained. "He might figure he was fixed for life in a place, and then suddenly get the call to go to China. We don't know. A wife has got to be prepared for that when she marries a preacher. Then again, I asked to go out to India, but I could be refused. No use getting all steamed up about it for nothing."

But he'd tell a perfect stranger like me, and then not discuss it with the girl he was going to marry, thought Dan. Carefully he poured the steaming drink into two thick mugs. Philip took one, holding it in both hands, warming himself on the hot china. Slowly he sipped the nourishing chocolate, while shadows gradually filled the room so that the two young men could scarcely see each other.

"So I told her, after the baby was born, we'd go," Philip went on. "Make a new life together, away from Gottlieb, away from the gossip. But she couldn't see it."

"How did she take it?"

"Cried a lot . . . I thought it was her condition . . . Can you tell me one thing? Should a man set aside all his hopes and ambitions, or in my case, the call of God, because the woman he married wants to stay home? Can you answer me that?"

"I—I don't know," said Dan uneasily. "I think I'd tell

her before getting married. But it's easy to have hind sight," he added quickly. " I just don't know."

" We could of had a wonderful life together if she had been different. I loved my work, Dan Root. I loved my sermons. Riding over the prairie on horseback and suddenly getting a good idea . . . Shaping it up in my mind with the right bits of scripture to go with it . . . Making people listen so you could hear a pin drop. I had the power . . . But it's all over now. The light is gone out of it. I don't believe . . . It's back to the farm and the thistles and the dust for me."

But you could go on to India, Dan thought. It would be easier to go than to stay. A lesser man, Dan realised, could live a life of pretence in the matter of faith. But not Philip.

" And she's gone, my lovely Fenna! " cried Philip. " I loved her, Dan Root. Maybe I didn't know how to make love to a girl like Gottlieb would, but I loved her. How can I go on living without Fenna?"

" Time will help," Dan insisted. " I lost my father," he said slowly.

" I lost my father too," Philip shot back. " And that was what set me free. Set us all free. He was hard as nails to Mother and the girls. He wasn't cold in his grave before I was on my way to Bible School."

" My father and I were about as close as father and son could be, I think," persisted Dan humbly. " When he died, it was so sudden I couldn't believe it. I thought about it every day, all day long at first. Then I found I wasn't thinking about it all the time, and gradually it didn't crush me so much. Now I remember him often, and I think how good he was, but I don't grieve any more . . ."

" You think I can forget a hanging?"

" I know it can't compare with what you're going through," said Dan compassionately. " But I think you'll find it will lessen as time goes on." His tone carried conviction. " Even your faith may come back," he suggested. " It's mainly the shock that makes you feel as you do now . . . You must go to bed," Dan said, striking a match to the coal-oil lamp. " Sleep in my bed in the other room. I often sit up by the stove on a cold night. I'm used to it. Come along."

" Why do you treat me like this?" cried Philip. " You heap

coals of fire on my head, Dan Root. Oh damn the scriptures coming through! But why, Dan Root? You loved her too . . ."

"Get some sleep," said Dan gently, supporting Philip with a skinny arm, wiry and strong. "Sleep will be the best thing for you."

He helped Philip out of his jacket, laid a warm quilt over his prone figure stretched out on the bed. The preacher raised suffering eyes.

"There's a light in you, Dan Root," he said. Then he dropped heavy lids, turning his face to the wall.

Chapter Fifteen

I

BEFORE the end of April, Gottlieb's crop was in. From the time he had started seeding, he had been living in his bachelor's shack, a granary converted to a one-roomed house. It faced the road, its two small windows blinking like eyes in the sunlight, its crooked stove-pipe giving it a devil-may-care appearance as though it were thumbing its nose at passers-by. In the adjacent pasture where the pump stood, handle leaning rakishly upwards, Patches drank dreamily from the water trough, or grazed lazily, his mane streaming in the wind.

One morning Gottlieb was spading a small piece of land at one side of his shack. The sun felt unseasonably warm, and he soon had a large sweaty area showing on his shirt between the shoulder blades. Leaning the spade against the wall, he studied the sky, which though blue and giving no promise of rain, had a dusty look. A breeze blew in snatches, sometimes making a black whirlwind out in the fields and then dying down again. He took off his hat, mopping the sweat from his face with his sleeve. Then, tunelessly whistling between his teeth, he went into the shack.

At one end, he had flung his saddle down on the floor, while other bits of harness hung on hooks on the wall along with various garments. Tins containing nails and screws and wire lay on the window ledges. Set up on bricks was the stove, and beside it cupboards made from apple boxes, containing stores of food and tin dishes. Near the bed stood a table covered with oilcloth on which a tin of tobacco and one of syrup, a pair of pliers and the heel of a loaf kept curious company. Linoleum covered the floor, swept clean by a stub of broom which leaned in one corner. There was a basin with a piece of carbolic soap beside it, and on the wall a small distorting mirror. The place looked clean, utilitarian, and uncomfortable.

Reaching under the bed, Gottlieb brought out a boxful of rustling packages of garden seeds. Seated on the bed he began turning them over, still whistling between his teeth, when he heard the roar of an approaching truck, and Herman's truck stopped in a cloud of dust at the door.

"Mind if I get some water?" Herman asked, climbing down with a pail in his hand as Gottlieb came outside.

Gottlieb flung out an arm in the direction of the pump.

"Help yourself."

He moved closer to the truck with some curiosity, for it was not Sarah, but Leota who sat up front beside the driver.

"So! You and Herm, eloping?" Gottlieb grinned, pushing back his sweaty hat. "You're all dressed up fit to kill."

Leota smiled, looking elegant in a soft blue suit and white lacy blouse. Gottlieb noticed a small trunk. He saw that she wore gloves and carried a handbag.

"Where you off to?" he demanded.

In the background the pump began to squeak protestingly.

"I'm catching the train to Calgary," said Leota shyly. "I'm going to meet Reuben there. We're getting married."

"Jees!" Gottlieb stared at her. Now he saw that she was beautiful, radiant. "Well, Reube's a lucky guy," he said at last in obvious admiration. Yet he could not resist a final dig at her. "But you don't need to think you fooled nobody," he teased. "Ada Pearl seen all them letters coming to you in Reuben's writing. She don't steam open letters like her old lady used to, but she's sure wise to what goes on. And I told Joe way back in the winter, I says, 'You got no more chance with Leota than a snowball in hell!' Yep, Leota, you're not so smart as you think you are!"

The pump squealed a long final note.

"Gottlieb," said Leota quietly, not in the least perturbed by his remarks, "Naomi wants to see you . . . Gottlieb, I think she's in trouble . . ."

The teasing smile left his face; his laugh died. His gaze fell under her searching liquid look.

"Why the heck you don't oil up your pump?" cried Herman, hurrying back. "Squeals like a dying hog!"

o

"I hear you're taking Leota off to her wedding," said Gottlieb, somehow subdued.

"If I ever get to town," Herman smiled, pouring water. "We got to pick up Florrie still."

"Well, best of luck!" said Gottlieb, seizing Leota's hand through the cab window. "Like I said, he's a lucky guy."

When the truck had disappeared, rolling dust behind it, Gottlieb picked up the spade again, and once more began to dig, turning the earth quickly and efficiently. Then he methodically raked and planted, covering the seeds, patting the earth down with the flat side of the hoe. All through the morning he worked, stopping only for long draughts of water at the pump.

In the afternoon, the wind blew more strongly, and again he watched the black whirlwinds out in the fields, and the dusty blueness of the sky. Inside the shack, he could hear the plaintive note in the wind as it rounded the corners, rattled the windows, knocked mockingly at the door, and went moaning past. Gottlieb poured water into the basin, washing his hands and face with the stinging red soap. Selecting a clean blue denim shirt from the clothes hanging among the harness, he changed, ran a comb through his hair, and put on his windbreaker. He took a hurried meal of bread and cheese. Patches came running to the gate in answer to his sharp whistle, and when he had watered the big black and white horse, he saddled up and rode off.

How dry it all was, with dust following the hoofs, with a teasing wind blowing flurries of dust in front of him. The newly sown fields no longer looked rich and black with damp turned loam, but grey with lack of moisture. Gottlieb rode on at a steady jog-trot for some time. Then, thinking he heard something, he pulled Patches to a walk, even to a standstill. Perhaps he heard a car or a truck, still out of sight. He listened intently. The dull roar that came to his ears had a deep undertone not heard from an engine. At the same time, the wind struck savagely with the force of a giant fist, while the deep roar increased in volume like the waters of a flood bursting a dam.

For minutes, Gottlieb waited, his horse restive beneath him. Then, on the western horizon, he saw a huge black cloud

Honey in the Rock

approaching, rolling forward with incredible swiftness along the ground, darkening the day so that the sky was half black, half blue. The roar was the wind driving a blizzard of dust before it.

Digging his heels into Patches, Gottlieb galloped to the pasture fence, and leaping down, let his horse go free. Growing in immensity, the storm darkened the sun, blackening out the sky with a roar like thunder. Gottlieb wrapped his windbreaker around his head, and flattening himself on the ground, lay hugging the fenceline. With stifling blackness the wind hit him, soil and seed flooding past. At his side, above the terrible crashing of the storm, he heard Patches plunge and squeal. He thought he himself would be torn from the ground, but he clung hard to the fenceline, stones and clods of earth striking him, the whine of the wind in his ears, thick choking darkness blotting out sight.

Suffocating in his jacket, Gottlieb lost all sense of time. He would think the wind was slackening and begin to move, only to retreat again at a new onslaught of the storm. Only the fenceline had any reality; only the squealing of the horse seemed to link him with things living. But eventually the blackness turned to grey, and in the greyness, giant Russian thistles, like twisted ghosts in another world, went whirling over the land. The wind at last lost its sinister note; gradually a sickly sun shone through the grey haze. The storm had spent itself. Seeing through the sleeve of his jacket that it was about over, Gottlieb stirred, unwinding himself from the posts and the wire.

He was all but buried in the drifting soil which showered about him as he stood up, stiff and battered. Patches was running aimlessly along the fenceline, but he turned back at Gottlieb's whistle. Gottlieb shook out his jacket, whacked at the rest of his clothes with the flat of his hand. In his earthy face, black as though he had been working in a coal mine, his teeth and the whites of his eyes glittered strangely. He pulled out his shirt tail, letting the loose dirt sift down his back. Then, pulling himself together again, he mounted Patches.

Slowly he rode along the way he had come, examining his fields. They had become desert, robbed and wind-torn, rocks sticking up in them like the bones of a dead animal half picked by a carrion bird who had beat its dark wings over the land. At his shack, the stove pipe had been blown off, but he was thankful that the fire had been dead in the stove. Everything in the one room was covered by a layer of dirt. Outside, the garden too had been stripped of its seed. Once more he got up on Patches and turned down the same road as before.

2

At Leniuk's house, the women had started on the task of cleaning up after the storm. With bits of wet newspaper scattered around on the floor of the kitchen, Naomi began to sweep, poking at the drifts of dust piled up in the corners. A layer of fine silt covered each piece of furniture and the window-sills, and hung in the folds of the curtains. In the cupboards, dishes and pots and pans were shadowed over with the soil that had drifted in from the fields. Naomi's eyes smarted from the dust. It made her scalp prickle, and smeared her face and neck when she wiped away the sweat with a grimy hand. Dust gritted between her teeth and caught at her throat. In the sitting-room she could hear her mother coughing and choking as she lifted the braided rugs from the floor. Although the storm had gone over, through the window, Naomi saw that the sky had a dirty look and the sun shone but bleakly through a haze, while the wind still went moaning past.

Sweeping up the wet mushy papers, leaving streaks of mud on the linoleum, she straightened to reach for a cardboard carton to put the rubbish into, when she saw Gottlieb ride across the yard. Leaning on the broom handle, she stood quite still, watching him through the window. Man and horse looked greyed. Gottlieb got down, giving Patches a thump on the flank that brought out a cloud of dust, and sent the horse to the barn, reins trailing. Then he went to the water trough, and setting the windmill in motion, lowered his head under the pipe as the water gushed forth. Naomi shoved the wet newspapers aside violently with the broom. She took a towel from a pile of laundry, and shaking the grit from it, went down the back steps and out into the wind.

Silently she handed Gottlieb the towel as he lifted his dripping head. Without a word, he dried himself, flung the towel over one shoulder, and stilled the windmill with its clamour and its rushing of water. Then he looked at her out of red, dust-grimed eyes.

"Where's Jonas?" he asked.

"He went on horseback to look around at things. We're just cleaning up." With a filthy hand she tried to keep the tangled hair from blowing into her face. "The garden's gone too."

"My crop's sure gone."

"Get relief seed and put it in again," she said patiently.

"Yeah."

They gazed around at the ruined fields.

"Did you see Leota go by this morning?" Naomi asked anxiously. "She was catching the train to Calgary to marry Reuben there. Herm took her."

"To marry Reuben!" Gottlieb faked utter astonishment.

"She was going to stop by your place . . ."

"I never seen them go by! I been stuck out there like a gopher in a hole, missing all the news!"

"Did you come to see Jonas?"

"Know what I was coming here for, Naomi? It's a joke." He gave a hard laugh. "I got my crop in, so I was coming to ask you to marry me."

"To marry you!"

Turning away, he trailed his hand in the water of the trough

"I didn't know you was still a good girl."

"You're insulting me."

"I know."

"I says to you, 'No, no, Gottlieb, please!' But did you listen?"

"I didn't hear you," muttered Gottlieb. "But I sure hear you now. Nights, when I can't sleep."

She stared. "You been worrying? It was my fault too."

He flashed a look at her, green eyes glinting like the water in the trough under the weakly shining sun.

"But you wouldn't marry a guy like me."

"Sure I would."

He brushed his head against Naomi's arm like a colt.

"Will you marry me, then?" he asked.

"Sure, I'll marry you."

"And live in a shack?"

"Why not?"

"How about getting married right away?"

"Oh yes, Gottlieb . . . Because I'm going to have a baby, and we could get married before it starts to show too much . . ."

"A baby! Show! My God, why didn't you tell me?"

"I wanted you to come."

"What if I didn't ask you?"

"But you did ask me first, before I told you."

"That'll be another girl, just like all the Leniuks," he laughed, holding her hard.

"You're glad? Everybody will talk . . . They'll count the months."

"Let them talk. I'm glad," he said defiantly. "Maybe it'll be a boy after all. I kept my boots on, you remember."

She smiled to see how puffed up he was to think he could beget a child so easily.

"Here comes Jonas," she laughed with her old drawl. "You better tell him, now he seen us kissing."

Stiffly, Jonas dismounted beside them, while Zoe drank deeply. Jonas slowly shook his head, gazing over the dreary landscape.

"I just got finished seeding yesterday," Gottlieb told him. "I was on my way over here when the dust hit. I lay down by the fenceline till it went past."

"It's tore out everything," Jonas rumbled. "All to do again."

"I was just on my way over to ask Naomi to marry me, Uncle. I asked her anyways, crop or no crop."

Zoe lifted her head, water streaming from between her lips. Jonas turned to his nephew, his look piercing him through.

"Funny time to ask a girl to marry you."

Gottlieb stood his ground doggedly.

"Yeah, but if you keep putting it off, you never ask her."

"That's true," said Jonas, sardonically.

"We figure on getting married right away, if it's O.K. with you."

Jonas stood there, heavily weary, while the wind whipped past them.

"Tell Mama," he said at last.

Taking Zoe's reins, he watched Naomi and Gottlieb walking

to the house, holding hands, their heads bent together. They would be married, and soon. The Zwick's land adjoined that of the Leniuk's, and the two young people were both good farmers. Jonas leaned against the watertrough, remembering the day of horror, seeing again Gottlieb slithering down out of the loft, his face streaming with tears, seeing Patches unaccountably in the barn. Jonas was not deluded. In Gottlieb, he saw himself again as a young man, headstrong, wild, attractive to women. He saw himself young again, spending his youth as he regarded it now, sinfully and wastefully, to find himself suddenly middle-aged and alone, lonely and full of self-loathing. Well, he had managed to solve his problems, returning to his faith, marrying a woman who needed him, who had brought life and laughter, song and voices into his emptiness. A child of his own, even.

He sighed. Naomi must have a baby on the way. Nothing else could hurry Gottlieb into marriage like that. But they would be married, and soon. And the land adjoined. Jonas hoped for a houseful of children. Maybe that would steady Gottlieb down; maybe the wildness was finished with already.

3

Sarah and Herman were among the first arrivals at the wedding. After they had unhitched their team, Kazmiri and Jonas welcomed them on the church porch. Florrie was just ahead of them, bearing a large vase with sprays of pussy willow and of saskatoon stems leafing into greenery in one hand, and in the other a low dish of wild mauve and yellow crocuses.

"Best we can do for flowers at this time of year," she said cheerily.

"Lucky to get those, even," said Sarah stiffly as Florrie went into the church to arrange them.

Kazmiri held on to her husband's arm with both hands, almost lovingly, it seemed to Sarah.

"Lots of people coming?" she inquired.

"Just a few neighbours," her mother answered, anxiously studying her daughter's sullen face. "Everybody is so busy. And of course you're coming to the wedding supper, Sarah?"

"I don't like to say I hope it won't rain." Herman glanced

at the sky where clouds boiled up over the sun in a boisterous wind, "But maybe rain would be lucky for them."

"Even felt a drop or two on our way over," Jonas remarked hopefully.

"Well, let's go in, Herman," said Sarah impatiently.

"They aren't ready yet," said her mother.

But Sarah had already opened the door and started in.

"Still dolling up the bride," remarked Florrie who was just coming out again. "What a year this is for weddings!"

"Sarah, they're not ready," whispered Herman, following her inside.

In the cool dimness of the church, Gottlieb and Naomi stood together near the entrance to the vestry. She wore a long white wedding dress, a present from Prolet and Nathan. On her glistening dark hair lay a wreath of imitation flowers fashioned by Prolet's clever fingers. Gottlieb looked unfamiliar and uncomfortable in his suit which he had hardly ever worn, and a new white shirt and gay tie.

"I'll sure be glad when this shebang is over," he muttered nervously.

Prolet put her head out the vestry door.

"You shouldn't come and see the bride before the wedding, you know. It's bad luck. Come on, Naomi. There's still pins in the hem, and I have to fix your flowers so they won't fall off."

"It's the bride who's supposed to be nervous," said Naomi cracking her gum as she straightened Gottlieb's tie.

"You better spit out your gum right now before you forget," Prolet admonished. "Come on, Naomi. People are here, and you're not ready . . . Hullo Sair. Well, here goes the last Leniuk girl to the altar!"

Naomi brushed some dust from Gottlieb's shoulder.

"You'll be O.K.," she told him, smiling.

Suddenly he clung to her.

"Holy cow, Naomi. I swore I wouldn't take a drink before this wedding, but I sure could do with one right now."

Sarah's look flashed scornfully, jealously, over the pair of them.

"There'll be lots of apple cider up at the house, after," teased Naomi. "Think you can last out?"

"Naomi! You must come!"

Prolet seized her sister's arm and pulled her away.

"Be seeing you," grinned Gottlieb as he turned, becoming aware of Sarah's presence for the first time.

"She shouldn't be wearing flowers in her hair," sneered Sarah, her dimples coming and going. "In the Brethren in Christ Church, the bride don't wear flowers in her hair when there's a baby on the way! I'll have to tell the preacher."

Gottlieb turned white. He did not answer, but strode out of the door. Stifled laughter came from within the vestry, while Herman, with averted face, moved tiredly towards the front of the church as though to look at the flowers Florrie had placed there. As the ugly words hung on the air, Sarah rushed away, past her mother and Jonas on the porch, and away from neighbours who were gathering jovially in the churchyard, across the road to Fenna's grave. She stood there with bowed head, in horror at what she had done.

Thus Herman found her.

"You must hate me now, I guess," she said.

"No, you feel bad enough. But Sair," he said sternly, "you're not telling the preacher nothing about Naomi."

She shook her head.

"No," she said. "I could do it to Gottlieb, but I couldn't do that to Naomi."

"Come now. We go back to the church like everybody else. And when they're married, we wish them luck and go to their wedding feast."

With downcast eyes, Sarah took her husband's arm. A cool wind sprang up as they crossed the road back to the churchyard. A bit of gold sunlight struggled through the gathering darkness of the clouds, and in spite of the gusts of dust that blew into their faces, the smell of distant rain and wet earth flowed around them like a blessing. The drone of an unseen tractor far off to the west reminded them that Philip was seeding his crop, working like a madman through Sabbath day and every day. Herman pressed steadily on with just the briefest of greetings to friends as they passed, Sarah thrilled by his strength and determination. And he came to find me even, she thought in wonderment.

Seeing Gottlieb talking with some of the men, she was surprised to notice that in his suit he was actually awkward, gauche, not the thrilling figure who had filled her dreams for years. She stopped a moment, looking up at her husband, so distinguished in his best clothes.

"He'll never be knee high to you, Herm," she declared clinging to his arm. "I'm glad I never married Gottlieb. I'd never be happy, like we are."

Herman stood still. It was a good moment for him. Suddenly a few huge drops of rain pitted the dust at their feet.

"We'd better get in," he said happily, hurrying Sarah along.

Thudding into the deep dust, the rain beat with a steadily increasing rhythm, sending the wedding guests scurrying to the porch and into the church.

"Just a shower, I think!" cried Florrie. "Lay the dust and freshen things up."

Gottlieb stood at the altar with the best man beside him. Prolet played the wedding music, and as Naomi went up the aisle on Jonas's arm, Sarah tightening her lips, thought, I'm not jealous. He'll never stand knee high to Herman. And I'm going to have a baby too . . . Her look softened, and she smiled dreamily to herself while the rain dinned on the roof and the Hosanna preacher performed the ceremony. Then as the married couple came back through the church, Sarah thought sadly and contritely how lovely the flowers looked in her sister's dark hair.

Chapter Sixteen

I

DAN ROOT sat on the steps of the Lily of the Valley School. His bedroll and his large battered suitcase, packed, strapped, and locked, lay ready beside him. It was the last day of June. He had balanced the figures in the register, swept the school, and set the teacherage in order. Gottlieb would soon drive by to take him to the station and the train which would transport him to the north and to his new job with Reuben's uncle. Dan plucked a grass stem to chew at, thinking that now he knew enough not to stand waiting expectantly for Gottlieb, but to sit down and relax. The sun had sunk low in the sky, making the shadow of the church oddly elongated as though it stretched out in one long stride to claim the whole area.

Dan breathed deeply the prairie smells, trying to identify them. The buffalo beans. Blue vetch. Sweet clover, And new green wheat. A three-day rain had soaked the land, and there was great hope for the crop after its second seeding. In the distance he heard the roar of a motor, and soon he could see the truck, far down the road. He waited until he was sure that it was Gottlieb before getting slowly to his feet and picking up his things. Standing at the gate, with his shoes crushing tender green blades of grass amidst the prairie wool, he looked back at the school and the teacherage, at what had been his domain for the past term. Now that it was over, a pang of sorrow caught him unawares. He listened while a meadow lark sang, hidden but close. He took a last look at the school, dwarfed by the vast arc of prairie sky with the evening clouds rolled up in a purple mass near the sinking sun.

And the truck ground to a stop beside him.

"Right on time!" Dan grinned as Gottlieb jumped out of the cab.

"Anything breakable?" Gottlieb asked, picking up the suitcase to fling it and the bedroll unceremoniously into the back of the truck. "Hope you don't get all messed up," he added, glancing at Dan's clean shirt and grey flannel trousers. He himself looked as if he had been underneath the truck for a good part of the day, as in fact he had. "Well, come on, Teacher. Don't sit too close to me."

The noise of the truck making conversation next to impossible on the fourteen-mile trip to town, Dan was left to his own thoughts, and once again the pain of leaving bewildered him, even the idea of parting with Gottlieb who had grown dearly familiar, part of his life. He watched him now, for the last time, the brown ruddy face, the flash of green eyes looking alertly this way and that as the steady hands drove the truck along the impossible road.

"I'll take you to the hotel!" Gottlieb shouted to him as they came near to Ulna. "Got a piece of machinery to pick up. I'll come around before you go."

"So you're leaving us," said Joe heartily as Dan came into the waiting-room.

"Yes," the other returned, setting down his heavy luggage.

"What's in it? Bricks?"

"Books, mostly."

"I'll get somebody to take your things over to the station on the dray. Come and have a drink."

As Dan hesitated, Joe clapped a hand on his thin shoulder.

"Come on, have one on the house."

In the waiting-room, they could hear the muted sounds of the beer parlour, the clash of glassware, shouts and loud male laughter, snatches of song.

"Don't mind if I do," said Dan shyly.

Joe opened the heavy door. After the smell of the fields and the cool rainwashed evening, came the acrid sourness of beer, mingled with tobacco smoke, horse, sweat. The place was crowded with men, their heads bent together over the little tables. While Joe roared at the beer slinger, Dan sat down quickly just inside, a slender conspicuous figure in his clean blue shirt. Presently, out of the rumble of talk, a single male voice detached itself in a fragment of song:

> I am like a Russian thistle
> In the wind blown along . . .

At once two or three more voices joined in:

> Rolling o'er and o'er the prairie
> In the wind blown along . . .

"There's your song, kid!" shouted Joe. "Give it the works, boys!"

> Torn up from my watered roots
> In the wind blown along:
> Without a home, without a guide,
> In the wind blown along . . .

It came out now in slightly drunken harmonising, lonely and heart-catching. Dan sat with bent head, a hot mist before his eyes, a lump in his throat. Will I ever see it again, he wondered. Those rough hills . . . That vast rim of prairie and sky . . . it gets you . . .

> He is like the fenceline sure,
> Hand outstretched for to save . . .

Some of those voices are good . . . Hand outstretched for to save . . . They stretched out their hands to me . . . Florrie . . . Jud . . . Herman . . . Reuben . . . They took me out of the pit and held me up until I could walk alone . . .

> In the dust-storm or the blizzard
> Hands outstretched for to save . . .

It doesn't matter what the future holds. I can face it now . . .

> Though I'm an outcast, still He's there
> Hand outstretched for to save . . .

Dan glanced up, deeply flushed, his heart pounding painfully. Through the thick curtain of blue smoke, the men were looking over at him from their various tables, curious, friendly. Across from him Joe smiled a twisted smile, close to tears. I used to feel like an outcast, an outsider, but not now, Dan thought, surprised. And look, they're singing my song. They like it. They know I fell in love with a Leniuk girl too, and lost her. He felt a wrench at the heart. Pain . . . suffering . . . loneliness . . . I wasn't specially marked out for them as I used to believe . . . They are only what all men know . . . and endure. The memory of Philip's agony crossed his mind like a shadow, and as Reuben had done he thought gratefully, I'm lucky. Luckier than most.

The song thundered to a close:

> And I'm not too lost or lowly
> For His outstretched hand to save!

The single voice which had started it, added a last plaintive phrase:

> For His outstretched hand to save!

Too brimful of emotion to speak, Dan waved a hand at the room in general, and then swung up his glass of tomato juice for a long cooling drink. He knew he would remember this moment as long as he lived. The tawdry beer parlour. These rough men, drunken and noisy, ready to fight at the drop of a cowboy hat. Lonely men. Singing his song. Paying tribute to the city slicker in whom they had found neither sham nor cowardice. It was one of those rewards, rich and rare, that Dan was to find at intervals throughout his life.

It was indeed the very honey in the rock.

Suddenly he heard a roar of laughter, and looked up to see Gottlieb sauntering in.

"Oh here you are," said Gottlieb, ignoring the teasing laughter of the men, his wandering gaze coming to rest on Dan. "Figured you'd lost yourself some place."

"Everybody getting married. Even Reuben, marrying my Leota," mourned Joe, setting down his glass, his lips red and wet. "Well, he can have her, that wildcat!"

"He gentled her," said Gottlieb blandly. "He gentled her . . . I got to shove off," he told Dan. "But they say the train will be on time. If you hurry, I'll get you over there now."

"Yeah, you better hurry, Gottlieb," Joe drawled, following them out of the beer parlour. "Little wifykins is looking out of the window, waiting for you to come home."

"Shut up!" snarled Gottlieb.

As Dan and Gottlieb approached the truck in the darkening street, Ada Pearl was just passing the hotel on her way home to supper.

"Hi Gottlieb!" she shrilled. "Long time no see!"

"He got hooked, that's why," said Joe, leaning in the doorway.

"You poor guy. Well, drop by some time for some coffee."

Gottlieb put a cigarette between his lips.

"Maybe I'll do that." His eyes gleamed at her in the flame of the match which he cupped in his hands.

"Hell, you're a married man now," Joe reminded him.

"There's nothing wrong with a cup of coffee, is there, Gottlieb?" crooned Ada Pearl.

"Wait a minute, Teacher." Philip, after tying his horse, appeared out of the shadows looking handsome and gloomy. "Just want to tell you good-bye."

They shook hands warmly.

"Don't let them give you any wooden nickels up there in Edmonton, Teacher," Joe called out. "Come on, Preacher, come and have a drink."

"No thanks," said Philip dourly.

"Walk a piece down the street, Philip," Ada Pearl suggested, chummily taking his arm. "Tell me your troubles like you did the other night. It's such a treat to me to have somebody educated to talk to."

"Well, look at that." Joe laughed softly, watching them go off together.

Gottlieb got into the truck, slamming the door savagely.

"Want to miss your train?" he growled at Dan.

Joe stood in the doorway of the waiting-room until the truck had driven off. Then he returned to the noise and the life of the beer parlour.

"Gimme a beer!" he yelled at the beerslinger. "And be quick about it!"

THE END